12/15

27 JAN 2016

28 OCT 2020

22 JUL 2021

12 SEP 2024

21 OCT 2022

Suffolk Libraries

Please return/renew this item
by the last date shown.

Suffolk Libraries
01473 263838
www.suffolklibraries.co.uk

Copyright © 2014 Natasha Preston
All rights reserved.

The right of Natasha Preston to be identified as the Author of the Work has been asserted by her in accordance with the Copyright, Designs and Patents Act 1988.

All rights reserved. No part of this publication may be reproduced, stored in a retrieval system, or transmitted, in any form or by any means without the prior written consent of the publisher, nor be otherwise circulated in any form of binding or cover other than that in which it is published and without a similar condition being imposed on the subsequent purchaser.

All characters in this publication are fictional and any resemblance to real persons, living or dead is purely coincidental.

ISBN: 1499199392
ISBN-13: 978-1499199390

Acknowledgements

There are five girls that I could not have done this without. They helped shape the story and, well, their 'yes there should be more smut, Tasha' made this book so much better and utterly inappropriate for my grandad to read! So thank you Kirsty, Whairigail, Emma, Adelaine and Hilda.

The gorgeous cover, that's made me squeal a few times, was made by Mollie Wilson from MJWilson Design.

And last but not least, thank you to my fabulous editors, Debz Hobbs-Wyatt and Eileen Proksch.

Dedication

For Kerry

CHAPTER ONE

Chloe

"Lift your leg higher," Logan said in full, annoying trainer mode. It was alright for him, he was a sodding fitness instructor. I hadn't exercised properly in *years*. Narrowing my eyes at him, I pushed myself a little more, laying my leg on his shoulder. *Should muscles burn this bloody much?* He grinned. "Better, Chlo."

I hadn't stretched like this for ages and I was already dreading the aching and stiffness that was going to kill me tomorrow. I'd just started my crazy exercise regime again two weeks ago, and I was so out of shape, it was embarrassing. I used to be able to keep up with Logan, but now I was like a little old lady.

"I hate you," I huffed, gritting my teeth, brushing my dark brown hair out of my face. Even if I tied it up, after working out for a while it started to fall out of the ponytail. Annoyingly, Logan's hair never looked any different. The sides were cut just a tiny bit shorter than the top, which was styled and flopped over his forehead a little.

He arched his eyebrow, the corner of his mouth pulled into a smirk, and I knew he had more in store for me.

"We've barely started, sweetheart." I couldn't help smiling. Not many young men could make *sweetheart* work. Logan definitely could and it made plenty of women turn into mush.

"Barely started my arse!" Logan's idea of having *barely started* was so far away from mine it wasn't even funny. We'd already stretched, skipped, lifted light weights and done half an hour of yoga. That wasn't *barely starting*, that was sodding barely breathing!

"A couple more and we'll go for a run." He pushed my leg back a few times, stretching out the muscle, again.

"Okay, okay," I said, shoving his chest and dropping my leg to the floor, "let's just get this damn run over with."

Logan sighed. "Chloe, if you don't want to do this…"

"I do." It was time to get my life fully back on track. I couldn't have it on hold a second longer. Fitness was important to me and I wanted to be back in my old routine. Gulping down almost a whole bottle of water, I wiped my forehead. "Come on." I sprinted off, knowing it would only be seconds before he caught up.

And as I thought, Logan overtook me less than five seconds later. I hated that I let myself get so unfit. "You okay?" he asked, turning left at the Post Office instead of right. We had two main routes we would run and both involved turning right.

"Yeah," I replied breathlessly. "Where are we going?"

"Scenic route, lots of trees, more shade for you so you don't *die a slow and painful death, burning in the blistering heat of the ridiculous sun*." He laughed as he repeated my words from a few days ago. The midday sun had been incredibly hot that day, shining right down on us.

I laughed, too, and pushed his shoulder, making him stumble to the side. Logan was probably the only person who could have made me do normal things again, although I was beginning to regret asking him to train me again.

We ran, Logan gracefully, and me less so. My lungs

started to burn long before they used to, another sign of how unfit I'd become over the last few years. Getting my fitness back was another step towards getting the old Chloe back.

I turned left and heard Logan stop and then follow my new direction. He'd intended to go straight ahead but I was pulled through the gates.

The hairs on the back of my neck stood up as his head stone came into view.

It had been three years and six days since he died, and I still missed him every day. We had been together for two and a half years before he was taken from me. Jace was my first and only love. We were close – annoyingly close if you asked my best friend, Nell – even though we had absolutely nothing in common.

Logan smacked straight into my back, his arms shooting out to stop me from being thrown to the floor. I gasped as the air was knocked out of my lungs. "Don't just stop!" he cried, chuckling in amusement. Then he stopped laughing, and I knew he'd seen it, too, his younger brother's grave. "Sorry, Chlo, I should've taken one of our usual routes."

I rolled my eyes at him and swatted his arm. It had been a while since I'd broke down over his death. I felt both relief and guilt for that. "I'm fine coming here, you know I am."

"Yeah, I know," he muttered under his breath, looking over to Jace. I'd always got along well with Logan, at twenty-two he was just two years older than me and Jace.

Logan and I liked a lot of the same things, like keeping fit, which was why we started exercising together. Logan was a personal trainer at a small but posh and expensive gym so he'd also helped me plan an exercise regime to stay in shape.

"Do you want to go over?" I asked. Logan didn't come often. He always said he hated the thought of Jace being stuck underground, cold and motionless. I used to come all the time but now it was only a couple times a month. I loved Jace but he was gone, and I had a chance at a new life. It wasn't the one I thought I would have but that didn't mean it couldn't be great.

A shallow crease formed between his eyebrows as he frowned slightly, thinking about it. The few times he'd been here I was with him. "Alright," he responded. It took him a minute to move. I stood still, knowing he should be the one to make the first move if he really wanted to. He walked slowly.

"Logan, if you really don't want to…"

"No, it's fine," he replied, stopping about three feet from the grave.

"Hi, Jace," I said, sitting down and pulling a stray weed from the ground above him.

It had been just over three years since he went on a trip with his college class to London to look at architecture. It was just over three years that the bomb went off and killed him, his whole class and fifty-four other people.

The whole thing was senseless. A hate group of two, brothers Richard and Alexander Gregson, that didn't like a Mosque being built so they bombed it. They killed more British people than anyone else. No one won in terrorism. There was only ever loss.

Out of the corner of my eye, I saw Logan frowning. "Do you want to leave?" I asked. I didn't want him to be here if he was uncomfortable. Just because Jace was here didn't mean this was the only place to be close to him.

Logan shook his head and lowered himself to the floor. He grabbed my hand and held it in a death grip. "I hate this. He should be upstairs continuing to waste his life on his Xbox."

I laughed and nodded. "Yeah, he loved that stupid thing." Jace was a gamer. He could play for hours, easily all day if I wasn't over. I never understood how anyone could do that. It was so flat and dull. I preferred to be outside with the natural smells, sounds and all things three-dimensional.

"He loved you more."

"You think? I mean, he did buy it more accessories than me," I joked, bumping my shoulder against his.

Logan chuckled and shook his head. His deep topaz eyes lit up when he laughed. "He pissed so much money away on it. I think he had a delivery every week of some new part or game." He shook his head. "I miss the fucking idiot."

"Me too."

"You're okay, though?" he asked.

"I really am now. Does that make me a bad person?"

"No, it makes you human. It happens, right?"

"Death?"

He nodded. "Can't escape it and if you're the one left behind you have to carry on."

"Yeah." It was true. The world didn't stop. I wanted it to for so long and with every new day I wanted to scream, but now I looked forward to it. I wanted to get up and achieve something, and I wanted to be happy again. "Wow, this is depressing."

"It is. Wanna carry on?" he asked, tapping his fingers against his knee, impatient and eager to get away.

I stood up and it came as no surprise when he jumped to his feet. "Come on, I'll give you a head start so you have a chance this time," I teased.

"Oh you think *I* need a head start, Miss *I need to rest for a minute*," he said in what was supposed to be my voice.

"Firstly, I don't sound like that. Secondly, I needed to stop *once*. One time, Logan, and that was ages ago."

"It was four years ago," he said and shrugged.

I stared at him. "That you remember, but your mum's birthday…"

"Okay," he shouted loudly, holding his hands up. "I get that enough from her. In my defence, I knew the date it was just the month I got mixed up. They both begin with a J."

"Good argument," I said sarcastically.

"You wanna stay here and argue some more or can we

move it along?"

"We can move it along."

"Good, move your tiny arse then!"

Whoa. "Tiny?"

"No, it's not tiny, tiny. Not big either. I'm not saying it's big *at all*, I swear," he rambled, looking like a rabbit caught in the headlights. I knew exactly what he meant but I *really* enjoyed making him squirm. He swung his arm around my neck as I started laughing. "Wasn't funny, loser," he whispered in my ear, trying not to laugh himself.

"Yes, it was. Admit it." I pushed him away, still laughing, blew Jace a kiss and ran off towards his house. I didn't look back.

***

"Have I ever told you that I hate you?" I said, breathing heavily, bending over and leaning against my knees as we got back to his house. Why didn't I just go shopping with Nell? It was a Saturday and I was torturing myself by letting Logan train me.

Exercise always made me feel good after but before and during it was my enemy. I honestly didn't know how Logan could do it all day and train other people too.

"Frequently," he muttered dryly. "In fact, the last time before today was a week ago, you know, when I threw water on you?"

I narrowed my eyes at him. "That was *not* funny." When his mum had asked him to wake me up I doubt that was what she had meant.

Jace and I spent most nights together at his house, and I couldn't bring myself to stop that little routine. Since I got out of my hermit state, I'd slept in Jace's room more than my own and his family had no issue with it at all. It was all I had left of him, but I knew I would have to give it up eventually, and I wanted to.

Logan grinned wide, the shallow scar just below his bottom lip from when he flew over his bike's handlebars disappeared, the way it always did when the skin was stretched. "It was."

"I need water, to *drink*."

Logan waved his water bottle out in front of me, eyebrow raised and mouth curved, smug. "I keep telling you that you should take water with you when we run." He did tell me that, *all* the time. Logan did everything properly when it came to exercise, even when he wasn't at the gym and even though I wasn't a paying client.

"Shut up and give me that." I grabbed it out of his hand and drained the remainder of the bottle.

"Right, the usual stretches to cool down and then you're done." I groaned and followed him to the back garden to die again.

"Do you think I should take it slower since I've been out of action a while?" We worked out together three times a week when Jace was alive but I stopped doing it when he died.

"Nice try but you're doing fine now. I don't think you should slow down on anything."

"Why do I get the feeling there's a double meaning there?"

He looked away. "There is. I've spoken to Cassie."

Siblings were supposed to fight, not talk! "You think I should move on?"

"It's been three years, Chlo, you deserve to. You want to, don't you?"

"Yeah. I'm ready."

He smiled. "Good. Now, smoothie?"

"Oh, definitely," I replied, my mouth watering at the thought. Logan always made his famous strawberry and banana smoothies after a workout. That was my favourite part of our routine and made it worth the pain.

CHAPTER TWO

Chloe

"How was the run, crazies?" Cassie asked. Like with the rest of the family, I got along really well with her, too, she was like a sister. She didn't like exercise though, the same as Jace, so they always let us get on with it and would make faces when we returned.

I groaned. "Good-ish." She shook her head, looking at me as if I were actually crazy. I think the last time she had done anything sporty was when she was at school, nine years ago.

Cassie looked very much like Logan with the same colour blue eyes and dark blonde hair. Hers was dead straight and just below her shoulders but she often shoved mousse in it to make it do something. She was just a little taller than me but then most of the people in my circle were.

"You two want Chinese?" she asked, glancing at the Golden King Chinese menu in front of her.

Logan raised his eyebrows at her. "Cass, it's half past four in the afternoon." Usually, his mum would serve dinner at half past six every night but it was the anniversary of their first date so Daryl was taking Julia to some posh hotel in the city. They deserved to celebrate after being together for thirty years.

"Yeah?" she questioned, staring at her younger brother blankly, waiting for a good explanation as to why she couldn't have Chinese so early. "And?"

"Nothing. Never mind."

"If you think I'm playing mum just because they're away, you are seriously mistaken. Now, what do you two want? Chlo, you're staying, right?"

"Yes, thanks. My usual?" Cassie nodded and scribbled down my order on a scrap piece of paper.

My house was too quiet. Since my parents set up a car rental place four years ago they had spent most of their time at work, leaving me at home. I was plenty old enough to take care of myself but I now found the silence suffocating.

Logan reeled off a list of what he wanted and went off to have a shower.

I sat down opposite Cassie on the kitchen stool and waited for the inevitable Jace conversation. "So, how's everything going?" I asked, trying to steer things into her life rather than mine.

Cassie thought that hanging on to Jace was unhealthy. The problem I had was I didn't quite know how to live my new life without him. We'd spent years practically glued to each other's side. It was hard to fully let go of my old life.

She sighed and it was then that I noticed how tired she looked. She'd been having a shit time too. "Okay, I guess. Hopefully the divorce will be sorted soon and the house will sell. Then I can move on."

Cassie and her bastard husband, Rick, had recently separated so she was living back with her parents. Arsehole-Rick's new slut girlfriend keeps contacting her to whine about how long the divorce papers were taking, like it was Cassie's fault.

"I just want it over now. It's hard moving back in with your parents, you know? Especially living with Logan again!"

"Yeah, he can be a pain."

"It's good to see you so much again, though."

I frowned. *So much?* "Do I stay here *too* much?"

Cassie laughed and shook her head. "No. Not enough, actually. We love having you here. You're part of the family, you know that."

I let out a sigh of relief. I did still hang at theirs a lot but I didn't want to if they thought it was too much. Part of me felt like, because I was moving on I shouldn't be here, but they were family to me, and I didn't ever want to give that up. Cassie said I was part of the family, and I felt like it, too, but technically, I wasn't anymore. I just hoped that when I eventually found someone else they wouldn't think any differently of me.

"Thanks, Cassie."

"What's new with you anyway?"

"Hmm, not a lot. Some guy at work asked me out, but I'm not going." He was nice and very good-looking but it didn't feel right, I think.

"Why not?" I shrugged. "Chloe, it's been ages and you said yourself you *want* to move forward. You can date whenever you like, there's no set time you have to wait before you can be happy again."

I squirmed on the seat. "Yeah, I know. I do feel ready to date again but…"

"But," she prompted.

"I'm not sure."

"Well, there's no rush but why not just go for a drink? Something casual. You don't have to marry the guy." I smiled, chewing on my lip. Maybe she was right. It was only a date; I wasn't committing myself to anything.

"Doesn't have to marry who?" Logan questioned, suddenly appearing back in the kitchen. He rubbed a hand towel over his short, dark blonde hair.

"Chloe's got a date."

My heart stopped as I waited for Logan's reaction. I had

spoken to Cassie and Julia in depth about new guys, but not Logan. I could talk to Logan about absolutely everything else but he was close to Jace – they were more like twins – so it felt weird.

He frowned and turned his intense gaze to me. "With who?" It was a simple question but it felt like the Spanish inquisition.

"Um, Rhys from work."

I felt like a child waiting for its parents' permission to do something. What if Logan hated me for it? Would he see it as me betraying his brother? But he wouldn't expect me to be alone forever, surely? He smiled tightly.

"Have a good time." *That's it?* "You ordered yet?" he asked Cassie, turning away from me.

"About to. Will probably be about half an hour."

Logan nodded and grabbed a beer from the fridge, while I sat frozen, trying to figure out what his response really meant. Why did it bother me so much anyway? Well, because he brought me back to life after Jace died, that was why. Logan meant so much to me. I hated the thought that he could be angry with me.

I watched silently as Logan popped the top off the beer and took a long swig. What the hell was going on in his head? He then put it down and got two wine glasses from the cupboard. "Are you staying overnight, Chlo?" He started pouring the wine without waiting for my response. *Looks like it.*

"Yeah, thanks." He put the glass of rosé down and sat opposite me. Awkward. It had never been awkward between us before. With Jace it was at first but with Logan there was no pressure. I was just his little brother's friend and then girlfriend, so we hit it off straight away. I had no preparation for awkwardness with Logan. Usually, if I knew I was meeting people I would think of a few random things to ask, but I had nothing here.

If Cassie wasn't in the room, I would have made and

excuse and gone home. "I'm starting spinning," Cassie announced. *Okay*...

"You don't do *any* exercise, Cass, you should start with something less physical," Logan advised. "Spinning is pretty full on."

Cassie nodded. "I know. I want full on." Oh, this was about Rick. She wanted to take her mind off everything that was going on. I went the opposite way when Jace died, there were no distractions that could have worked. I became a hermit and just existed. "Wanna come, Chloe?"

"Sure." I'd been spinning before and it was complete hell but it worked. Logan was right though, someone who wasn't used to exercise really shouldn't start with that. "Your legs are going to *kill* you. You sure you want to go straight in with spinning?"

"I'm sure. I'll call tomorrow and book it for next Sunday."

Logan smirked. "I'm *so* glad I'm working that night."

"Oh, shut up! I'll be fine, Mr Muscles," she teased, throwing a plastic lemon at Logan from the *for show* fruit bowl. She was so not going to be fine.

***

The second Cass left with her wine, I turned to Logan. He had a bottle of beer in each hand and smiled innocently when I spotted them. I needed to talk to him about Rhys and clear the air, but I was nervous. My heart rate increased, and I had butterflies. "Logan?" I said quickly before I could back out.

He turned to me. "Yeah."

"Earlier, when I told you about Rhys…"

"What about it?" he responded. *Poker face.* I hated when he showed nothing, he was so good at it. Usually, I could tell what Logan was thinking from his expression but when he shut down he was a complete mystery.

Chewing on the side of my mouth, I turned my whole

body so I was facing him. "You acted… strange. I didn't expect that."

"I acted strange?"

"Logan, stop. Please, just tell me what you're thinking."

He shrugged with one shoulder, not even bothering to put the effort in for a full shrug. "You can do what you want, Chloe. You're a big girl now."

"Don't be like that. Do you think it's too soon? Do you think I should wait longer? It's not that I don't still love Jace because I do. I just want to be happy again. I'm ready to move on but I don't want to hurt you or piss you off if you think I shouldn't—"

"Chloe," he cut in. I took a breath. Maybe I went overboard but I opened my mouth and it all poured out. He sighed and put his arm around my shoulder. "I don't think it's too soon. I'm sorry I was a dick earlier. Go on the date if it's what will make you happy." He wrapped his other arm around me, holding me tight. "I just want you to be happy."

"Thank you. I think I'll go. Can't hurt to have a drink or something, can it?"

He pulled back and smiled. "No, can't hurt at all."

CHAPTER THREE

Chloe

"Thank you," I whispered and laid my head on his shoulder. Thank goodness that was sorted out. I hated the thought that Logan would be hurt or disappointed because of something I'd done. We were too close now. Besides my parents and Cass, he was the most important person in my life and the sole reason I wasn't still hiding out in my room between work and university.

"Anytime. I am going to check this guy out, though. You said he works with you, right? Do I know him?"

"Logan," I groaned. "I'm twenty years old. I think I can take care of myself now."

"I know you can." I sighed in relief. Logan quizzing Rhys would be really awkward. "I'm still doing it, Chlo. I don't want you to get hurt, you've been hurt enough."

Okay, that was sweet. "It's a completely different thing. If anything happened with Rhys and he broke it off it wouldn't be on the same level as losing Jace."

"I don't care. I was there when you cried so much you were sick. I don't ever want to see you cry again and if that fucker thinks he can just play around and use you, I'll ball his eyes out with a spoon."

I laughed. What was that? "Ah, she laughs. Your face is hilarious by the way, sweetheart. I meant it, though. I don't want you to get hurt again. That was hard to watch."

It was hard to go through.

"I don't want that either. I'm not going to rush into anything or do anything stupid. It's just one drink to see how it goes."

He nodded once. "And you like him?"

"He's a nice guy, but I don't know if I like him in any way other than a work colleague, sort of friend. Hence the drink."

"When are you next working?"

I narrowed my eyes. "I'm working Monday morning."

"And Rex?"

"Rhys," I corrected.

"Whatever."

Laughing, I rolled my eyes. "Monday as well."

"I might be thirsty on Monday."

I swept my long hair out of my face. *What a surprise!* "I have no doubt you will." Christ, he was acting like my brother. Was that what he was trying to be? No. We weren't like siblings. Not once had I ever seen Logan as a brother.

"Hey, I just want to make sure the guy isn't a prick."

"He's not. I wouldn't even consider going out with him if he was, but thanks for looking out for me, as always."

He was always there. I'd always been able to talk to him about absolutely anything. Even when Jace was alive I went to Logan more, not that I didn't tell Jace my problems, I did, but Logan was able to look at situations logically and find solutions quickly. Until Jace died and he didn't have any answers anymore, not for himself or me, not until he saw me disappearing in grief and loneliness.

"I thought you'd tell me to stop stressing over it and let you make your own decisions. What've you done with Chloe?"

"Funny. You do stress about me, far too much. I'm

okay, Logan. You need to concentrate on you now."

"What's wrong with me? I think I'm pretty close to perfection." He frowned and pouted his lip adorably.

Deflecting, always deflecting and making everything seem okay. Truth was, he was still a little lost. Logan had all these plans for the future, too. He should be in his own place by now but Jace's death had taken over his life for a while as well. Now Logan had a big hole where his savings used to be and he was stuck at home until his bank balance looked healthier.

"You're alright, I guess," I said, turning my nose up. Logan *was* pretty perfect, as much as a person could be anyway. He was loyal and if he loved a person there was nothing he wouldn't do for them. If it wasn't for him I don't know what I would be like now. Probably still curled up in bed, stuck grieving a life I'd never have.

"Fuck off, you love me."

I hugged him because I did love him. "You know I do and that's why I'm going to be as annoying about you achieving your goals as you are about me achieving mine."

"Oh, good," he said sarcastically. "Seriously, I don't need saving. I'm fine, will be back on track soon."

"Uh huh. So the girl at the gym the other day wasn't pissed at you because you'd slept with her and ditched her?"

He held his hand up. "That happened months ago. I'm laying off women for a while, you know this."

"I do. I just worry that while you're so busy pushing me and holding Cassie together you're going to relapse." It was only six months ago that he was drinking himself stupid and sleeping with anything that crossed his path. I'd forced him to a sexual health clinic once – thankfully, he hadn't caught anything – and was not keen to repeat the experience.

"Not gonna happen, sweetheart. I have no desire to wake up feeling like I've been run over or worrying who the fuck is next to me ever again. I can keep myself on the straight and narrow."

"Promise me."

"I promise," he said.

"Okay. And you'll come to me if you ever need to talk, right?"

He smiled tightly. Logan wasn't a *load his problems onto someone else* person. It was one of the things I loved about him, but it frustrated me to no end. I wanted to be to him what he was to me. I wanted him to know he could rely on me for anything and to get him through anything.

"Sure. Now we gonna eat so much Chinese food we need to run an extra fifty miles tomorrow, or what?"

"Yes to stuffing our faces, no to running more. I'll deal with the extra pound. You should still run though, you're looking a little fat," I joked, poking his very toned, very not fat chest. Practically the entire female race converted to the Church of Gym when they saw Logan's body. Male fitness was a religion I really could get on board with.

"You wound me," he said, smirking and bumping my shoulder with his.

CHAPTER FOUR

Logan

"Chlo, really?" I couldn't help but laugh as she lay starfished out on the gym floor.

She groaned and covered her eyes with her arm. "Oh God, my legs hurt so bad. I hate you. I really... just... *hate* you."

I smiled wider. "You wanted to get back into shape."

Not that there had ever been anything wrong with her shape, not at all. Her legs were perfectly toned and the object of many, many of my fantasies. She had a tiny little waist that was begging my tongue to trace every inch of it. Or maybe it was my tongue begging for it. Either way, she was fucking perfect and I wanted her so badly I had to take at least one ice cold shower every damn day.

"I take it back. A toned body is so overrated. No more, Logan. If you so much as want me to look at a cross trainer I *will* kill you."

"Well," I said and clapped my hands, "it's good that you're not overreacting."

"You don't understand the pain."

I did. I understood perfectly and she knew that but she did like to get a little dramatic. It was cute and just another thing to add to the list of *Things Logan Adores About Chloe*.

The list was long, and I was going to hell.

When Jace died I either worked out until my muscles screamed in pain or drank until my liver did. Chloe brought me back without knowing it at the time and stopped me fathering about seventy kids, too, I imagine. If I kept on the way I was going – whisky and women – I would be dishing out thousands in child support by now. The alcohol relieved the guilt but since I'd given it up – mostly – I felt like a proper bastard every second of the day.

"You want to hit the shower, then go home?"

"No. I want to lay here until I can feel my legs again. Possibly until morning."

"People are looking at you."

She shrugged one shoulder lazily. "Right now I don't care if they're dancing around me singing Kumbaya."

I laughed, staring down at her and trying to keep my eyes off her cleavage and that sexy gap between her legs. "If you don't get up I'll sing Kumbaya."

"So? You have a nice voice, that won't get me up."

She was being impossible. "I'll pick you up, strip you and chuck you in the shower if I have to."

And I would like that very, very much.

I held my breath as I waited for a reply. If she told me to I would. There was no fucking way if she asked me to strip her down to her birthday suit and get her all wet I would be able to resist. I was the lowest of the low.

Brother's girl. Brother's fucking girl.

"You can carry me to the changing rooms but I'm pretty sure you'll get fired if you come in."

I literally don't care.

"Fine," I huffed, pretending to be annoyed. Reaching down, I scooped her into my arms and carried her to the ladies' changing room.

My supervisor didn't bat an eyelid as I walked past, probably because I'd worked here forever and had covered his arse when he was off screwing the January women. Most people felt down in January, Christmas was over and it was still freezing. January brought women that wanted to get fit – for what usually lasted one to two months tops. January was Patrick's Christmas.

I put her down outside the door and she groaned as her feet touched the floor. The sound was almost erotic and alongside the mental image of her naked in the shower, I was not doing well to keep my hormones in check.

"Gotta shower, too," I said and got the hell out of there as fast as I could. Today's cold shower was going to be lot earlier than usual.

***

I met Chloe by my car. She was curled up *on* the bonnet. "Good thing you weigh nothing," I said, unlocking the doors.

"If you ever suggest a heavy workout again…"

Holding my hands up, I replied, "Got it. You used to do that all the time, Chlo."

"I used to be fit."

You've always been fit.

"You'll get there again."

She flicked her hand in my direction. "Especially with the drill sergeant training me."

"Hey, *you* asked for this."

"Yeah, nice one, Chloe," she muttered. "Can we go back to yours and not move off the sofa until Cass feeds us?"

"Sounds like a plan to me."

"And I'll need a smoothie," she said, rolling off my car onto her feet. "And a blanket."

"Wow, you're going to milk this all day, aren't you?"

"Yes."

I drove us back to mine and took photos of Chlo hobbling to the door like a little old lady, earning me a slap on the chest and the second death threat of the day.

"Chloe, are you okay?" Mum asked her.

I rolled my eyes. *Here we go...*

"No. Logan is evil."

Mum smiled. "Oh, you've just been to the gym."

"Gym, hell, it's all the same," Chloe replied and sank down on the sofa.

"She's handling it really well," I said sarcastically. "Banana and strawberry or cherry and kiwi?"

"Banana and strawberry, please."

Mum followed me into the kitchen.

"It's good she's getting back into fitness."

"Yeah, it is."

"It's because of you, you know."

I carried on shoving the strawberries in the blender. "What?"

"You brought her back."

I smiled up at Mum. "I owed her one."

"Oh, come on, Logan. No need to play it down. That girl is happy again because you wouldn't let her wallow anymore. I'm proud of you."

Yeah, well, I love her so I don't really have a choice. I needed her to be okay. Jace would have needed her to be okay.

"Thanks," I said, peeling a banana. "Something had to change or Chloe was going to waste her life away hiding at home and I was going to die of alcohol poisoning."

"I was so worried about you, Logan. Your dad, too."

"I'm sorry. I shouldn't have put you both through that. It's just... the guilt..."

"I understand. It's all worked out for the best now. I've got my son and my surrogate daughter back." I would've preferred daughter-in-law.

"Yeah, things are good." They had been for a few months now. Finally. Well, apart from her wanting to see other guys. I wanted her to be happy and not drown in depression from missing Jace, but I didn't want her to be with anyone but me.

If Jace didn't hate me for the last things I'd said to him he had every right to for how I felt about Chloe. Only I knew he wouldn't. He loved me and her and if it couldn't be him he'd want it to be me. If it was the other way around I'd want the woman I loved to be with a person I trusted with my life. It was hard to detach that knowledge from the guilt of wanting his girl, though.

"Smoothie?" I asked.

"No, thanks, love. What's next for you then?"

Ah, I loved that question when I was so far away from reaching my goals. It was like a little kick in the balls every time someone asked.

"Save money. Buy a house. You want me out soon or something?" I drank a lot of my savings after Jace died. All I cared about was going out and getting so drunk I didn't remember my brother had died, I'd been a dick to him and wanted to kiss his girlfriend.

"Of course not. This is your home and you'll always be welcome here, same as Cassie. I just like to know what's going on in my son's head."

God, she did not want to know that. Truth was, she probably knew already. Not once had she ever said anything about me having feelings for Chloe but there had been looks. Looks that made me want to bash my head against the wall. She knew. I wasn't sure if it was a good thing that she never questioned me on it.

I flicked the blender on and watched for the perfect consistency. Mum didn't leave and I was starting to feel a bit awkward.

"Work okay?"

I turned the blender off. "Spit it out, Mum."

Sighing, she sat down on the stool. "Are you really okay?"

"I'm fine."

"Chloe mentioned she might have a date."

"Yeah, she does have a date. Rhys from work. I'm gonna check him out with Ollie tomorrow, make sure he's alright."

"It's going to be strange, isn't it?"

"Seeing her with someone that isn't Jace?"

"Yes. They came as a package for so long."

I poured the smoothie into a tall glass, contemplating smashing it over my head. "Yeah, they did."

"Do you think she'll still come here?"

Oh, that's what's wrong. Chloe was like a daughter to her and she didn't want to lose her, too.

"I don't think we're ever getting rid of that girl." Mostly because I would never let her leave. Like a deranged stalker I would keep her in our lives.

Mum smiled, seemingly satisfied by my answer. "Yes, good. Things were awful without her."

I could barely remember, but when I was sober I know I'd missed her. Then I drank more because I felt even guiltier.

Mum followed me back into the living room and sat in her chair by the window.

"Back in the gym tomorrow, Chloe?" she asked.

Chlo laughed. "Not a chance."

I handed her the smoothie and received one of her heart-stopping smiles that I would do anything for. "Come on, you'll seize up if you don't continue."

"Logan, my muscles feel like they're on fire. I can barely walk. The only exercise I'll be doing tomorrow is lifting the TV remote." She laughed then. "Okay, I sound like Jace."

I loved that she could laugh when she spoke about him now. We all could. It was such a huge difference to crying, drinking, hiding, pretending it hadn't happened and screaming. We all dealt with it in different ways.

"You do. You know every time you and Logan went on a run or to the gym he'd call you both crazy, grab a snack and sit down in front of the TV."

"The little… He told me he was doing college work," Chloe said. "I should've known really."

I kicked my feet up on the coffee table. "I think he was allergic to exercise. He should've been fat, eating junk all the time and laying around the house."

"That was probably all down to Chloe," Mum said, wiggling her eyebrows.

I tried to keep a straight face as my lunch came back up to meet my throat. It bothered me back then and it still did. She was always supposed to be with me and if I hadn't been such a dick trying to deny it I could've told Jace that I liked her and he never would have gone there. I didn't, so he did and then all I could do was keep my mouth shut and let my brother be happy.

Chloe blushed and laughed along with Mum. I knew if I forced out a laugh it'd sound wrong so I kept quiet. He was my brother after all so I could get away with thinking that was gross.

Dad hopped over the arm of the sofa and sat beside Mum. "Me and Daryl have been speaking and we'd like to do something for his birthday."

The last two birthdays were hell. It'd be good to do something that would honour his memory.

"That sounds really nice," Chlo said. "What were you thinking?"

"London," she replied.

I frowned. Why the fuck would we visit the city where he died for his birthday? Then I got it. "Right. The architecture." Mum nodded. Jace loved big, fancy buildings and wanted to do something in that line of work when he was older. It was also what killed him. If he hadn't been on that stupid fucking college trip he would still be here today.

Chloe nodded. "He wanted to go for a week, do the tourist bit and take pictures of the architecture. We planned to go after uni."

Mum reached over and squeezed her hand as if she expected Chlo to fall apart. She really was okay now. I was so fucking proud of how far she'd come and how she handled Jace's death.

"We'll go for the weekend and do what he wanted. He mentioned a few places."

"He has a list. We planned the trip quite thoroughly. Well, he did, I just wanted to go to Madam Tussauds and have a photo with David Beckham," Chlo said. "I have the list at home."

I threw my arm over the back of the sofa. "I'm sure we can find time to take you to the creepy wax place." I'd actually love to take her there. There weren't many things I could do with her that she hadn't already done with Jace, especially as friends. I bet there was a whole load of things I could do with and to her that she hadn't done with him if we were more than friends.

"Of course," Mum said, forcing me back to reality and away from the place in my mind where Chloe was handcuffed to my bed, naked. "We can go on the London Eye, too."

Cassie walked into the room and snorted. "I'll wait for you guys at the bottom."

Big fucking baby.

"So you'll all come?" Mum asked. "I understand that it's an odd choice but I'd really like to do something that was important to him."

We agreed, of course, and Mum started to tear up.

"See, Julia, there was no way they wouldn't want to do this for him, too. You were fretting over nothing, love," Dad said, giving her a side hug.

Yeah, it was going to be... great...?

CHAPTER FIVE

Logan

"So we're cock blocking this Rhys guy?" Oliver asked, sitting on a stool in Sam's Bar and Grill where Chloe worked. I'd known Ollie since we were in high school and hit it off straight away, neither of us responded well to authority and we both hated pretty much every subject.

"Not cock blocking," I replied.

It was. I didn't just want to cock block I wanted to castrate. The thought of that prick anywhere near her made me fucking violent. Chlo wasn't mine, we weren't together, but in my heart she'd been mine since the second I laid eyes on her. Therefore, I wanted to be around to make sure he didn't come within three feet of her.

He shoved his fingers though his dark hair, pushing it to the side over his even darker eyes. "Sure, man."

"Shut up, Ollie," I snapped, earning a toothy grin from the twat.

Chloe came from the back and leant on the other side of the bar. Her long chestnut hair was pulled back and messy. She wore her uniform shirt and never looked so pissing beautiful.

"Thirsty?" she asked, tilting her head and smirking.

I leant in a little closer. "Beer, please."

She frowned. "Logan, it's quarter to ten in the morning. Take a seat. I'll bring you both coffee and a fry up."

"You're the best, Chloe," Ollie said, pushing off the bar and heading for a table.

"Where's this guy then?" I asked.

"He'll be in at ten," she replied. "Be. Nice."

Backing up, I made a cross over my heart. "Always." With one last look at her amber eyes, I followed Oliver to the table he'd picked.

Ollie tapped his fingers on the table. "She's a good girl, huh?"

I leant back in the chair, stretching my legs out. "Yeah." Me and Chlo had always go on. Jace was punching well above his weight but I was glad it was her because compared to the rough, bunny boiler thing he was with before, Chloe was a fucking diamond. We liked most of the same things. She was the girl version of me, only smarter, gorgeous and full of ridiculous, female, unpredictable hormones.

"What's the story there, man? Don't give me this friend shit either."

"We are friends."

Ollie was hard to bullshit so I held eye contact and hoped the little bastard accepted my reply.

He gave one lazy shrug of his shoulder. "As long as you're telling yourself the truth."

Cocky wanker!

Chloe picked the moment I almost reached over the table to punch Ollie to bring us coffee. "Thanks, Chlo," I said, making quick eye contact.

"Yeah, thanks, Chlo," Ollie said.

She looked up as someone walked through the door. The stupid smile on his ugly mug made me realise he was *him*. I knew of him but had never had a conversation past giving him my order. Had she already accepted a date? "That him?" I said.

"Be nice," she replied.

"I'm always nice."

"Logan!"

"I haven't done anything."

Damn, she knew me well.

Sighing, she straightened her back. "Your food will be about five minutes. Let me know if you want a refill."

Ollie leant in the second she was gone. "What're you gonna do about the guy then?"

"Nothing. Why would I do anything?"

"Fucking hell, Logan, come on! I'm not stupid. You know how you feel, I know how you feel, you know I know how you feel."

"I think I've got a headache."

"Stop diverting. You like her."

"She's Jace's girl."

"Was, man. Look, I'm sorry, I don't mean for that to sound harsh but Jace is gone and you two are still here."

I rubbed my eyebrow. "Do you know how shitty of me that'd be?"

"No. It'd be shitty if he was still here and you stole her away. What's happening here is nothing like that."

"He's my brother." There were lines you just shouldn't cross and as much as I wanted her I couldn't go there.

"I know who he is and I know how much he loved you and her. If you guys have a chance of being happy – and with a chick like that, man, whoa – he'd want that too."

The logical part of me agreed. Jace was a good person, he wanted the people he loved to be happy, he never judged, but I couldn't help bringing it back to the sacred, unwritten guy rules: thou shall not screw a brother's girl.

"Hmm," I muttered, hoping he'd change the subject.

"You're a proper stubborn twat, Logan."

"Cheers, *mate*."

Sighing harshly, Ollie stuck his middle finger up. "You're being a dick. I don't understand why you don't just ask her out."

"You had a recent head injury?"

"C'mon, you know what I mean."

"Okay. One, and I'm getting sick of saying this one now, she was with my brother. And two, I don't even know if she'd want to."

"That's what's really bothering you. You know Jace would want it to be you. You're worried she'll turn you down and you'll be left eating ice cream from the tub and watching *Pretty Woman*."

There wasn't much chance of that happening anyway; I was the pickle your liver type. "Fine. I don't want to hear her tell me she only sees me as a friend. I don't want to see the look of disgust in her eye when she realises her ex's brother wants her."

"You're gonna die alone, man."

"Chlo isn't the only woman in the world." That was a shit argument. She wasn't the only woman but the only one I wanted, so I was definitely headed for living alone with rats or snakes.

He shrugged. "You can come to mine at Christmas."

"I am not going to fucking die alone!"

Chloe put two plates piled high with greasy food down on the table. "Why would you die alone?" she asked, grinning.

"He's a whore," Ollie said.

I wanted to shove him off the fucking seat. *Was* a whore.

"He's changed," Chlo said. "Right?"

I frowned. "Right." There was nothing I wanted less than to go back to being drunk constantly and screwing random women. I could deal with the guilt without needing something to take the edge off now.

"See. He won't die alone and, anyway, I'd buy you cats if—"

I lurched forwards and she jumped back laughing. "Kidding," she said, holding her hands up. "Eat your food before it gets cold or someone notices I put extra sausages and bacon on the plates."

She left us to it and Ollie stared at me, one eyebrow raised in an obnoxious way that made me punch him. "What?" I growled.

"She's the perfect woman. If you don't ask her out I will." He wouldn't and we both knew it. Still, I kicked him pretty hard under the table, making him laugh.

Out of the corner of my eye I could see Chloe and Rhys talking at the bar. Laughing, she was laughing. He didn't look like he could do funny; he looked like a bit of a prick. Chlo arched forwards slightly, twisting her body to face him more. She was flirting. *Why is she flirting?*

I was having a hard time keeping my food down. I understood that she was ready to move on and I was all for that, she deserved it, but I didn't like it one bit. As well as I knew it shouldn't be me she moved on with, I couldn't help wanting it with every fucking ounce of my being.

"You're staring," Ollie said all too casually, between mouthfuls.

"I was not staring." Shovelling another rasher of bacon in whole, I made myself concentrate on my food and Ollie. He would love it if looked over there again. I'd hoped that by ignoring them behind me I'd forget about it, but although I couldn't see them I knew they were there. Was he touching her hand? Her arm? Did she put her hand on his scrawny little chest?

Even I was aware that I was stabbing my food as if it was alive and I had to murder it first but I was too pissed.

Ollie's hand gripped my wrist. "You wanna calm the fuck down?"

"No, I'm fine."

"You're fine with her and him then?"

I smiled tightly. "Of course."

"That's good because he's kissing her."

"Fuck," I hissed under my breath, snapping my head

around so quick I pulled a muscle. My hands clenched with rage. How fucking dare he touch her?

Only he wasn't. She'd disappeared somewhere out the back and he was taking money for drinks he'd just made.

Behind me Ollie laughed, proud. "I'm going to rip your head off!"

He laughed more.

"Hey, at least now I know how much you like her."

"I violently dislike you, you twat."

"And you're a pussy. This is why we get on."

"We don't get on," I said, taking a big gulp of my coffee. I was still wound pretty tightly after thinking she was kissing that guy. One day she was going to kiss someone else and there wouldn't be anything I could do about it. I wanted to tell her how I felt but how could I be *that* person?

"Excuse me," Ollie said, lifting a hand to the bar.

"What're you doing?" I asked.

His only reply was an unsettling smile just as date twat stopped at our table. If he said one thing about Chloe I was gong to strangle the fucker.

"What can I help you with?" he asked. I had about a dozen answers for that question.

"Could we get some more coffee, please?"

Little prick.

"Yeah, sure thing," he replied.

"I've got it, Rhys," Chloe said, coffee pot in one hand and taking Ollie's mug with the other.

I got the disgusting full force of them together, sides touching as he hadn't fucked off yet. It left a bad taste in my mouth.

"So you've asked her out then?" I said.

Chloe froze mid pour and her eyes widened. Yeah, it was my turn to be the prick. I hated myself the second the words left my mouth. I shouldn't be interfering with this. He might make her happy. All I'd ever wanted was to see her smiling and laughing. Well, that wasn't exactly true, I wanted to see her smile at me the way she used to at Jace.

Date twat looked like a rabbit caught in the headlights for about five seconds and then he nodded. "Yeah, I have. Not got an answer yet, though." He turned to her and smiled.

She was embarrassed and I was in trouble.

Turning her attention to *him*, she smiled. "I know, sorry. I'd love to go out sometime."

And just like that my heart felt as dead as the day I saw her first kissing my brother.

CHAPTER SIX

Chloe

Me and Cass walked into the gym and I said hello to a few of Logan's colleagues that I knew.

"You really do come here a lot, don't you?" Cass said.

I flexed the teeny, tiny almost non-existent muscles in my arms. "Yep."

She smirked. "It doesn't seem to be doing anything."

"I don't come to lift weights and bulk up, I do cardio to keep fit. Your brother is the one lifting stupidly heavy stuff."

"I don't understand how he's not body builder big," she said.

"Duh, because he's not a body builder." Logan was ripped and looked like he'd been carved from stone but he wasn't huge.

Waving her hand, she pushed the main hall door open. "Whatever."

Logan was standing by the spinning instructor, no doubt waiting for us. A few of the women that had already arrived were openly gawping at him. He saw us and a huge grin spread across his face. I'd done enough exercising recently for this not to kill but Cassie hadn't.

He said something else to the woman with legs that

went on forever and strolled towards us. "You ready for this?"

"Yes," Cass replied, glaring at him.

"Good. I'll be in today's class."

I narrowed my eyes. "Why?"

"Adele wanted help with the equipment."

Glancing around the room, I pursed my lips, ready to fight back. "Looks like the equipment is set up. Good job helping, now you won't be needed for another hour so why don't you go train someone or lift something heavy."

"But then I'll miss you and my sister gasping for breath and cursing the bikes, sweetheart."

"That's the point!" Cassie snapped, cutting in. "You're being a crap brother right now and you're meant to be the supportive one."

Jace was supportive but I knew what she meant, Logan was a pusher whereas Jace sat back and said *go for it* from his gaming chair.

"I'm here for support," he replied.

"You're here to gloat, Logan." I pointed to the door. "Out."

He pointed up to a camera in the corner of the room. "I'll be watching, ladies. Good luck, Cass."

Without planning it me and Cassie slapped either arm as he walked past.

"He is so my least favourite brother," she said.

Smiling, I took my jacket off and chucked it behind one of the bikes. "That used to be the other way around."

"Yeah, well, since Jace died Logan's taken it upon himself to make up for Jace's half of *annoy the fuck outta Cassie*. I swear if I have a boy first…" She stopped talking as she realised what she was about to say. The likeliness of Cass ever having a biological child was very slim. She had cysts on her ovaries and was told it was almost impossible for her to conceive naturally.

"Hey, don't do that. You'll have a child one day."

"Yeah, I will. And, hey, I can stroll into that adoption centre and pick out the least awkward looking ones from the cages." She cracked a smile.

"Yep, I'm sure it happens just like rehoming a dog."

She knew exactly how adoption – humans – worked. She had enough material and books on the subject. Before she found out about Rick cheating she was all ready to approach social services and get the ball rolling.

The impossibly gorgeous and long legged woman – who introduced herself as Amy – started the class. Cassie, bless her, looked so confident as she climbed on the bike. She was kitted out in a long length t-shirt and leggings. I knew how physical it got so I wore a tank top and shorts. Cass was going to bake.

It took all of seven minutes for Cassie to turn from stylish gym goer to hot, sweaty mess. Her hair was damp, sweat dripped down her face, she was beetroot red and breathing like she'd smoked fifty a day since she was nine.

"What. The. Fuck. Is. Wrong. With. Spinning," she huffed, wheezing so hard I was sure she'd pass out any second.

My legs and lungs burned but I was nowhere near as bad as her.

"Cass, stop," I said.

She shook her head, staring at the clock on the wall with a look of pure determination in her eyes. This was because Logan said she couldn't, or shouldn't, start exercise with something that was pretty full on. He was right but there was no way she was ever going to let him know that. Cass would collapse from exhaustion before she admitted that and it looked like she was headed right there.

"Come on, Cassie, take a few minutes to get your breath back."

"If I stop… I won't… start again."

"Yeah, maybe that's a good thing, hun."

"He will not be… right, Chlo." She gritted her teeth,

wincing through the pain.

Christ, I was carrying her to the car.

I was surprised when Cass kept up until the end of the session. She did, however, slump to the floor as she got off her bike. I took a long swig of water before helping her up, supporting almost her entire weight.

"How you feeling there?"

"Take me to the spa," she replied, groaning as we took just one step towards the changing rooms. "If I ever, *ever* suggest doing any form of exercise again, please, punch me really hard in the face."

Laughing, I guided her to the other exit so we'd miss Logan gloating.

***

"This is a much better idea," I said as we soaked our feet in the foot spa.

"It really is. I'm coming back tomorrow, my legs are going to kill even more then."

"Yeah, they really are. So will you admit Logan's right and you should have started anything else before spinning?"

"Absolutely."

I laughed. "To his face?"

"Not a chance in hell!" *That's what I thought.* "He would *love* that."

"He would."

She groaned and closed her eyes. "Are your legs not hurting at all, Chlo?"

"They ache but Logan's been training me well. I'm starting to feel like the old me again."

"I am *so* glad to hear that. And Logan is the old him again, which isn't always a good thing, the idiot. You did that, you know."

I shook my head. "No, he did that. He saw that I wasn't getting it together and getting me back to the world of the living gave him something else to focus on. He healed himself."

"Hmm," she murmured. "I still think you had a lot to do with it."

"Indirectly, I did. I was in no state to help anyone back then."

"What was it like? Sorry, you don't have to talk about it if you don't want but we've never really had that conversation."

"It's fine, I can talk about it. I was stuck, completely stuck and couldn't see past everything I'd lost. For years I had literally no idea what I was going to do and it scared me. I missed Jace so much and could only concentrate on what we'd never get the chance to do. I'll always love him but I don't want to waste another second of my life, it's far too short to not to live it."

"We missed you at home."

"I'm sorry."

"No, it's okay. We're all so glad you're back now, the last five months have been a complete change, mostly for the better."

"Hey, you're definitely better off without that idiot. I know Rick hurt you but you'll find someone that'll treat you right." Someone that didn't think having a biological child right away was more important than their wife. There were far too many kids out there without parents and there were other options available to them to have a child of their own. Rick was just an arsehole.

She smiled. "One day. I'm done with men for now and just want to concentrate on getting my life back on track."

I could identify with that but now my life was back on track I wanted to get back out there and see if I could form a connection with anyone. Jace had been it for me for so long and he was my first serious boyfriend so I didn't know how dating was going to go. Would I compare them to him?

"Your perfect man will come along when you least

expect it."

"Did Jace come along when you least expected it? You were friends first."

I tilted my head and smiled. "Yeah, he was definitely unexpected. Gamers weren't usually my type but there was something about him, like you could never feel down because he was such a joker, that I was drawn to."

"Do you ever wonder what it'd have been like if you'd remained friends?" I could tell she was thinking about wishing she'd never been more with Rick.

"No. It would have been a hell of a lot less painful if I'd never fallen in love with him but I would never wish it hadn't happened."

"So it really is better to have loved and lost than to never have loved at all?"

That was hard but it was right. Losing Jace was unbearable but I had the most amazing memories. "I guess so. I'd go through the pain of losing him all over again to remember him telling me he loves me and generally being a big idiot."

"Aww. Do you think the next guy you fall for will be enough? It's hard enough sometimes living up to your new love's ex but one that has died…"

"I'm not worried. I love Jace but I don't want a replica. There is no replacing him. It'll be different but equally as good." *I hope.* Honestly, that terrified me. What if I never felt that in love again? I'd have to live the rest of my life knowing my one big love had come and gone and all I had left was consolation love. That sucked on so many levels, especially for the guy. "Is it weird talking about this stuff?"

She laid her head back, tilting it towards me. "Not at all. Why would it be?"

"You're sitting there, listening to me tell you I'll love my next… love the same amount as your brother." Didn't she feel some sort of loyalty to Jace where she didn't want me to love anyone as much as him?

"Don't be silly. You're like a sister and thank God I have you because I'm left with Logan!"

"You love Logan."

"Of course I do but brothers are a pain in the neck."

I wouldn't know being an only child and all.

Our feet were removed from the spa and the pedicure commenced. It was so nice to be pampered. I hadn't been to a spa since before Jace died.

"I worry about Logan," I said.

"That makes two of us but he's getting there, Chlo."

He was but sometimes his eyes would drift and he'd get a look of pure agony in his eyes and I had no idea where he was in those moments. I cared about him too much to let him drown in grief, guilt or whisky.

"Yeah, I just wish he'd open up more. All he really says is that he feels guilty over the argument with Jace and that *I'm doing fine, sweetheart*."

"He's a guy."

"Not a good enough excuse for me. I might have to organise an intervention."

She laughed, picking out a striking orange nail polish for her fingers and toes. "He'll probably just laugh his way through that. Seriously, don't stress over it. He's alright."

"He's holding something back."

"Isn't he allowed his secrets?"

"No."

Laughing again, she shook her head. "You two are like an old married couple."

I frowned and bit my lip. We were, I suppose, we bickered and leaned on each other when we needed to – although that was more one-sided thanks to Mr I'm Fine, Sweetheart.

"I guess we are."

That felt weird. Logan, along with Cass and Nell, was my best friend, the person I went to first, so to think we were like a married couple was strange. Not to mention the fact that he was Jace's brother.

"Poor you!" she said. "Hey, at least I'll still get you as a sister-in-law, huh?" Her face fell with mine. "'Cause that's not weird at all."

"Yeah, little too close to home I think."

"Hmm…" She looked at me for a second too long and I had no idea what was going on in that blonde head of hers. "Anyway, what colour are you getting? I'm going for this bright orange for the almost beginning of summer."

"Candy pink," I replied. Not a colour I'd worn much in the last few years but things were looking up and I was feeling more and more like the colourful Chloe I missed.

"Will it go with your outfit for your date?"

"Yep, wearing a white sundress."

"Cute."

I winced. "I hope so."

CHAPTER SEVEN

Chloe

Thankfully, Mum and Dad were out when Rhys rang the doorbell. I was nervous enough as it was and did not want to deal with Dad's cold, hard stare at the poor boy. Rhys was the first person I'd be going on a date with since Jace and I still felt a little bit odd about it. But I was determined to give it a try because he was nice and I wanted to see if it could go anywhere.

Opening the front door, I did a double take. "Logan," I said, a little dazed. "What're you doing here?" He was supposed to be Rhys.

"You said your parents were out."

"Yes, but I'm often in the house alone, you know, since I'm twenty and all."

"I remember your age, sweetheart."

Groaning, I stepped back so he could come in. "You're here to do the stare at Rhys, aren't you?"

"Bingo. I spoke to your dad." Of course, he did. Sodding men. "You look good, Chlo, you should change."

I rolled my eyes.

"Logan, I'm not changing so you should just leave."

"Do you have anything with a high neck?" he asked,

ignoring my question and heading for the stairs.

"Where are you going?"

He looked over his shoulder as he walked up the stairs. "Come on, you can't get changed from there."

Following, I shouted, "I am *not* changing." Jesus, he was acting as if I had on a transparent tutu and Basque. "Logan Michael Scott!"

"If you think using my full name is stopping me finding you a snow suit you're sadly mistaken."

He was rummaging in my wardrobe when I stomped into my room. I stood still for a few seconds, trying to work out if this was actually happening. Logan had his head in my clothes.

"Okay, what the fuck?" I snapped.

"He's going to want to get in your pants."

I threw my arms up. "So?"

He stilled, back to me, in the wardrobe still. What the hell was going through that pretty head of his?

"Logan?" I whispered.

Turning around slowly, he took a deep breath. "He'd want me to look out for you."

Ah, this was about Jace.

"You do look out for me. I doubt Jace would expect you to pick out my outfits."

"How much do you really know this Riley?"

"Rhys."

"Whatever, begins with an R."

"I've known him for about three and a half or four years, but I guess I don't really know him much at all. That's the point of dating though, to get to know each other. Not that you'd really know that, your idea of dating doesn't involve much talking."

"I'll have you know they're very vocal."

Good thing I didn't have lunch. "Lovely," I muttered dryly.

Reaching back into the wardrobe, Logan pulled out an

oversized, cream knitted jumper. "I like this."

"I'd be too hot. My outfit is fine, Logan. Rhys isn't an animal. I'll be fine."

"Can you at least not do that thing with your lips."

"What thing with my lips?"

"Where you kind of purse them, just a tiny bit. You do it when you concentrate or really listen or are just million miles away."

"Right." Great, I was going to be self-conscious of that now.

"It'll make him want to bite it."

"My lip?"

"Yes. Don't do it."

Talking to Logan had never given me a headache before.

"Alright. No lip pursing that I don't even know I do, got it. Is there anything else I should or should not do? Sir."

His mouth twitched into a smile. "You shouldn't have *any* physical contact with him. At all. In fact, why don't I chaperone?"

"No, and no."

"You're planning physical contact?"

I sighed, exasperated. "No, I'm not but it's likely at some point."

The doorbell rang again.

"That'll be Ryan," he said.

"Rhys," I corrected. He was doing it on bloody purpose now, the awkward arse! "Please, stay here until I leave. You don't have to check him out, mostly because you've already done that. Please, Logan."

"Fine. I'll stay here. I won't even look in your underwear drawer."

There was nothing I could calmly reply to that so I gave him my stern glare and turned to leave.

"Chlo," he said, gaining my attention again.

"Yes, Logan?"

"You look beautiful. Have a nice time."

My heart warmed. "Thank you. I'll call you when I get home."

I left Logan in my room, hopefully not going through my underwear, and answered the door.

"Hey," I said.

Rhys gave me a charming smile. "Hi. You look gorgeous."

"Thank you. You don't look so bad yourself." He really didn't in a simple blue shirt and jeans. Rhys was handsome enough to pull off pretty much anything; he had striking light green eyes that meant even the plainest outfits still made him stand out.

"Ready?" he asked.

Closing the front door, I replied, "Yes. Where are we going?"

"Somewhere."

"What?" I said.

He unlocked his car. "You'll find out soon enough."

I hated surprises, always had and always would. I didn't like the unknown. I had on my knee length white sundress, glamming it up a bit with accessories because I didn't know what we were doing. Surely, he would have told me if I was dressed inappropriately for whatever he had planned.

"Nothing dangerous."

His laughter echoed as we got in his car. "No, nothing dangerous. I'll have you home in one piece, I promise."

"Okay. I trust you."

Rhys pulled out of the drive and I caught a glimpse of Logan watching us from my bedroom window. At least his spying meant he wasn't perving, yet anyway.

The drive was taking entirely too long. Silences, when they were awkward, made time almost stand still. This was one of those times. Outside of work, me and Rhys never socialised and that was hard to force now. *Say something, Chloe.*

I managed to hold off on the awkward small talk or filling the silences with crap until we arrived at the local nature park.

"Picnic," he said. "It's a nice evening and I thought we could do something a little different to a drink at the local. I hope that's okay?"

I was impressed. It was certainly a thoughtful first date and nice change from a pub. "This is great. I love picnics."

He relaxed. "Good. I was worried for a second that you'd hate the idea and want to go back. There's a really nice spot I used to go to with my family as a kid."

"Lead the way then."

Rhys grabbed the basket from the boot and we walked along one of the nature trails. I'd been along a few of them but this one was new to me. It was one of the shortest and if I was walking I usually wanted to get away for a good few hours.

"You been here before?" he asked.

"Yeah, I like the walks. Me and Logan have run a couple of them."

"You run?"

"I love running and keeping fit in general. Not overly keen on the gym, I prefer to be outside."

He was watching me a little too closely. "Wow, my last girlfriend was allergic to the outdoors. Not that I think you're my girlfriend," he added quickly, his eyes widening.

"It's okay," I replied, laughing.

It was way, way too early for anything like that. I didn't even know if I liked him yet. Sure, he was handsome and at work we'd had a laugh but good looking and a giggle wasn't enough. I needed a connection.

"You said you came here for picnics with your family, have you always lived here then?"

"Yep, I was born in the house my parents are still in. A bit boring really."

"It's not boring. If you find somewhere you love why

would you want to move? Do you have your own place?"

He nodded. "Moved out three months ago."

"How's that going for ya?"

"It's different. I like my space but not having to do my own washing!"

His mum still did his washing?

"Parents tend not to want to clean your house for you, huh."

He shook his head. "What about you?"

"Still with the parents, at least until I finish uni."

"How long do you have left?"

"Another year. I like it but I can't wait to be done with education."

We reached a picnic spot with wooden tables and plenty of grass for if you wanted to sit on a blanket. I let Rhys choose as this was something he used to do. He went to the table furthest away from the few people dotted around.

"I got sandwiches, pasta, chicken, fruit, chocolate, and juice." He opened the basket and laid the food out.

I sat down. "This looks great, Rhys."

He looked up as he poured us a glass of juice. "I hope you like it." He took the seat opposite me. "So what's the plan once uni's finished?"

"Well, I want to be an event organiser. I've not decided if that's weddings or general. There are plenty of hotels and venues around I could apply to if I choose weddings but not so much with general so I'd be looking at starting something up myself."

"Yeah? Being your own boss would be great."

"It would. A bit scary straight out of uni though, so I might see if I can get a little experience then maybe go on my own after a year or two. My course covers managing a business but it's quite a big leap."

"You'll be great at that. You can get us organised at work in two seconds flat. I've lost count of the amount of times you've solved a problem before I've even processed what's going on."

Yeah, I was great at organising events and problem solving for other people. It was myself that I still struggled with.

"I love it but it's one thing taking on staff of six, a big corporate event or someone's wedding…"

"You'll be fine."

"What about you? What's your grand plan?" I asked, tucking into a cheese sandwich.

He shrugged. "Now there's a question. I have no idea. Still not figured that one out. It's frustrating seeing my friends going off doing what they want and achieving something when I'm still working at the little pub I've been at since I was eighteen."

How old was he? I'd put him no older than twenty-four.

"Plenty of people still don't know what they want to do. You've got time to figure it out."

"Yeah, that's true." He shrugged. "Would be nice to have even the smallest idea, though."

"This is really good," I said, changing the subject. I couldn't identify with that, I'd had a plan since I was about thirteen. I knew what I wanted to do and what I wanted my life to be. He probably had the better idea though, if you didn't plan you couldn't be disappointed.

"I'm glad you're enjoying it. When you didn't agree to the date straight off I was worried you didn't want to."

"Sorry about that. I've not done this since Jace and it was just a little strange to begin with."

He winced and I saw him practically kick himself. "I'm sorry, Chloe, I should've thought."

I took a sip of the juice. "No, it's fine, no need to apologise. I wouldn't be here if I wasn't ready or didn't want to be."

We fell into a slightly awkward silence. My dead boyfriend was always going to be a tough subject, no matter what the situation.

The sun broke through the clouds and I looked up, raising my arms. "I better get a tan this year," I said almost absentmindedly.

"You're already tanned," he replied.

He was back smiling and the awkwardness had passed, thankfully. Rhys really was handsome. His pale green eyes looked almost translucent in direct sunlight. I liked that they were so unique; I'd never seen a colour like it before. Jace's eyes were gorgeous too, although I'd always preferred Cassie and Logan's slightly lighter shade of blue.

It was getting dark when we finally walked back to the car. Rhys had run the basket back earlier and then we'd gone on a long walk. It was really nice and I felt myself relaxing around him more and more.

"So, Chloe," he said, leaning against his car, "am I going to get a second date or are you blowing me off?"

I couldn't keep a straight face. "You're very forward."

His eyes widened. "Whoa, not what I meant! Shit, that really did sound wrong, didn't it?"

"Yeah, but I know what you meant, and I'd love to go out with you again."

This was the part where he was going to kiss me, I could sense it before he started to lean in. I hadn't kissed anyone since Jace so my stomach was fluttering with nerves.

He tucked my hair behind my ear and pulled me closer to him with the other hand. I placed my hands on his chest, not quite sure if I wanted to push him away. This was unchartered territory. Since I was fifteen the only person that I'd kissed was Jace. That was five years of my lips belonging to him only.

When he was just an inch away I'd finally made up my mind. I was just a tad scared but I did want to know what kissing this gorgeous guy felt like. I lowered my arms, wrapping them around his waist as his lips finally met mine.

The kiss was sweet and made me arch into his body but there was something missing. Rhys was a good kisser but I didn't feel like I wanted to do it all day. It was early days, though. I had to give it a chance and try not to compare everything to Jace. This was different, I was in love with Jace, and me and Rhys had been on one date.

He pulled away first, smiling down at me. "I guess I should get you home then."

"Yeah, you probably should." I could have easily stayed out with him longer; once we'd passed awkward silences we got along well. It was dark now though, so I knew I had to get back.

Rhys started the car up and I gasped. "It's eleven o'clock!"

Laughing at me, he placed his hand on my thigh. "Time flies, huh?"

That was an understatement. We'd been at the park for four and a half hours. I knew it was late but I had no idea it was that late. I checked my phone and apart from a text from Logan that I was not going to open until I got home, I had nothing else there. My parents would be asleep, although they would sleep lightly until they hear me come home.

Rhys pulled up outside my house and gave me a chaste kiss on the lips. "Thanks for tonight."

"I think that's my line," I said.

"Yeah, well, I'm just glad you said yes."

"Me too. Night, Rhys."

"Night."

I tried not to look back at the car as I walked down the path. Once I'd opened the door I gave him a little wave and went inside. He'd waited until he saw me go in before leaving. I liked men that did that; it showed they cared. That could pretty much be a deal breaker for me. I needed to know a man at least cared enough to make sure I got home okay.

Smiling to myself, I practically skipped up to my room. There were no big fireworks between us – possibly because it was still early days – but I'd just been on a date and I didn't feel guilty for moving on. That was a big step and I couldn't keep the moronic grin off my face. Things really were going to be alright.

CHAPTER EIGHT

Chloe

By the time I'd gotten out of the shower, dried my hair and put on my pyjamas I was exhausted and just wanted to crawl into bed. I still had that *post great date* glow but fatigue was taking over and I needed to curl up under my quilt.

I left the bathroom, tiptoeing across the hall, careful not to disturb my parents. Another date conversation with my mother would tip me over the edge. Hearing details of your parents' dates was not something I wanted to hear – especially some of the dates they'd been on. I shuddered.

I walked into my bedroom and jumped out of my skin. Logan sat on my bed, flicking through my magazine. He looked up as I tried to slow my erratic heart. *It's Logan, not a burglar.*

"Good, you're finished in the bathroom."

I stared blankly, literally not knowing what to say to him. *Who sneaks into someone's home and waits for them in their bedroom?*

"How was the date?"

My brain caught up with what was happening right now and I threw my hands up. "We are not skipping over the part where you explain what the hell you're doing in my room!"

"I'm waiting for you, what else would I be doing?"
Is he serious?

With a deep breath, I replied, "No, Logan. *Why* are you here in the middle of the night with no warning?"

"Oh. You didn't answer your phone."

"So you came over and let yourself in? You didn't think that maybe I was in the bathroom or asleep?"

"No, and that's a pretty accurate description of—" I held my hand up and he stopped talking, breaking into a huge, mischievous smile. "So did the date go well or not?"

Since he was clearly not leaving like any normal person would have done, I shoved him over the other side so I could get to my favourite spot in the bed – the middle.

We're really doing this right now. "Yes, Logan, the date went well. Rhys is perfectly nice, not an axe murderer, so you can calm down about that one. We had fun."

He was silent for a minute. His gorgeous blue eyes were guarded. I hated when I couldn't tell what he was thinking or feeling. After years of pretending he was fine, Logan had gotten really good at fooling people.

"That's good. I'm glad you had a nice time, Chlo."

"Thank you. It was strange at first and I kinda felt like I shouldn't be there but as soon as we got talking more, and walking, I relaxed and didn't feel… guilty."

"Good, I'm glad of that. You shouldn't feel guilty."

"I know. I've spent so long feeling guilty for living, for thinking about a future without Jace, for wanting to date again and just about everything else I could feel bad about. I'm tired of it and I know it gets me nowhere."

He frowned and flicked the magazine closed. We'd be talking about him reading a *How To Boost Your Bust* article later. "Do you not feel guilty about moving on anymore or do you just think you shouldn't. There's a huge difference, Chloe."

"I don't feel guilty. I loved Jace and he died, there's nothing I can do about it and I don't want to be the way I was anymore. I deserve a second chance."

"You do."

"Do you still feel guilty?" I asked.

His eyes clouded and jaw clenched. Finally, he replied, "Every day."

"Logan," I said breathlessly. The pain in his voice was so real and so raw that I felt it, too. He sat tense on my bed, refusing to meet my eyes. I shoved myself up and wrapped my arms around him. I felt the muscles in his back and shoulders bunch. They were rock solid and I couldn't help admiring his dedication to his fitness.

"Please, talk to me," I whispered.

He hadn't hugged me back, just sat deathly still with his arms fisted by his sides.

"Logan, please, I can't stand it."

Slowly releasing a deep breath, he raised his arms and clamped me flush with his body. It was a little more intimate than we'd been before with me straddling his hips but there wasn't anything sexual about it. He was hurting over the death of his brother and I needed to help him.

"I'm alright, sweetheart," he said into my hair.

"No, you're not. Talk to me. I can help."

He released me and I wanted to cling on for dear life. I wanted to hold him until he stopped hurting, until all the broken pieces knitted back together. I wanted him to hold me and let me in all the way. I wanted to be the one who gave him the power to stop the guilt. I wanted to do all of that, just like he'd done for me.

I didn't leave his lap when he'd stopped our embrace. "You're talking to me, Logan." I felt a tear slither down my cheek. "I'm not moving until you talk."

He shrugged. "Beautiful girl sitting on my lap. I got time for that."

"Come on," I said, lightly slapping his chest with the back of my hand. "Why do you feel guilty every day?"

"Me and Jace argued."

"You and Jace argued regularly, Logan. Neither one of you apologised, you both knew the other one didn't mean it and you moved on. Jace had forgiven you before he'd even closed the front door. Stop agonising over it."

"I get that, Chlo, but the *last* words I ever said to him were…"

"Were what? What was so bad about what you said?"

"Nothing really. He was pissing me off and I snapped."

I didn't get it. They'd snapped at each other and told each other to piss off at least once a week. Jace knew Logan loved him and he never held a grudge, especially not against his brother.

"Is there more to it?"

He blinked a few times before replying, "No. I just feel like crap for how it ended. I wish I could go back in time and—"

"Don't. Please, don't do that. I've thought about going back in time constantly and it won't get you anywhere. Logan, there is nothing you can do about what happened; you can only change what happens next. He wouldn't want you to stress over it when he probably forgot all about your fight five seconds after it happened."

"Yeah, you're right," he said. That was far too easy and I knew he only said it to shut me up but to him the conversation was over so I didn't push it. That didn't mean it was over. I was determined to get him to forgive himself. This was merely an interval.

"I want you to stay here tonight." *So you don't drink yourself stupid at home.*

His mouth popped open. "How inappropriate. I'm feeling quite vulnerable right now."

Logan's back. I rolled my eyes and removed myself from his lap. "Shut up and go get ready for bed."

"I don't need babysitting, sweetheart. I'll be fine on my own."

Staring into his eyes, I said, "Maybe I'm not fine on my

own." Truth was, I was terrified of leaving him alone. I wouldn't be able to settle properly if I was worrying about him finding a bottle of whisky and drinking until he drifted off to sleep.

My words were all he needed to hear to pull his t-shirt over his head. I laid down and rolled onto my side, giving him some privacy while he took his jeans off. We'd spent the night in the same bed before but that was when one of us – usually me – was a complete mess and the other stayed to comfort. I'd never shared a bed with him where I was wearing little shorts and a spaghetti strap top and he was just in boxers.

I had a huge moment of doubt but then he slipped beneath the covers and wrapped me in his arms. I felt safe and protected and prayed that he felt that, too. It would be fine, no different to all those other times I'd fallen asleep in his strong arms as he held me together.

"I'm the one that should be holding you."

"Nah, more manly like this," he said.

Completely back to pretending he was okay. The boy drove me nuts! Why couldn't he just open up without thinking of it as a weakness?

Resigning myself to the inevitable, I snuggled back against his chest and let it go – he wasn't going to talk anyway.

"Are you going to see him again?"

"He asked me on a second date," I replied.

"To which you replied…?"

"I said yes. We're going to the comedy club next weekend." Logan stilled and I felt his muscles tense around me. "What?"

"That's our thing. Me, you, Cassie, and Rick the Prick before he was the prick."

And Jace before he died.

"Do you not want me to go there with Rhys?"

"No, you can go with who you like, Chlo. It's just weird

you doing a Scott thing with someone else. I'm being an idiot, ignore me."

I didn't realise it would be weird before Logan said it. I was taking a date somewhere I used to go with my boyfriend and his siblings. "No, it is weird. I'll tell him I want to go somewhere else."

His arms loosened but didn't relax and he started tracing patterns on my arm with his fingers. It felt *really* nice. I closed my eyes and unconsciously snuggled back against him. I felt his touch everywhere, from the top of my head to the very tips of my toes. It was the most comforting thing I'd felt in a very long time and didn't ever want him to stop.

"Don't do that. I don't own the comedy club. You can go with whoever you want. We can go with Cass next month," he said against the back of my head. His breath tickling the sensitive skin at the back of my neck.

"That sounds good," I whispered, flicking off the lamp and closing my eyes again, enjoying having him slowly sending me to sleep with his magical fingers.

I yawned. "I'm exhausted and need sleep. Night, Logan."

"Night, sweetheart," he whispered in the darkness.

CHAPTER NINE

Logan

I woke up with a human on my chest and it took me a few seconds to realise it was Chloe; I was in her room and hadn't left last night like I'd planned. Out of all the women I'd woken up next to this was by far the most pleasant. The least being the charming woman that stumbled to the corner of her room, crouched down and pissed on the floor. She was still off her face drunk, but still, I was out of there before she'd pulled her thong back up.

Waking up to Chloe felt about a million times better every time it'd happened, which wasn't a lot. We'd fallen asleep in the same bed or on a sofa but this was different. There were no tears or anger. Neither of us was really there for comfort. Well, maybe I was after her fucking *date*.

She spent the evening with him but the night with me. I needed that night. I wondered what he'd think if he knew we'd shared a bed – not doing what I was desperate to do in it. She wasn't his but I wanted to tell him and it'd be a deal breaker for him.

Fuck, I was a selfish bastard.

Chloe breathed heavily and balled her hand in a loose fist, dragging her fingertips over my chest before they curled under her palm. I closed my eyes and counted to ten, slowly.

The bottom half of her was beside me on the bed but the top half was almost completely on me. Her breasts were pressed pretty firmly against my chest, which made calming the fuck down almost impossible.

She was everything I'd wanted for the last six and a half years but she'd always been within my reach yet completely unreachable and I didn't know how much longer I could pretend like it wasn't killing me.

Her lips were facing me, soft and ready and I wanted to attack them more than I wanted anything else. She might scream if I just went for it. I could pretend I was still half asleep and disorientated, speak a load or rubbish that didn't make sense so she thought I was sleep kissing if she shoved me off. Like that thought hadn't ever entered my mind, every time I'd had a drink I'd wanted to kiss her so I could blame the alcohol if it went wrong. The thing that stopped me every time was the possibility that it could be awkward after. I didn't want awkward with Chloe. I wanted everything with her. I could settle for an agonising fucking *friendship,* but I couldn't do awkward.

I wanted to lay in her bed all day with her but I knew she'd wake up soon and I wasn't sure how she'd handle the intimate position, the closest we'd been before was waking up with her elbow in my side or one of her legs against mine.

I kissed the top of her head, closing my eyes and savouring the moment for a second. *I fucking love you.*

Against every instinct I had when it came to her, I rolled her over, laid on my side and leant on my hand. "Morning, Chlo," I said much too loud and much too cheerfully.

She gasped awake, jumping and clinging to the cover. "Logan! What're you doing?"

"Waking you up, you've been sleeping too long. Want to go for a run?"

First she looked lost, then she looked murderous. "You woke me up to ask if I want a run at…" Her eyes flicked to the alarm clock on the bedside table, "seven in the morning?"

"Yeah, you up for it?"

"No, I am *not* up for it. What's wrong with you?"

Now that was a question I wouldn't mind the answer to as well.

"You like running in the morning."

"Not this morning. We weren't supposed to run today."

"So is that a no?"

She groaned and flopped back on the bed. "Logan, go home."

"I don't want to. We could go get breakfast somewhere or you could cook for me here." I'd already put my hands out to protect whatever she was about to hit. I caught her wrist before it came into contact with my shoulder and laughed. "I was joking. I'm a modern man; I'll cook for you. What do you fancy?"

"Why're you so happy?"

The answer was pretty fucking obvious to me and it was currently glaring at me.

I shrugged. "It's a lovely day, Chlo. Come on, sweetheart, cheer up."

"You can cook for me here. I want bacon."

That was what I'd hoped because there was no way her mum would let me loose in her kitchen so I wouldn't end up being the one that cooked anyway.

I got out of bed. "Alright, miss grumpy, bacon is coming up. You want it in bed or are you getting that arse up?" Actually, I quite liked the idea of bringing her breakfast in bed.

"I'll get up. Give me five minutes to get ready and I'll be down."

"Alright. See you in a minute." I opened her door and looked back over my shoulder. "And, Chlo, the messy bed hair is pretty hot." I got out and closed the door as she frantically looked for something to throw at me.

***

"Morning, Bethany," I said to Chloe's mum as I walked into the kitchen.

"Logan, hi," she replied, shocked to see me. "I didn't know you were here."

"Yeah, sorry, popped over to see Chlo after her date and fell asleep."

She nodded, having no issue with the fact that I'd spent the night in her daughter's bed. But that was because I was Jace's brother and she would never think anything would happen, so it kind of sucked.

"I'm making bacon, you want?" I asked her.

She laughed and shooed me to the table. "You sit, *I'll* be making breakfast."

"Will you ever let me cook in that fancy kitchen?"

"Not a chance, mister! I don't even let Bill cook in my kitchen."

"I'll make the coffee then."

She pointed in my direction, already getting pans out to cook. "That you can do. How did Chloe's date go? She tell you?"

Oh, yeah, she told me. "It went alright, they're going out again." I tried, really tried, to sound happy for her.

"That's good. For a while there I wasn't sure if we'd ever get her back. She relied on the plan she'd made with Jace far too much."

"She just needed a kick up the butt. Honestly, I think she was getting there herself, she was healing but couldn't see a way of planning for a different future."

Bethany ripped open the pack of bacon. "She needed you. You're good for each other, you've always bounced off each other."

She didn't mean it in the way I wanted her to or she did but knew it was about as likely as pigs flying. Either way, someone saying me and Chlo were good for each other did things to my heart that I'd only admit out loud if I turned into a teen girl.

"Yeah, we've always got along."

"Until last night," Chloe said, walking into the kitchen and glaring at me again. "Scare me or wake me again and I'll have your balls, Scott."

That would've frightened me but I really wanted her to have my balls.

I held my hands up, playing along. "Noted, sweetheart. No more surprise visits or wake ups."

"Ugh, you so don't mean that." She sat on a chair and rested her head on her arms. I wanted to sit down next to her and pull her into my arms while her mum cooked. I wanted to be able to hold her, just to fucking hold her.

So I wouldn't make a tit of myself, drop to my knees and proclaim my undying love for her, I went back to making coffee.

"Tell me about your date, love," Bethany said.

If I got details I was pouring the kettle out over my head.

"It was good. He made a picnic, we ate at the park and then had a long walk. He's taking me out next weekend."

"That's great."

I wanted to make a puking sound but refrained.

"Yeah. It was a little awkward at first, we've never spent any time together outside of work, but he's really nice."

"Nice but awkward. Winner!" I said before I could stop myself. Chloe stuck her finger up. "Sorry, I'm sure he's your prince charming."

"I'm not looking to marry the guy, Logan. We're just getting to know each other. There might not even be anything that comes out of it."

There fucking better not be!

"There's no pressure, Chloe, just go with the flow and

see what happens. You never know, you may well end up marrying him," Bethany said, wiggling her eyebrows.

I thought she'd end up marrying Jace and that hurt enough but some random guy... As much as I wanted her to be happy I didn't want to watch her walk down the aisle and take the hand of someone else. The thought of sitting there while she recited vows to another man made me want to hurl.

I poured boiling water in three mugs, trying to push away the image of her in a white dress dancing her first dance with a guy that wasn't me. Marriage wasn't something I thought much about but I'd marry her right now, no hesitation.

Shit, I had problems.

"Bill's at work?" I asked.

"Yeah, he'll be home in an hour, he just had to sort something out for Monday."

"Mum, what are the chances you and Dad'll get me a new car for my birthday?" Chloe asked.

I turned around, really wanting to see this.

"Hmm..." Bethany said, pretending to think. I couldn't help a big, fat grin. This wasn't going to go in Chloe's favour.

"Come on, Mum. Please?"

"There's nothing wrong with your car."

"It broke last month."

"For the first and only time in the three years you've had it."

She pouted and I almost offered to buy her a fucking car.

"Please? I'm a poor student and can't afford one."

Bethany rolled her eyes, turning around to continue cooking a shit load of bacon. "Chloe, when your car breaks we'll replace it, that was the deal."

"Okay, fine, but you'll have to get me a birthday present and a car. I was saving you money here!"

Women logic.

"Nice try, love. Dad wants to get you something special, we're both so proud of how well you've been doing this year, but don't hold your breath for a car."

"This year's been a lot easier. It's nice to think about Jace and not feel total despair. Still not too sure about what happens after uni but I'm working on it."

"After uni you get a job and a house," I said, handing Bethany her coffee before taking mine and Chlo's to the table and sitting down. "Like the rest of us."

"You didn't go to uni," she replied. She looked smug and pouted her lips in that sexy, unknowing way. It got me every time.

"Alright, smartarse. I mean you do everything you wanted to do, just…"

She chewed her lip and then released it to say, "Do it without Jace."

"Yeah. You have to do it without him." We all had to do everything without him. It fucking sucked.

CHAPTER TEN

Logan

"It's been an hour. Actually, it's been an hour and twelve minutes, Chloe—"

She waved her hand at me like a mad woman. "Alright, alright, you slave driver. I'm up. See!" Standing up, she narrowed those pretty amber eyes for the millionth time today. "You're being an arse today... and yesterday, actually. What's up, Logan?"

"Nothing's up. I wanted to hang out, should there be something wrong for me to want that?"

Her frown slowly slipped from her forehead and her features softened. "When we spend the night together like that, yeah, usually there's something wrong. I hope there's not, you know I don't want you to be unhappy, but from experience there's something else going on. Is it Jace's birthday coming up?"

That day was going to be awful but for the first time since he died I wasn't feeling shitty because of that. It was because she was moving on. It was because I was soon going to have to watch her be with someone else and put him first, and I wanted every second I could get until that happened.

But I couldn't tell her that, so I took the coward's way out and nodded. "Yeah, it's just a shitty time."

It took her less than a second to be in my arms, hugging me tight. "It'll be okay, Logan. We're both stronger this year. It'll always be hard but we can smile this time. It'll be his twenty-first, a big one, so let's try to make it a happy day, yeah?"

I held her petite frame tight against my chest and buried my head in her hair. "Sure, sweetheart," I whispered. "We can try to make it a happy day."

"Still want to go for that stupid run?" she asked against my collarbone. That was sexy as hell.

"Yep, you're not getting out of that one. Nice try, though."

Pulling back, she slapped my chest and huffed. "Fine. Let's go then."

***

"What was the car thing about with your mum this morning? You love your shit heap of a car." Who buys a Citroen C3? Tiny little roller skate of a car that's marked 'a great run around' and that was probably because the fucking things broke so much running was the only way you were getting anywhere. And it was a steal at a grand. Women should never shop for cars alone.

"Oi, don't speak ill of Ellie, thank you very much!"

"See, you've even named the heap."

She shoved me as we jogged down the path but didn't manage to move me much. "I knew Mum would go on about Rhys and I didn't want to deal with it. Plus, I thought it was worth a try, could've gotten a new car out of it."

"What do you mean?"

She picked up the pace, clearly uncomfortable with where this was headed. I wasn't going to let it go. If there was something about this guy she was unsure of I wanted to know and I wanted to revel in it.

"I'm not going anywhere, sweetheart."

Groaning, she said, "It's just a little weird, okay. I'm not sure how I really feel about Rhys right now and I don't want to have to keep talking about how things might go with him in the future. Right now my future is blank and it scares the hell out of me. I've never had that, Logan, there's always been a plan."

"You plan too much."

"I know I do, but I like knowing what I'm doing and working towards. The unknown scares the crap outta me."

"I like it. Not knowing where I'll be doesn't bother me. You have to leave room for change, Chlo, or you'll forever be disappointed."

"I can't help it. You're so laid back and I wish I could just go with the flow more but I can't."

"Can't or don't want to?"

"Can't, I think. I don't like the feeling of everything being out of my control. I can't control life and death but I can control what I do in between."

She couldn't, though. Chloe could plan right up until the day she died but it wouldn't all go how she wanted it to. Life was constantly ready to throw more and more shit surprises at you. Control was an illusion, something people claimed to have to make reality seem that much more bearable. No one was in control of anything; in every situation you were either lucky or unlucky.

I didn't want to bring her down with my cheerful theories so I took the easy road and kept my mouth shut. "Which route?"

"Cemetery," she replied, making me almost lose my footing.

Back to Jace. I didn't want to go there. I hated it. You were supposed to die in old age, starting with the eldest. I shouldn't have buried my brother; it was backwards. He was just a fucking kid, not quite eighteen.

"Really?" I asked. "Any reason?"

"Yes. No. I don't…" She stopped suddenly and I almost

rammed into her. "I went on a date last night."

Oh, I was painfully aware of that fun fact.

"And?"

She bit her lip, which made her look sexier.

"Not too sure actually."

"Right." I scratched my forehead. I rarely understood women when they said what the fuck was going on so guessing was impossible. "You feel guilty? You said you didn't."

"Not guilty. Maybe like I should, though." She shrugged. "I just feel like I should talk to him."

That was impossible, too.

"Alright, cemetery is it, but if it's cool with you I'll run a lap while you're talking."

She touched my arm, rubbing her thumb over my skin that was oversensitive to her touch. I fucking felt it right where I wanted to. "Of course. I don't expect you to stay."

"Do you want me to stay?"

"I think I need to talk to him alone."

Thank fuck for that.

It was my turn to speak but there was little left to say other than *let's go* and I knew if I said that she'd stop the touching. She didn't touch me nearly enough and I was getting greedier.

"Well," she said, blowing out a big breath and lowering her hand. "Let's go or this run will never end."

I stopped at the gate to the cemetery. Chloe gave me a fleeting smile before jogging to Jace's grave. I envied her for the way she approached him and sat down. No hesitation.

My brother was over there and it was the last place on earth I wanted to be. I couldn't even pretend it was just because I hated the thought of him in the ground. I was in love with his girl, what right did I have to go over there and pour my heart out to him? I could pretend while he was alive but I couldn't now that he was dead. He would know and I couldn't face him. There was nothing he could do, he couldn't call me out or tell me to get out of his life, but I still could not face him.

Fuck guilt and fuck wanting what you shouldn't.

***

I read the text again. 'Can't do today, going to lunch with Rhys. Tomorrow? x'

Then just because I was a masochist, I read it once more. She was out with that prick two days after the first date. They weren't even supposed to be going out until the weekend. I was meant to have a week to meddle in some way and break it off, show her how wrong he was for her.

As a result of their early second fucking date I was in a foul mood, wanted to get drunk, smash something, and find a way to stop loving her. If I could just switch it off it would make my life a million times easier.

If there was a button you could press to stop yourself loving someone I would have pressed it years ago. Or I wouldn't because I loved how she made me feel when it wasn't like I was suffocating. Basically, I was screwed and I was a sick arsehole.

"Earth to Logan!" Cassie shouted. My eyes shot up to meet carbon copies of mine staring back at me. "Where were you?"

"Sorry. What's up?"

"I asked if you want Indian. Mum doesn't want to cook, I don't want to cook, Dad can't, and it'll be a cold day in hell before you get off your arse to do it, so…?"

"Yeah, sure, whatever."

"What's gotten to you?"

"Nothin', just tired." If it wouldn't be too obvious I would've asked her about this Rhys guy and got her opinion on the two of them. I could see he wasn't right for Chloe, but could Cass?

"K. Fancy getting the guys together for a night out

soon? It's been ages since we've done anything."

"Saturday?"

"We can but Chlo has a date so she wouldn't be able to come. Unless they meet us after."

Not happening.

I tried to keep an even, *I don't give a shit* expression but I was sure I was looking at my sister like she'd just suggested we sacrifice a whole Maternity Ward of newborns.

"I'll speak to Chlo and see when she's free."

"Sounds good. I need to get some action soon."

I could feel lunch coming back up. "Ugh, what the fuck is wrong with you, Cass?"

She laughed. "Least I got a proper reaction out of you. And I was kidding; I'm so done with men. They're all arseholes."

"I'm offended. We're not all arseholes."

"Really? I challenge you to recite the names of just five of the women you've slept with."

I gripped the edge of the worktop. "I can give you three."

"Thought as much."

"That doesn't make me an arsehole. The last three years have been… difficult. I didn't forget them because I didn't want to know, I'm not sure I got the names in the first place."

"Oh, much better."

"Cheers for making me feel like an dickhead."

"I'm sorry." She held her hands up. "I know it's been hard and the things you've done weren't exactly planned. You're not an dickhead, Logan. You've never lied or cheated."

I've lied. I lied to Jace every time he asked me what was up and I gave him some shitty reply about having a bad day at work or being tired. I lied to Chloe when she asked if I was cool with her dating – like it was even up to me.

"That's done with now. And anyway, I don't know if I

slept with them all, I might've just *slept*."

She bit the insides of her lips together, trying to force herself to keep a straight face. She looked ridiculous.

"Alright, fine, those odds aren't great. Fact is, I did it and I regret it. I've got no diseases – thankfully – and I have no desire to play STI roulette again."

"I know. I'm sorry, I really am. I didn't want to make you feel bad. We all know you regret what you did."

I regretted a lot, not just the women but there was nothing I could do about that now.

"Can we change the subject from my fuckups, please?"

"Sure. Why aren't you dating? You're not that hideous and to other women you're not even that annoying."

"Thanks," I said sarcastically. "Having a girlfriend is hard work and I don't need that shit right now." And the only person I wanted for anything more than a night of fun was currently getting ready to have lunch with some other guy. That kind of put a damper on it.

"How would you know?"

"I've had girlfriends before, Cassie, I'm not a monk."

She laughed so hard tears leaked out of the corners of her eyes. I rolled mine.

"Shit, even the mention of you and a monk in the same sentence…"

"You're not funny," I said. She didn't stop laughing. "Alright, I'm outta here." I left the kitchen and wished I'd swiped a bottle on my way through. The ache left behind by Chloe was getting harder to ignore and harder to mask.

CHAPTER ELEVEN

Chloe

I met Nell outside the library at the end of my lecture. The whole uni was buzzing with end of year exam nerves. Mine started next week and I was quietly confident. One thing being a practical hermit for three years did for me was boost my grades. I'd spent a lot of time studying because I was determined that while the rest of my life had been thrust into the unknown, my education wouldn't be.

It wouldn't be long until exams were over and I'd have a long summer to look forward to. Then it was back to uni for just one more year and I would've finally finished my Events Management course.

"Hey," I said as she stomped outside, slamming the library door open. "Problem, Nell?"

She huffed and her leafy green eyes darkened. The girl was gorgeous with cheekbones that look liked they'd been sculpted from stone, big bright eyes and rosebud lips. Her hair was the darkest shade of black I'd ever seen; everything about her stood out in the most striking way against her porcelain skin.

She was also very angry about something.

"They don't have the book I need to study for finals,"

she replied, shouting the last part at the door.

I grabbed her arm, leading her towards the car park. "Okay, let's calm down. Why are you only just getting books to study for finals?"

She threw her hands up. "Is that the most important part, Chloe?" Well, yeah. "They don't have it and now I'm going to have to go into town or order online. This is wasting valuable time and that whore of a librarian doesn't care."

Wow. "Aaaaand we're going to town," I said. Who only sorted their revision books less than a week before the exams?

"I'm going to fail, Chlo."

"You're not. You just need to get these books and spend the rest of the week reading them. No Damon."

She rolled her eyes. "As if I want to talk to that prick."

I didn't even want to ask why he was a prick now. I was pretty sure last week they were getting in each other's pants again. They gave me a headache.

"Well, that's good then, you'll be able to concentrate."

I drove us into town and followed Nell as she headed straight for the bookshop. My phone beeped with a text as we looked for the book she needed.

Rhys: Fancy dinner tonight?

"Who's that?" Nell asked, not being one to worry about something not being her business.

"Rhys," I replied. "He wants to know if I want dinner tonight."

"You look thrilled he asked," she said sarcastically.

Wasn't I? "He's nice and we have a good time."

"Nice and good. If Damon used either of those words to describe anything about me I'd kick him in the balls."

"Ugh, I don't know. Maybe it's just because we're getting to know each other outside work. We've only had two dates."

"Exactly! You've only just started dating, you should want to see him, your face should have lit up when he just texted you."

"Yeah, maybe. Or maybe I'm expecting too much. Maybe I'm looking to feel about Rhys the way I felt about Jace."

"You'll love someone as much as you did Jace but not right away."

"I know. I fully appreciate that but how do I know if that person is Rhys? What if I break things off and it turns out that I would've loved him?"

"Jesus, Chloe, you analyse things to death, girl. If you're not feeling anything now you're probably not going to. You should at least want to go on this date and right now you look like you could take it or leave it."

I could, that was the problem. I don't think it would bother me if Rhys said at lunch on Monday that he didn't want to go on another date. But I wanted it to bother me.

"Look, he's the first guy you've been out with since Jace and I get that you want it to go somewhere so it wasn't pointless or meaningless but you shouldn't feel bad for that. You made the decision to date again so stop second-guessing it. You're not doing anything wrong."

Was that what I was doing? Seeing someone new was a big deal to me and I didn't want it to mean nothing. I couldn't force things with Rhys though, that wasn't fair to either of us.

"Yeah, you might be right."

"Of course, I'm right! Go on the date and if you still just think he's a *nice* guy that you have *fun* with then ditch him."

"I will." This would be date number three; I couldn't let it go past tonight if it didn't even have a chance at going somewhere.

"Ooh, here's my book. Text him back while I pay thirteen pounds to fail my exam next week."

I rolled my eyes and replied to Rhys, setting up dinner.

***

I wasn't feeling it. Not even a little bit. When he kissed me it was nice but there was still no spark. I didn't want to deepen the kiss, to have him touch me and take me back to his. It was just… nice.

We were supposed to be going to the comedy club at the weekend. I couldn't go on that date. I wasn't even sure what had happened, our first date was good but it was my first date since Jace and it had gone well. I think I was over enthusiastic because I'd come away not feeling horrible but feeling hopeful.

Rhys smiled from across the table. "Know what you want yet?" he asked.

Yeah, I did – excitement. I wanted to get a thrill every time I even thought about him. I wanted to want to be around him all the time, but I didn't and it was nothing he'd done, I just wasn't into him.

"I'm not sure yet. You?"

"Steak," he replied.

My phone rang in my handbag. "Sorry," I said, reaching for it. "I thought I'd put it on silent."

"That's okay, answer it."

I shook my head and pulled the phone out – it was Logan. I bit my lip, I wanted to answer but I wouldn't. I'd call him back later.

"No, it's fine. I'll ring him back tonight." I hated when people answered calls and texts when they were at dinner with others. It was rude and there was no way I was doing it.

He smiled and ran his hand through his dark copper hair. He looked like he was trying to think of something to say. We'd reached the point where we were forcing it. If we'd have come out as friends we'd probably be chatting away.

By the time dessert was brought out I think Rhys knew this was the last date, too. I dug into my chocolate cake and couldn't hold it in any longer. It was becoming painfully hard work.

"Rhys," I said.

"Don't. I know what you're about to say. At lunch yesterday you were distant and today you're even more distant. I'm getting the brush off, aren't I?"

I squirmed in my seat. *This is so awkward.* "I'm sorry." Breathing deeply, I managed to stop myself churning out all the clichés like 'it's not you, it's me.' Truth was, it wasn't really either of us. He was great and I liked him but there was nothing romantic between us at all.

"It's okay. Not gonna lie, I had hoped this would go differently but I get it. For the last few years at work you've kind of been like a zombie, it was nice to see you back to your old self for the last six months. Even though this isn't working out for you I hope, and my God, this is going to sound so cheesy, that we can still be friends."

"I'd like that. I've missed messing around with you and the other guys in the kitchen."

Smiling sadly, he replied, "So have I."

Dessert flew by since we decided to be friends and I finally relaxed with him again. He didn't mention wanting to give it another go or hoping it would've worked out again so that led me to believe he wasn't really into me either. We were definitely supposed to be friends.

CHAPTER TWELVE

Chloe

After dinner and the slightly awkward sort of break-up, I called Logan's phone on the walk back to my car to see what he wanted earlier. Cassie answered and something inside me twisted. Why didn't he answer? That was so unlike him.

"Thank God, Chlo! I wanted to call earlier but I remembered you were out with Rhys," she said.

"What's going on? Logan called but I was at dinner. Where is he?"

"He came home about ten minutes ago drunk and covered in lipstick."

"What?" He was past that. He'd been doing so well. Shit, he'd called me an hour ago, was that before he'd lost it?

"I don't know what's happened, all I know is that he's relapsed and barely making sense."

I picked up my pace, jogging to my car. Rhys peeled away but I didn't have enough time to worry if he just drove like a crazy person when he was alone or if I'd really hurt his feelings. "Is he awake?"

"Yeah, laying on the sofa having a full conversation with my dad about random crap."

"Good. Keep him awake; kicking his arse will be so much more effective if he's aware of it. I'll be there in ten minutes." I hung up, ripping my car door open so hard I almost knocked it into the car next to me. Bloody boy!

As mad at him as I was it also worried me why he was drinking again. There was no way on earth he was going back there. Recently, he'd been a much better person, better than before Jace died even. He didn't use women at all now, well, until this evening, apparently.

It took me a little over ten minutes to get to his house, I'd purposefully driven a little slower so I could think, try to work out why he'd fallen and what I was going to do about it. He didn't let me lose myself to grief and my hermit-like state and I sure as hell wasn't letting him lose himself again.

I stormed through the front door, ready to kill him. In the kitchen I could hear Julia and Cassie talking but my focus was on Logan, laying on the sofa with Daryl holding out a bottle of water to him.

Daryl looked up and smiled, relieved. Somehow, after being the ones to save each other, we knew what to do to keep the other in check. He'd done it for me a lot and hadn't given me many opportunities to need to pick him up but now he had and I wasn't going to let him down.

"What are you doing, Logan?" I asked, folding my arms over.

As mad as I was I couldn't help admiring how adorable he looked with glossy topaz eyes and a lopsided smile. He looked like a naughty kid.

"What're you doing, Chlo?"

"I'm here to kick your arse." I dropped to the sofa he was on and sighed. "You're better than this. What happened?" Daryl got up and left for the kitchen, giving us privacy.

"I don't know." He scrubbed his face with his hands. "I really don't know. We all fall off the wagon, right?"

He was right. There had been times since the first time

he pulled me from my pit that I'd not wanted to get out again. I couldn't be too mad at him, everyone had setbacks. "Do you want to talk about why you picked up a bottle?"

"I only had a few glasses."

"You're drunk."

He grinned. "Well, they were big glasses."

I was back to being so pissed off that he'd got himself into this state – although not as bad as it had been, apparently – that I had to take a few seconds to breathe.

"Logan, sit the fuck up and drink the fucking water."

With the curve of his mouth and humorous glint in his eye, he sat up and said, "Chloe's got a potty mouth tonight."

Chloe's seconds from pouring the water on your head.

He slumped back on the sofa and held his hand out. "Alright, water me."

"Don't tempt me, Logan." I handed him the drink, which he drained in one.

"Why're you so pissed? It wasn't that long ago that I was holding your hair back."

"We were on a night out and I had one too many, I wasn't drowning my sorrows at home alone."

"Po-tay-to, po-tah-to."

I rubbed my forehead. "I am so not in the mood for this tonight."

"What happened tonight?"

Removing my hand from my face, I looked down at him. All trace of humour had gone and he was watching me with curiosity and concern. "I had the awkward *let's just be friends* conversation with Rhys."

"The prick broke up with you?" His voice actually went up a couple octaves.

"He's not a prick. I broke up with him and technically, it wasn't really breaking up, we weren't official."

He stared at me with a completely blank expression. I *hated* when I couldn't read him. "Ohhhh." Tilting his head to the side, he added, "That makes sense. You can do better."

"There was nothing wrong with him at all. It just wasn't working out."

"He's not sexy enough."

I did a double take. "Sorry?"

"You're a ten and he's a four, max." Rhys was good looking but the drunken idiot was biased.

"Can we not number people, please?" At school guys would call out numbers, scoring girls as they walked by, it was so pathetic and actually made one girl cry once. Since then it bothered me. Also, Logan was rating men?

"Number me," he said, and smiled wide, showing his pearly white teeth.

I couldn't keep a straight face. "Looking like that?"

"I can't help sexy. I was born like this, sweetheart."

"Okay, there is no getting sense out of you when you're like this. I'm just gonna put you to bed and do the arse kicking in the morning."

"Shall I list the pros and cons?"

Again, I was stumped and slowly losing patience. "What?"

He held up a finger. "Con, my family will hear you scream." My eyes bulged. Where the hell was his head tonight? "Con, you'll get awkward in the morning. Con, in my drunken state I might feel a little violated in the morning." Now why didn't I believe that? "Con, people will ask you who is better in the sack and you'll have to refrain from shouting out my name, which will be hard."

"Okay, there we have it. All cons and no pros so let's just get you upstairs so you can *sleep*." I hooked my arm under his.

"There is a pro," he said, not moving an inch to help me get him up. He was damn heavy.

I sighed in frustration. "Go on then! Pro...?"

He leant forward and whispered, "It will be fucking mind-blowing." His breath cascaded across my neck and I shuddered.

And what in the world do I say to that? I gulped, goose bumps prickled all the way along my arms. What was he doing? He didn't say things like that and I certainly didn't react to him the way I was.

Just when looking into those deep topaz eyes was getting too much, he chuckled. "But," he said, shoving himself forward, "an awkward Chloe would suck, so please stop begging and we'll forget this conversation ever happened."

With a devilish smile over his shoulder, he walked upstairs and left me speechless in the living room. I'd forgotten what drunk Logan was like. Pretty amusing if you weren't the one that had to deal with him and if you weren't the one whose heart rate was all over the place.

"Is he okay?" Julia asked.

I snapped out of it and turned to her, plastering on a smile and rolling my eyes. "Yeah, he drank the water so I sent him to bed."

"Good. Are you staying tonight?"

"That okay?"

She pointed at me and arched a perfectly plucked eyebrow. "I'll pretend I didn't hear you ask. Night."

Smiling for real, I replied, "Night, Julia, Daryl." Daryl nodded and followed his wife up to bed. Cass hadn't come out of the kitchen so I went in. "You okay?"

She looked up from staring at the worktop. "Yeah, sorry. I've not seen him like that in a while. Thought it was behind him."

"Like he said to me, people have setbacks. Like you've told me before, he'll be fine."

"Don't let him fall, Chloe."

"Don't plan to."

I sat down and she opened the fridge, pulling out a bottle of white wine. "This late?" I asked.

"Oh, yes."

"Logan's good, Cass."

"I hope so. Want a glass?"

Why not? "Please."

"I'm worried about him. I lost one brother and I'm not prepared to lose another."

I ran my finger around the bottom of the empty wine glasses on the counter. "You won't lose him." *I won't lose him.* "It was a one off. We stopped by Jace's grave a few days ago, that's probably why he's not dealing so well. I shouldn't have suggested we stopped."

"Don't blame yourself for his drinking, he's perfectly old enough to not get smashed." She poured two very generous glasses of wine and immediately took a long sip.

"Thanks, Cass. I know he's old enough to handle it but sometimes he just doesn't. I'll talk to him in the morning."

"You think he'll tell you more than *I'm fine*?"

I shook my head. "Not at all, but I'll try anyway."

"You're good for him. He wouldn't listen to any of us."

"Not convinced he listens to me the whole time either. Guys are a nightmare."

She laughed. "Yeah, don't I know it? Fucking Rick."

"Sorry, Cass. How's everything going there?"

"Nothing new. I can't wait for all this to be over, to go back to my maiden name and put him firmly in the past. I must've had a six year brain meltdown."

"You didn't. He was great before he turned into a selfish wanker."

She blinked hard and opened her eyes wide. "I don't think I've ever heard you say the word wanker before."

"Don't think I've used it much. Rick thoroughly deserves that title."

She held her glass up and I did the same, ready to toast to whatever she wanted. "To moving on from wankers."

I clinked my glass against hers. "To the next man in your life being worthy of your love."

"Back atcha, chick," she said. "Never know, maybe we'll both get lucky this year."

"I'll definitely drink to that!"

CHAPTER THIRTEEN

Chloe

Nell leant in, shouting over the music, "So no more Rhys?"

I shook my head. "No, he's nice and everything but—"

"You don't want to rip his clothes off?"

"I was going to go with *there's no spark* but that works too." I sat back, taking a sip of my vodka and lemonade. The whole situation was irritating. Here I was completely ready to move on and date again but I didn't want anyone. The only guy I wanted to spend time with was Logan. Perhaps not wanting anyone was my punishment for moving on from Jace.

"Don't fret, Chlo, you'll find your Mr Right."

"Hey," Ollie said, holding out his arms, "you could always settle for a Mr Right Now."

Logan kindly slapped the back of Ollie's head for me.

"I think I'll pass, Ollie, but thanks."

"Yeah, got someone else in mind?"

Logan thrust his empty glass at Ollie. "Your round, mate."

He stood and rolled his eyes. "Same again, ladies?"

Not being ones to turn down free drinks, me and Nell accepted and downed our last few mouthfuls.

"Oh, I know what we can do!" Nell said. "Me and Logan can set you up with someone in here."

"I don't think so," I replied.

"Oh, come on, Chloe. You'll never find someone if you don't meet anyone new."

"I thought we came for a drink, not to pimp Chlo out," Logan said.

I pointed to him. "Exactly, thank you!"

"Don't be antisocial."

"I'm not, Nell, if someone approaches me I'll talk to them and if I like them maybe something will happen but I'm *not* walking around this club looking for a man." Dating was something I wanted to do again but I wasn't desperate. I had at least another ten years before I started worrying about that.

"Okay, well, after this drink we'll go dance and I'm sure you'll be approached by loads of gorgeous, eligible bachelors."

"Or slimy, dirt bags with pregnant girlfriends back at home," Logan said, earning a glare from Nell.

"Right, let's slow down, shall we. I'm perfectly fine hanging out with you guys. In fact that's all I want to do tonight, so no more talk of setting me up." I stared pointedly at Nell.

She raised her hands. "Fine. It's up to you."

"Can't resist playing Cupid, can ya?"

"I just want to see you happy, Chlo."

"I *am* happy. I miss Jace and that'll never change but I'm happy again. I don't need a man for that, okay."

She gave me a one sided hug. "I'm glad you're happy and I promise there will be no more man talk tonight."

***

So I was drunk. That happy, everything's just dandy drunk, and I was loving it. Logan had made himself my bloody babysitter for the night but I didn't really care because he was good to look at and smelt great.

He was the designated driver because after I'd yelled at him for about twenty minutes for getting wasted alone like he used to he agreed to give drinking a miss for this weekend. I did feel bad about being mean to him but he worried me so I didn't feel bad enough to suggest a taxi.

Nell had been trying to get me to dance with her for the last ten minutes but I was content sitting at our table, laughing with Logan. I wish Ollie didn't have his tongue down some girl's mouth and hand up her skirt because then he could dance with Nell and leave me and Logan alone.

"Chloe, come on, I wanna dance," Nell said for the millionth time.

"I wanna do a shot with Logan!"

"Logan's driving," he said, smirking at me.

I like his smirk.

I held my finger up and pouted. "One teeny little shot?"

He was driving but one shot of something not too strong halfway through the night wasn't going to do any harm, especially not to someone as muscular as Logan.

I like his muscles.

Nell huffed and walked away.

"Please?" I added.

"*One*," he said, holding back a grin.

"Yay. I'll get it." Before I could hop off the stool he gripped my shoulders.

"You stay right here, little pisshead. I'll get the shot you *wanna do with Logan*."

Smug bastard.

He touched my arm as he left the table and I felt a shudder ripple through my body. It reminded me of the night I'd fallen asleep to his fingers gliding all over my arm.

I watched him walk over to the bar. Those light denim

jeans... Wow.
I like his backside.

The whole time he was at the bar I watched him. I watched the muscles in his forearms and silently thanked him for rolling his sleeves up. I watched him laugh and smile as he spoke to the bartender, and I watched those gorgeous blue eyes shimmer with the spotlights above the bar.

He walked back, smiling wider as he caught my eye.

I stopped breathing and for the first time since Jace died I felt the floor being whipped away from under me. I fell into darkness. *I like Jace's brother.*

Logan did a little bow as he handed me my shot.

Through the ringing in my ears and churning in my stomach, I managed to ask, "What is it?"

"Jager."

I nodded, not really registering his reply. Raising the glass, I clinked it against his and downed it in one. I liked Logan, and I needed another bloody shot!

"So what's with the heavy drinking tonight, Chlo? Not that I'm not enjoying you being drunk."

"Just needed a night out."

"That didn't answer the question."

"I don't know. I've not been drunk in ages and I wanted to be a normal, almost twenty-one-year-old for a change. It's been three years since I was pissed and carefree."

"Hey, I'm not judging. I like drunk Chloe, remember?"

I like sober and drunk Logan.

What the hell was I going to do now? Ignore it and pretend it wasn't happening was about all I could do. He was Jace's brother for fuck sake, so nothing could happen, and I couldn't lose Logan, too. I could deal with it. It was fine. I was just feeling deflated and vulnerable after things didn't work out with Rhys. *Everything is fine.*

"Dance with me?" I asked, tilting my head to the side before my brain could register that it probably wasn't a good idea to dance with him.

"Sure. You can walk, right?"

"Yes!" I hopped down off the stool and the world tipped to the right. "Whoa!" Logan's arms were around me quicker than I could blink. "I can walk. I just got up too quickly."

"Sure you can, sweetheart."

I gripped his upper arms. "Don't let me fall."

"I won't."

"Promise?"

Letting go of me with one arm he made a cross over his heart and held onto me again. I kinda loved it when he did that. And when he called me sweetheart, it didn't at all sound like when your grandad said it. Logan made it sexy, painfully sexy.

Before I did something really stupid and kissed him, I pulled back, guiding us through the thick crowd to the dance floor. "We should find Nell," I shouted over the thudding music.

I expected him to agree and for us looking for her but he brought me further into his strong arms and swayed us to the beat of the song. My skin prickled from the heat of so many bodies in such a small space and the look of intensity in Logan's eye. I wasn't sure if it was the alcohol in my system or if he really was about to kiss me but it sure looked like he was going to.

We shouldn't. The last person in the world I should be kissing was Logan. He was the worst person I could pick to *like*, only I didn't pick. I didn't get a choice. It was what it was. And what it was, was pretty shit. What kind of person wants her dead ex's brother? What was wrong with me? I didn't do things like that.

Logan's hands were on my hips but I felt them everywhere. He was a good dancer, he could really move and the way he looked at me made me dizzy. He guided me around the dance floor, or as much of it was we could move through anyway.

I leant in just a little bit further and my breath caught in my throat as my chest pressed against his. There was no distance between us. I wanted nothing more than for him to kiss me. My eyes were focused on his lips and I knew I should move them but I couldn't.

"What's up?" he shouted in my ear.

I shook my head. There was absolutely no way on earth I was telling him that I was desperate for him to kiss me.

"You feeling okay? You look pale."

And there was my ticket to get out of being this close and wanting more without having to tell him what was going on.

"I need some air."

With a quick nod, he had me tucked under his arm and walked us towards the exit. We'd danced for one song and I couldn't handle even one more.

I sucked in a deep breath as soon as the cool night's air hit me. Logan still held on to me, worried that I would collapse, so I didn't get the full effect of the cold that I wanted. "You alright? Want me to take you home?"

"No, I'm fine. I don't feel ill or anything, just a little hot in there."

His gaze trapped me, drawing out the truth. I prayed that I looked and sounded convincing enough. It wasn't even a complete lie, I was too hot inside, but that was because he was pressed up against me, making me feel desire like I'd never experienced before. *It's the alcohol.*

"Sure?"

"Yeah," I replied and nodded. "I just need a couple minutes, then we can go back in. I'll let you buy me a cocktail."

"Wow, thanks," he said sarcastically.

"You're happier today," I said.

"Well, not hung over like Thursday. Feeling like shit really puts a downer on my mood. I'm out with friends and I don't have to work tomorrow."

I gripped his arm as the world slanted to the left. "You're working tomorrow. We're going for a run."

"That's not work, you don't pay me to train you."

"Hey!" I snapped. "You wouldn't let me."

"Damn straight, I wouldn't."

"Can we go back in now? I'm okay." *And I need another drink.*

***

"You can't walk in a straight line even a little bit, can you?" Logan said, leading me to his car. As designated driver he was the only sober one.

Gripping his muscular arm, I planted my feet where I planned to be in a straight line but even I knew I was stumbling.

Logan laughed, pulled my hands from gripping him and wrapped his arm around my waist. I didn't like not having something to cling to so I fisted the front of his shirt. If he let go I wanted something to keep me up. "You're a terrible drunk, Chlo."

"You're a terrible…" Giggling, I buried my head in his chest. "I don't know. I need to sleep."

"Wait until I've chucked you in my car, then you can sleep all you want."

Chuck me in?

"And, Chlo, you're one of my favourite people in the world but if you throw up in my car…"

I laughed again, stumbling sideways as I clung to Logan. "I won't be sick."

Nell hitched a ride on Ollie's back and they'd made it to the car while we were still walking through the car park. As much as my feet ached in my stupid heels I didn't want Logan to carry me. That probably would have brought on sickness.

***

We arrived back at Logan's, magically. Honestly, I remembered nothing of the car journey. I stumbled until my feet left the ground and I was in his arms. My stomach lurched but I managed to hold my breath and close my eyes before I met my stupid shots again.

Logan awkwardly unlocked and opened the front door and the first thing I heard was Cassie's laughter, followed by Julia and Daryl's. They were still up. Great.

"Someone had a few too many," Logan said, carefully depositing me on the sofa.

I reached over the back and pulled a blanket down, ready to get comfortable.

"Good night, Chlo?" Cass asked.

"I think so," I replied, looking at all three of her.

"Okay, I'm gonna get you some water," Logan said. "Don't throw up."

I gave him a thumbs up over my head. "What've you guys been doing tonight?"

"Figuring out Cassie's next step," Julia replied.

"Oh?"

"Rick has been posting pictures of Barbie's non-existent bump on Facebook," Cass explained. My mouth hit the floor. "Yep, that's right, she's pregnant."

"Bastard! I can't believe he did that. I'm so sorry, Cassie." She smiled sadly. I added, "Wait, you're still friends with him on Facebook?" My reply was a surprised slur but from the flush in her cheeks she understood.

Daryl scoffed. "That's exactly what I said."

"Not anymore! I removed him a little while ago. It will only driving me insane. I know he didn't do it to hurt me but that's how it feels. It's like he's flaunting his perfect new life in my face and I'm tired of letting it happen. He's having a *baby* with another woman and I wish her nothing but a healthy pregnancy, I would *never* wish a miscarriage on anyone, but it hurts so much to watch him be a dad when I couldn't give him that."

"You gave him you and that should have been enough," I said, burning with anger that she blamed herself. Logan sat beside me and instead of handing me my water he slammed it down on the coffee table. He was mad too. Rick promised to love her no matter what. There were other ways they could have had a child.

"Are you fucking serious, Cassie?" Logan growled, leaning around me. "He knocks this bitch up and you think—"

"Don't." I gripped his upper arm, or as much of it as I could. I was so not in the right state to referee Logan but it didn't look like I had a choice. He was fiercely protective of the people he loved, especially his siblings, so I knew how pissed off he was that Cass still blamed herself.

"Logan, calm down," Daryl said.

He took a deep breath, jaw clenched and I really didn't think he could calm down but eventually, he obeyed his dad. He leant over and handed me my water. I downed it in about five gulps.

"My head hurts."

"That'll be all the alcohol," Logan said, smirking at my discomfort. I was pretty sure my aching head was a direct result of the confusing spike of my heart whenever I looked at him. That wasn't supposed to happen.

CHAPTER FOURTEEN

Chloe

I woke up and instantly regretted drinking so much the night before. A marching band had taken up residence in my head, and I felt like I'd been eating sand. A bottle of water sat on Jace's bedside table. I reached for it and unscrewed the lid, drinking awkwardly on my side.

After draining the bottle and not feeling quite so horrendous, I got out of bed. I was in a pair of Jace's joggers and one of his t-shirts and my make-up had been removed. I remembered nothing so either I was *that* drunk or Cass had looked after me well.

I walked downstairs and came face to face with Logan, standing just outside the kitchen door, arms folded over his chest looking very amused.

"Not now," I said, holding my finger up. "I need more water and paracetamol. Make that happen, please."

He only looked more amused.

"Please, Logan, the marching band just won't quit it. Feel sorry for me!"

"Self-inflicted, sweetheart."

"I gave you sympathy when you were hung over."

A short burst of laugher made me glare. "Not once did

you give me any sympathy."

"Well, I am now. Please, Logan, just make it stop hurting."

His face turned serious and he stared at me for a little too long. He was either genuinely concerned that I was in pain or thinking of a comeback.

"Sit down and I'll fix your head."

"Thank you," I said, groaning and curling up on the sofa. Daryl, Julia and Cassie all asked how I was and I groaned in response to every one of their questions. I wasn't human enough to hold a conversation yet, plus, all I could think about was the confusing feelings I now had for Logan.

"Here, pisshead," Logan said, "drink this and take these."

"I prefer sweetheart or Chlo to pisshead but thank you." I sat up and took the pills and water, downing them in one go.

"Want something to eat?"

"I'm doing a fry up," Daryl said, walking into the kitchen. "You in, Chloe?"

"Please," I replied. My stomach turned inside out. I was so ready for food, especially greasy food.

***

I sat next to Logan at the table but felt like I shouldn't. His smile did things to me that had never happened before. What the fuck was wrong with me? I knew that I was more than ready to let someone else in again but not Jace's bloody brother.

Maybe it was because he was the one who dragged me out of my pit and made me get a grip on my life again? Maybe it was just a little crush on a man that meant so much to me and a man that I knew had a drool-worthy body. Or maybe I was just a big sodding bitch and I had real feelings for my dead ex's brother.

"Not hungry anymore, Chlo?" Logan asked, smirking at me pushing the food around my plate.

"Just feeling a little delicate." I felt sick, puke my guts up sick. But I wasn't entirely sure if that was from the alcohol or from wanting to lean closer and breathe him in. He was amazing, incredible and I owed him so much. I wanted nothing more than to snuggle up on his lap and feel his lips against mine.

"Drink your tea, that'll help."

I nodded, not looking at him and picked it up. Could something ever happen between us? Bile rushed up my throat but I gulped it down with a mouthful of tea. Logan was Jace's brother, of course, it couldn't. I couldn't be that person. I couldn't have his family hate me. I couldn't have the stares and bitchy comments whenever I was out. Logan, no matter what happened with this stupid crush from here, couldn't happen.

After lunch I felt human again. A human with an annoying background headache but at least I didn't want to curl into a ball and cry in a dark room anymore. Me and Cassie were laying on the sofas in the living room, watching old romance movies and not talking about Rick getting his new girlfriend pregnant. Cass was holding up well considering.

"London on Saturday," she said. "I can't wait."

"Yeah, it'll be good. Weird but good."

"I thought that too. I'm glad we're doing it though, it'd mean a lot to Jace."

"It would. Bet he'll be laughing watching us look at all those boring buildings," I said. "Me and Logan are going to go off and do some proper sightseeing too. Wanna come?"

Her eyebrows flicked up before she corrected it. What was she thinking? There was no way she could just guess what I was feeling... Was there? "Sounds good, I might do if I'm not in a spa."

Since her rubbish attempt at hiding her initial response,

which I still couldn't work out if it was surprise or something else entirely, I was worrying. She would say something if she felt I was getting too close to Logan. She was Jace's sister, too, for Christ sake! There was no way she wouldn't have it out with me if she thought I was betraying him. It was one thing for her to support me moving on with another man but an entirely different thing to support me moving on with the older brother.

Her eyes, which were the same as Logan's, gave nothing away at all. She didn't look mad. She didn't look any different. How was I going to find out what was going through her head if she gave me nothing?

"You're thinking of spa-ing it then?" I said.

"I'll do the Jace tourist bit the first day but I don't know how much *he would've loved this* I can take. It's easier now but not *that* easy."

Now that was true. I could talk about him, laugh and smile while thinking of him and be thankful for the time I got with him but it still hurt. Nothing was ever going to stop it hurting that little bit – not any amount of time.

Logan, as if he knew I was obsessing about him, came back into the room and lifted my feet, sitting down and putting them back over his lap. Innocent enough… before. It felt really nice. I wanted him to massage my feet, to rub those hands up my legs, anything affectionate. I wanted him to cross that boundary, and I hated myself for it.

I sat up, stretching my back so it looked like I was just getting comfortable. I couldn't be that close to him while I wanted him, while all I could think about was kissing him.

One night was all it had taken me to fuck things up in my head. How could I like Logan? I was probably being too hard on myself. It wasn't as if I chose to feel like this. There was no way I would choose to want Logan but I could choose to ignore it and that was exactly what I was going to do.

"What're you two chatting about and do we really have

to watch this shit?"

"*Grease* is a classic so, yes, we do," Cassie said. "And we were just talking about London. You two're going off and I'm going to a spa."

He frowned. "For the whole weekend?"

"No, just the second day."

"You don't want to do the shit Chlo wants to do with us?" he asked.

Cass's eyes flicked between us so quickly I almost didn't catch it. But I did so that was just one more thing to obsess over.

"Nah, think I'll need the pampering. It'll be a nice weekend but it'll be hard, too."

Logan looked away from us, his posture turning more hostile. He looked like he wanted to bolt for the door. What the hell was up with everyone today? I felt like I went out last night and everything was normal then I got drunk, started having fuzzy feelings for Logan and suddenly nothing made any bloody sense.

"You okay?" I asked.

He nodded and smiled at me, snapping back to us from wherever he was in his mind. "Fine. I'm gonna go for a run. I take it you're giving it a miss?" he said, already getting up. There was no way I wanted to stand up let a lone run anywhere but I got the feeling that he was only asking because he felt obligated to, not because he wanted me there. This was definitely a Logan only run.

"No, thanks," I replied.

He was already walking towards the stairs but grunted what sounded like *alright* before he disappeared upstairs.

Was I asleep still? I wanted to wake up and have everything be how it was. Most of all I wanted my stupid heart to stop jumping all over the place when he was around.

CHAPTER FIFTEEN

Logan

Chloe was hilarious. When she said she wanted to act like a tourist she wasn't kidding. Her phone, doubling up as her camera, was attached to her hand as she snapped a picture of every-fucking-thing we passed – in the car.

"You don't get out much, do you?" I said, laughing as she gasped at some statue and took a dozen pictures of it.

"Shut up! I'm excited, Mr Grumpy."

"I'm not grumpy, I'm just normal. This is kinda excessive and you know all those pictures are going to be blurry, right?"

"Yes, you are and no, they're not. I should've gone in your parents' car."

I snorted. "Please. My car is much more fun and you know it."

She rolled her eyes. "Sure. How long do you think we're going to look at buildings for?"

"Not long," I replied. "I want to do a couple for Jace but, fuck me, it's boring. I just need a pub and beer and I'll be happy." *And you naked and/or proclaiming your undying love for me.*

"Yeah, I definitely didn't share that passion with him. Actually, I didn't share any passions with him. We couldn't have been more different."

"Opposites attract."

Now why the fuck did I just say that? I was anti opposites and pro same. Same, same, same, same, same. We made so much sense I wanted to shake her for not seeing it now and almost seven years ago.

"I guess," she replied, frowning.

"You guess?"

"Yeah. I don't know. Recently, I've been feeling like…" She bit her lip and looked out of the window. If she thought there was any way I was letting that go then she really didn't know me at all.

"Spill, Chlo. It's just me and you in the car so out with it."

"I've been wondering if we would've made it. Sure, we were going to uni together and all but I think the further into the big, wide world we got the more we would grow apart. Growing up is inevitable. I'll never know but do you think we could've made it?"

"You two were so confident you would. Sickening really." Sickening. Agonising.

She looked back and gave me a shy smile. "We were one hundred per cent sure we'd be together forever and it's nice to think that maybe we could have been. Still, not a whole lot of people marry the person they were with when they were fifteen."

"Some do."

"Yeah. That was going to be us. I just wonder if it actually would have or if real life would've separated us eventually."

"Don't drive yourself crazy thinking about it, Chlo."

"Oh, I won't. Sometimes my mind wanders off into plenty of what ifs."

Mine too. What if she'd fallen for me and not him?

I slammed on my breaks as some idiot pulled out right in front of us. "What the fuck!"

Chlo had her hands on the dash, eyes wide. "We should've taken the train."

"And listened to you moaning about how crowded it is?"

"It *is* crowded. But at least we'd be alive."

I smirked at her. "We're fine. I just gotta allow for more pricks on the road."

"Might help if you watched the road, too," she said, pushing my head back around. "Where is this hotel anyway?"

"My instructions were to follow them." Mum, Dad and Cassie were in front, somewhere. I could just about see them a few cars up when the 4x4 prick that pulled out on us swayed to the side.

"It's a shame we couldn't be here for a full week. There's a lot to see and not just Jace's stuff."

I wanted to tell her I'd bring her back some other time but that seemed a little inappropriate, especially since I wanted to add that all she'd see was the inside of our hotel room.

"This won't be your only chance to explore London, Chlo."

"Yeah, I know. Me and Jace wanted to take a selfie in front of Big Ben. I'd really like to do that."

"Yeah, we can make sure you do that."

"*We* do that. I'm not doing it on my own!"

It shouldn't make me want to shout *fuck yeah* that she wanted a picture with me but it did. "You sure, sweetheart? Seems like it was a you and Jace thing. I'm cool to watch and laugh at you or take the picture for ya."

"No, I think he'd want you in it if he couldn't be."

Was that all he'd want me to do if he couldn't?

"You think?"

She smiled. "Of course. He loved you, Logan. He looked up to you more than anyone else."

"Then why did he never get off that fucking Xbox when

I told him to?"

Her laugher filled the car. "Not even I could get him off it and I could offer him things—"

"No! Thank you," I said, my stomach turning inside out.

I'd heard them before and it ripped me apart. After that one, gut wrenching time I was careful not to go to bed too close to them going up and if I heard anything I was out of my room and downstairs in a rush.

She laughed again and rolled her eyes. "So you'll do it with me?"

"Too easy, Chlo."

"Now, now. Not going back to your whore ways I hope?"

"No, thanks."

"Good. Hey, have you spoken to Cass?" she asked.

I gripped the steering wheel. Talking or even thinking about what that wanker did to my sister made me want to rip his limbs off.

"I have."

Chloe laughed. "And?"

"She's doing alright, considering."

"We'll get her through it."

"We will." I wasn't going to let anyone I loved drown in the darkness I knew only too well.

***

After checking into our hotel rooms we wasted no time in exploring London. Day one was all about Jace so we headed to Westminster Cathedral. Apparently, Jace liked the shapes of the building or some shit like that. He'd also wanted to visit Albert Memorial, the Royal Albert Hall, The White Tower and Tower Bridge. We had one day so we weren't going to spend too much time there, plus, we wouldn't really know much about what we were looking at.

Day two was going to involve actual fun. Mum and Dad were hitting a museum Jace'd wanted to visit and one they wanted, Cassie had already booked herself into a day spa and Chlo and me were being annoying tourists. Well, she was, I was just there for the view. The view being her.

We took taxis because Mum flat out refused to go on anything underground.

"Who gets enjoyment out of looking at a building?" I said, staring up at Westminster Cathedral.

"Our brother," Cass replied.

"Yeah, well, he spent ninety per cent of his time killing zombies or whatever he did on the computer, what did he know."

Chloe laughed and snapped a picture. "I think it's pretty."

Mum, Dad and Cass moved closer to the cathedral, talking about Jace.

"Are you going to take pictures all weekend?" I asked her.

"Yep," she replied. "I'm sending them to Nell as per her instructions and I'm also going to print the boring building ones off and give them to Jace. Think he'd like that."

"He would."

We walked around the outside of the building and Mum and Chloe got pictures from literally every angle.

"You know Jace has probably visited all this already, right?" I said as we got out of the taxi at The White Tower.

"Oh my God, you're the grumpiest!" Cassie said.

"I'm the realist," I replied. "I bet he's having such a laugh watching us right now." He was pissing himself for sure. Little wanker.

Chloe laughed, following my parents. She looked over her shoulder. "And you're putting on a great show."

CHAPTER SIXTEEN

Chloe

As much as I enjoyed yesterday, doing things Jace wanted to do, I was really looking forward to hanging out with Logan and doing something fun. I had a camera full of photos to show Jace but now it was time to fill it up with photos for me.

In three days it would be Jace's birthday and for the first time I didn't feel like hiding in bed all day. I was having a good time in London with Jace's family and it kind of felt like he was with us, too.

Cassie shoved her make-up bag in her suitcase and turned to me. "Sure you don't want to come to the spa?" she asked.

"No, thanks. Got a full day planned."

"You're dragging Logan to all of the tourist hot spots, he's going to strangle you by the end of the day."

Crossing my legs on the bed, I shrugged. "Pretty much. It's going to be fun."

She laughed. "You're evil."

"Hey, he volunteered to take me places."

"And he won't regret that," she replied, giving me her *I'm thinking more than I'm going to tell* expression. Logan would enjoy the day I planned and she knew it. Not that he'd ever admit it.

"I do feel bad that we're all going off doing our own thing and your parents are still doing Jace stuff."

"Only for the morning, then they're off, too. This weekend isn't just about him; it's about us as well. We all need to do something for ourselves. It feels like closure to me. I like that I can do something for him and for me."

"Yeah, I guess. I like that we can do this without it hurting too much."

"Feels good."

"Miss him," I said. "I often wonder where we'd be now."

She deadpanned. "You know exactly where you'd be, you had every second mapped out."

I stuck my finger up. "We did, but things have changed, besides the obvious, and I can't help wonder if we'd have stuck to it. I think we would." This conversation was the same one I'd had with Logan but I was keen to get a female's perspective.

"Things change, Chlo. People grow all the time, apart from my ex, he just turned into a bastard." Yes, he did. "Maybe you would've got that house, dream jobs in the same town, engaged, promoted, married, had a couple kids and died long into old age, or maybe you would've gone down different paths out of uni."

"Guess I'll never know." I didn't like the unknown. It was scary. I didn't feel free or exhilarated; I felt fear.

"You've got a second chance, Chlo. You've done that hard bit of getting over Jace so concentrate on what happens next for you. Go and have a good day with Logan and do it without feeling guilty for today not being all about Jace."

I wanted to say something in return, thank her and pretty much recite her speech, turning it around to her but there was an obnoxiously loud knock on the door.

"Well, that'll be Logan then," I said, getting off the bed

to open the door.

"Ready for this?" he said, skipping hello altogether.

"We're going to have a great day," I said, pushing his mouth up at the sides with my fingers. He raised an eyebrow but made no attempt to swat me away. I lowered my hands, grinning at him, earning a reluctant smile.

Behind me Cassie grabbed her handbag and pushed past us. "Have a good day you two."

"And you," I called after her as she walked down the stairs of the townhouse hotel. "Where to first, Mr Happy?"

"This is your day, sweetheart, you lead the way."

I grabbed my phone and shoved my coin purse in my coat pocket. "This isn't just about me. Logan, I don't want to drag you around London if you don't want to."

He held his hands up. "Ah, ah, ah, don't do that. I'm more than happy to escort you around London and do all that tourist shit you want to do. Besides, my other options are more buildings and museums, or a spa."

"You sure? We can do something you want to do instead."

I watched him breathe in and out three times before replying, "There's nothing else I want us to do. Let's get the tube and go to Westminster, Big Ben and the London Eye. Not sure where the fuck off creepy wax place is but we'll grab a map at the station."

I closed the door and locked it. It wasn't until we got to the bottom of the stairs that I realised Logan was so looking forward to today. But I wasn't going to say anything.

Stepping outside the hotel, I stopped dead. "So... the tube station is where?" I asked.

"Chloe, you have the worst sense of direction."

I threw my hands up. That was so not true. "It all looks the fucking same!" Rows and rows of townhouses were everywhere you looked. How was anyone supposed to find their way around? I was surprised there weren't more Londoners wandering the streets, scratching their heads.

"You're spending too much time with me," he said, touching my elbow and starting us walking along the path straight ahead.

"What?"

"You said fucking, you're always telling me I say that too much."

"Huh, you're definitely rubbing off on me." I regretted it the second the words left my mouth. I watched him struggle to hold it together with a bored expression. "Go on!"

Laughter burst from deep in his chest. "Sweetheart, it would be an honour to rub off on you."

My stomach fizzed. *Fizzed!* Like that popping candy. *Stay cool, Chloe.* "I walked right into that one, didn't I?"

He casually slung his arm over my shoulders as we walked towards where I hoped was the tube station. How did he just know where we were going?

I liked his arm around me a little too much. It felt really, really good.

Annoyingly, Logan found the station straight away and it took me all of zero seconds to realise I hated the underground. People were everywhere. Dirt, invisible dirt for the most part, was everywhere. Maps that made little to no sense mocked me on the walls.

Logan was a picture of ease, taking one glance at the routes and leading us through the stations. I clung to his hand, not even bothering to look where we were going by the second change.

"Almost there, Chlo," he said, holding onto the bar above my head. I gripped the one behind him, bringing us a lot closer together than what we'd usually stand. As the train wobbled on the tracks I wanted to wrap my arms around his chest. I was all over the place but he stood still, same as everyone else, apparently.

When we finally reached our stop I was ready to go back to the hotel. "Alright, if we can't get to all the places we want to go by foot we're not going there. Also, we're getting a taxi back."

"Don't be such a baby," he replied.

We walked upstairs, to holy ground level, still holding hands. It had started through fear but now I didn't want to let go. The same as his arm around me earlier, holding his hand felt nice.

He didn't let go so as long as he was cool with it I wasn't letting go.

I squealed as I saw Big Ben, and using my non-Logan hand, slipped my phone out of my pocket and took a couple pictures. "There's the London Eye! Let's do the picture with Big Ben and then go there!" It really was big. I mean, I knew it was big but seeing it, wow.

Logan laughed. "You're about to get really impossible, aren't you?" he asked, squeezing my hand.

I squeezed back. "Yep!"

Dragging Logan to the perfect spot, I turned us around and held my phone out. I rolled my eyes and looked up at him. "Logan!" He looked bored. I didn't want a picture of him looking bored. "Will you smile, please?"

He smiled too much but by the third picture the amusement of that must have worn off because we got a couple of really nice ones. I sent the best one to Nell, like I'd done with all the others. She wanted to know what I was doing all weekend but I bet by the end of the day she'd regret demanding pictures.

***

"Look, look, look! Buckingham Palace!" I pointed to the building from high up in the London Eye, but Logan was looking at me.

"Yes, Chloe," he replied, still not looking out of the big glass capsule that I kept reminding myself could absolutely not ever fall. He wasn't fooling me, I'd caught him looking out a few times when he thought I was distracted. Apparently, I was now hyper-aware of Logan so when he was around I was distracted; my mind on him constantly.

Not good, not good, not good!

I leant on the glass but before I could point out a street dance team, I was yanked back and Logan's hand was in mine again.

"Don't do that."

"It's safe, Logan." The glass was fine; it was whether the whole thing would stay attached to the big wheel that worried me.

"Still," he said, pulling me closer to his side, "don't do that."

For the rest of the way around I found it hard to watch the whole of London when Logan had me practically pinned to his side. I wanted to lean into him and already had done as much as I could get away with.

Cassie said this day was about us and I let it be. I forgot all about how much of a bad idea liking Logan was and just enjoyed being with him. I knew I would feel awful for it when the day was over but for a few hours I held Logan's hand, laughed and flirted with him as we made our way around the London.

For one day I let myself be with him and to steal a word from Logan, I fucking loved it.

CHAPTER SEVENTEEN

Logan

I wanted nothing more than to get blind drunk and forget today. I'd had a great time in London – the second day with Chloe where I was so close to her I could pretend she was mine, even if it was only for a few hours. That day seemed years ago compared to the absolute shit of a day Jace's birthday was.

Jace should be twenty-one. He should be here celebrating with a liquid breakfast, lunch and dinner. I should be planning a night out to get my properly grown up brother well and truly wankered. Instead I was standing at the gate to the cemetery, not able to take a step inside, like the fucking pussy I was.

Chloe had offered to come with me, Cass and my parents had offered to hang around until I arrived but I'd turned every one of them down because I wanted to *do it alone*. Well, I couldn't do it alone. There was nothing I could do to make my legs start working and walk up to his grave.

One of the shittiest things about this situation was him in this place. He was never alone when he was alive, never, but now he only had company when someone made the trip to sit above him and talk about mindless stuff that paled in comparison to him being in a box.

There were other people here, visiting their loved ones. At the minute Jace had no one with him. Mum, Dad, Cass and Chlo had left behind flowers. Jace's grave now looked like a fucking florist. He was a guy, he didn't even like flowers. I had a bottle of Jack in my hand but I couldn't get through the gate to have a drink with my brother.

Finally, I made my legs work and walked over to his grave. I sat down and froze up. On the rare occasions I'd been here I'd never known what to say. It didn't help that when I'd been here with anyone else they'd talked to him as if he was still here. I felt like shit that I couldn't do that.

Pouring a little Jack Daniels into the shot glass from my pocket, I downed it, filled it up again and sat it on the grass above him.

"Happy birthday, buddy." Jesus, I felt like I was going to ball like a baby and sounded like I was going to as well.

"Jace, you know I'm not good at this shit and I bet you're pissing yourself laughing from wherever you are right now, for which I will get you back one day, unless, of course, I don't die until I'm a little old man. Hey, at least you'll finally be able to beat me! Bloody pussy." I smiled at the memory of him trying to wrestle me to the floor.

I was being inappropriate, I think. What was protocol for talking to a dead person? Was it all about how much you loved and missed them? That kind of went without saying. He drove me crazy and loving Chloe while he was with her put a strain on my relationship with him but I would've died for him in a heartbeat. I would switch places with him right now.

"Sorry, bud. I don't even know if you can see what's going on from where you are, I assume you can, but I'm still sorry. I've been a shit brother for years. I envied you for years. I wanted to be the one who woke up beside her, who she looked at with *that* look, who she came to with a problem. I wanted to be the one who got to hold her and kiss her and make everything better. I watched you do that and it killed me, but I also want you to know that it only ever made me hate myself. I may have envied you and I may have wanted what you had but I could *never* hate you. Shit, Jace, I don't want her to affect me so much and I don't want to love her to the point where it suffocates me, but I have no idea how to make it stop. You know I would make it disappear if I could."

I gulped, tapping my fingers against my legs. "Half the time I don't know what I'm doing. It's a fucking miracle I helped her at all because I feel like I'm fucking up at every turn. I wish you were still here to keep the line firmly in place. I can't stop myself thinking about being with her, as hard as I try, I just can't fucking stop. God, if she was here right now I'd get told off for swearing so much. Her bloody fault though, right? Seriously, man, I just need you to know that I can't help any of it."

I downed a mouthful straight from the bottle as I felt a tear on my cheek.

"I'm so sorry, Jace," I whispered. "Don't hate me. Hey, does it help that it hurts like fuck to want her this badly but to know that I'll never get anywhere?" I tried to make it sound like a joke but I couldn't lift my voice enough. There was nothing funny about how much I wanted to be with her.

I took another long swig, swallowing a lump in my throat down with the whisky. A damn tear dropped onto my lap. "I miss you, bro. It might not seem like it but I do and I'd give anything to have you back. Chloe would, too, she'd want you." She'd wish I could switch places with Jace, too. I took a deep, broken breath and clenched my jaw. That hurt.

"Sorry, today's about you and I'm being a dick. You know I suck at this. I should've just stuck with I love you and I miss you, huh? I do, Jace."

The next gulp didn't burn anymore; the whisky slid down nicely and took the edge off how shitty I felt.

"We never really got the chance to go drinking together,

did we? You were always too busy on your bloody Xbox or with Chlo. Probably a good thing though, you didn't need to learn that alcohol can, temporarily, solve your problems. Thing is, you sober up eventually and you're left to deal with your shit with a hangover. Now I'm on drunk watch; someone's always waiting to stop me going over the edge," I said, waving the bottle around before downing a bit more.

"Oh no, you don't," Chloe said, snatching the bottle of Jack off me.

I turned back to my brother, waving my now empty hand. "See!"

She sat down, putting my drink as far out of my reach as she could. While her back was turned, I swiped my hands over my face. "What're you doing, Logan?"

I pointed to Jace's grave. "I'm having a drink with my brother on his birthday."

"That would be all well and good if this didn't have *falling off the wagon* written all over it. I'm not letting you drown your sorrows and get drunk, especially not here. Jace wouldn't want that either."

I shrugged. "I dunno, I think he might like it."

"Why're you really getting drunk, Logan?"

"Isn't it obvious, Chloe?"

She growled. "God, you're such a pain in the arse!" Her small, warm hand found its way around mine and I almost stopped breathing. I'd not had enough alcohol to think kissing her was a good idea – I don't think that amount of alcohol existed anyway – but, fuck me, I wanted to.

"Please, don't do this, Logan. This isn't going to help anyone. I know you miss him, I miss him, too, but there's nothing we can do and getting wasted isn't going to make you feel better, not in the long run."

"I hate it when you make sense."

She smiled and it made her eyes lighten. "I always make sense."

Yeah, she had always made sense. That was the fucking

problem.

"Sorry, I didn't mean to piss over today."

She squeezed my hand and I had a hard time restraining myself from grabbing her and wrapping my entire body around hers. I wanted her tucked against my chest, in my arms so we could grieve Jace together, support each other.

"How're you doing?" I asked. She looked okay, no redness around her eyes, no pain in her smile.

"I'm doing really good actually. This is the first time a birthday or anniversary has felt…" She trailed off, frowning and pouting her lip very slightly as she tried to find the right word. "I'm not sure how to explain it. Happy definitely isn't right. I can remember him and smile, I can wish him happy birthday without wanting to curl up in a ball and not exist for a while. I feel peaceful."

Good. I wished I could find that, too. I wished I didn't love her so damn much so I could stop feeling the crushing guilt on top of missing him. I couldn't forgive myself for wanting what I wanted so I couldn't just pure and simple miss him, there was all this guilt around it, tainting it.

Well, there was no way I wasn't holding her now, I needed it more than I'd ever needed anything. "Come here, sweetheart."

She shuffled closer, sitting by my side and laying her head on my shoulder as I wrapped my arm around her. "I'm so glad you're doing okay. I was worried about you."

"I think it's you we need to worry about now. You're the one that needs to make peace with what's happened. We can't change it; we can't control it. The past is set in stone, Logan, and all we can do is focus on the future. I want you to be able to come here and not want to drink. You and Jace deserve to still have a relationship that doesn't hurt you."

I'd never have that.

"Is that what you've got?"

"Yes. It's different, obviously, but I still feel close to him and I still talk to him a lot. I wish I could have him back,

I miss my best friend, but I can't."

My heart stuttered and I wondered if she'd picked up on the fact that she'd said she wanted him back as a best friend and not boyfriend. She was over him, if that was even the right way of explaining it, but I'd just assumed she would want everything the way it used to be if she could. Was Jace just a best friend now?

"I'm glad to hear that," I replied, leaning my head against hers. Closing my eyes, I added, "What about your birthday?"

"Nothing big. I feel like a quiet one this year."

It'd been a quiet one for the last couple years but I got it.

"Next year I'm throwing you a massive party."

She laughed quietly, snuggling that tiny bit closer and putting her hand on the grass above Jace. "Deal."

CHAPTER EIGHTEEN

Chloe

"Happy Birthday!"

I jumped awake, ready to murder my parents in cold blood. They stood by my door wearing ridiculous matching smiles.

Groaning, I pushed myself up on my elbows. "Yeah, thanks."

"It's almost ten, love, come on, up out of bed."

"Your Mum's cooked a full English and it's almost ready."

"Now that I'll get up for." I swung my legs out of bed. "And presents? There are presents, right?"

Mum shrugged, trying not to smile. "There might be one or two." That meant she'd gone a little mad again. I was an only child and although I was never spoilt to the point where I got whatever I demanded – I wouldn't ever dare demand! – she did like to go all out on my birthday and Christmas.

"Do you want to get dressed first?" Dad asked.

I looked down at my plan purple pyjama shorts and matching spaghetti strap top. "Not really. Do I look bad?" It was hot today already and I was at home. There was no need for me to get dressed before breakfast.

"Of course not, you never look bad," he replied. "Downstairs then."

My parents traipsed behind me; the excitement from Mum was palpable. Birthdays and holidays were her thing. She loved celebrating anything with family and friends.

I rounded the corner and almost jumped back, knocking them both over.

"Happy Birthday!" Nell, Logan, Cassie, Julia and Daryl shouted.

Now I got the *are you going to get dressed* question, it was a prompt. But these people were practically family, so I didn't really care.

"Thank you," I said, returning Julia's bear hug.

"Your parents invited us for breakfast, I hope you don't mind us tagging along?" she said.

"Of course not. I'm glad you're here."

I was ambushed by Logan next. Bracing myself, I wrapped my arms around his waist as he hugged me. "Happy birthday, sweetheart."

My heart did all kinds of somersaults.

"Thanks," I replied a little breathlessly.

Cass, Nell and Daryl gave me a quick hug and then we went to eat the food that was making my mouth water. I did notice a massive pile of presents on the coffee table. Most were wrapped in gorgeous metallic purple paper with silver ribbons and bows – from my parents. The rest were mismatched and I suspected from our new guests.

I sat down next to Logan by habit while the parents pottered around getting breakfast onto plates and making tea and coffee. Nell and Cassie gossiped about what they'd missed from each other's lives. They weren't really close but got along well when they were together.

That left me with the guy that I couldn't get out of my head, a guy that I really couldn't want.

"So what have you got planned for your birthday?" he

asked. "Wallowing in your lost youth? Crying because you're not just twenty anymore you're well into your twenties?"

"I'm twenty-one," I said dryly. "And no, I figured I'd make Cass and Nell take me out and get me good and drunk. Girls' night sounds perfect to me. You know I don't want anything big."

He nodded. "Also a good idea. Are men not invited?"

They would've been but being drunk around Logan wasn't a good idea. The other night I danced too close to him, was too drunken flirty. I was afraid of what I'd do if my inhibitions and let's face it, morals, were lowered by booze.

"Nope, sorry. *Girls'* night."

"I'm up for that," Nell said, cutting in quickly before going back to her conversation with Cass.

"Fine, have your stupid girls' night but you'd better have a naked pillow fight."

"Really? And you do know it's supposed to be an *underwear* pillow fight?"

He grinned like a naughty schoolboy and his topaz eyes brightened. "Not in my head."

Oh, I knew how to wipe that smile off his face. "It's me, Nell and *your sister*."

His smile to fall I expected. What I didn't expect was over the top gagging and him playfully shoving me. "You're disgusting, Chloe!"

"You said it."

"No, I didn't. You've ruined naked pillow fights for me now, I hope you're happy."

The rest of the table fell silent and we suddenly had the full attention of six people, who were also gaping at us.

I smiled. "Inside joke." Logan scowled into the distance.

***

"You're wearing that out?" Logan asked, eyeing me pretty closely. Heat bubbled under my skin, trailing the path of his gaze. *Stop it!*

"What's wrong with what I'm wearing?" I asked a little breathlessly. What was he anyway, my wardrobe police?

"Nothing. Everything."

His words gave me nothing but Logan was protective so my money was on the dress being tight and short.

"Why don't you wear that knee length dress with the sleeves?"

I raised my eyebrow. "Mmm, that'll look lovely out clubbing."

"Exactly. It's very nice and very... covering."

"Thank you for the concern, Logan, but I think I'll be alright."

"If any guys try to cop a feel?"

"Sharply jerk leg up between their legs."

"Then punch them in the face. Goes for you too, Cass."

She rolled her eyes.

"Come on," I said, linking my arm through Cassie's, "let's go get Nell."

***

Never again. I would never drink again and I would never speak to Cassie or Nell again. They'd promised me they wouldn't let me get drunk, and I knew logically that it wasn't their responsibility, but they were the ones buying me a new drink and a shot before I'd even finished the previous one.

My phone rang and the shrill noise made me want to launch it at the wall. It was Logan, which made me want to launch myself at the wall because my heart was still doing that thing where it went crazy at the thought of him.

I wanted to be able to blame it on alcohol or the fact that he was nice to look at and I was female but deep down I knew it was more than that. I was developing real, big feelings for him.

I let it go through to voicemail, too guilty to answer and face him. It didn't help that Jace was staring at me from the photo collage I had on my wall. I felt like he knew. His eyes, that at the time were smiling, now felt angry and judgemental.

Liking Logan was betraying Jace and I wasn't sure how to deal with that other than to take Logan out of the equation altogether. It wasn't a solid plan, I was too close to his family to be able to ignore him forever but right now it was the only plan I had.

Nell, who was now sleeping on my bedroom floor – when did she get up or fall out of bed? – stirred and groaned. "Chloe?" she said.

"Yeah."

"Why am I on the floor?"

"No idea, but I hope it's as uncomfortable as my head."

"I think it probably is. Did you have a good night, though?"

I shrugged even though she couldn't see me because her hands were over her eyes. "I think so." My phone started ringing again.

"Are you going to get that?"

Logan again. "It's too early and I'm too hung over to talk," I said, hoping that'd be it and she'd let it go. I flicked the damn thing on silent and put it down.

"Who is it?"

"Logan. I'll speak to him later."

"Wow, you don't usually cut him off. What did he do?"

He was Logan and made me like him. That was what he did.

"Nothing, I just feel like shit and I know he'll be cheerful and possibly smug." Definitely smug. "I don't want to be around cheerful right now."

"Mmm hmm," she murmured.

I wanted to leap out of bed, shine my computer lamp in her eyes and ask her what she knew. That *mmm hmm* was not innocent. She couldn't know how I was feeling about him. Could she? God, I'd turned so paranoid.

"What?"

"Huh? Oh, nothing. I need food pretty soon or I'll be seeing all that vodka again."

"Right," I replied, forcing my legs to work and get me out of bed. "I'll make us something. Do *not* throw up in my room."

I took my phone downstairs with me, she would answer it if she saw it flash. I had a text from Logan and Cassie. Groaning, I filled the kettle up and flicked it on before reading them both.

Logan: I take it since you're not answering you're dying. Call me back so I can make fun properly. And drink water!

I smiled and tried to calm the new feelings he was giving me.

Cassie: I don't like alcohol. Hope you had a good birthday. Xxx

I didn't reply to either of them because they lived in the same house. I didn't want Logan to know I was maybe a teeny bit avoiding him if Cassie mentioned I'd texted her.

With a brief pep talk about how everything was going to be fine and if I just kept to myself for a few days this little thing for Logan would disappear and order would be restored to the universe, I turned the oven on to warm some croissants for me and the sick one.

CHAPTER NINETEEN

Chloe

I walked along the aisle, picking up the things Mum needed for dinner and some things she didn't. I had successfully avoided Logan's house for a two whole days. I'd managed to keep contact to a minimum, claiming that I was busy helping my parents make plans for their big anniversary trip in October.

But that was all about to change because Cassie was at the end of the aisle, looking at ready-made sandwiches.

"Hey," I said, stopping beside her.

She looked up and threw her arms around me. "Hey! What are you doing in a supermarket?"

"Getting my car repaired," I replied sarcastically.

"Oh, ha ha."

"Mum needed some stuff."

Cassie pointed to my eyes. "You look tired."

"Wow, thanks!"

"Come on. You not sleeping well?"

"I've had a couple late nights, no biggie."

Two very late nights where I laid in bed until the early hours, scolding myself for liking Logan and wondering how the hell it happened in the first place.

"Late nights where? You've not been over in a couple days," she said.

I frowned. What was with the twenty questions? "I'll be over soon, the parents' trip is almost sorted. Kinda want to go with them. Everyone okay?"

"We're fine; we miss you!"

I grimaced. They were practically family and I missed them, too, but I didn't like the way Logan made me feel. Or I did but knew I shouldn't.

"Miss you guys, too."

"I better go, lunch break is almost over and I've not eaten yet," she said, holding up the sandwich she was buying. "Tomorrow, Chloe Holland, be at ours."

"Yes, sir!"

Smiling, she walked off towards the tills.

I felt awful for lying to her. I think the only time I'd lied to her was when Jace and I first started having sex and I told her I was too ill to meet her in town because we wanted to spend the day in bed. Even then I felt so bad I vowed never to lie to her again, even if it was only something small. Here I was shovelling crap out of my mouth to cover up the fact that I was the worst person ever.

I grabbed the things Mum needed and headed home. Cass had texted me, telling me to come over at six tomorrow evening. The thought of being around Logan right now made me feel sick with nerves, excitement and guilt so I replied, telling her that I'd forgotten something I'd planned with Nell and couldn't make it.

At some point I'd have to go over. I couldn't avoid them all forever and I really didn't want to, I just wanted to try and find a way of fixing whatever wire was loose in my brain that said Logan was a good idea. Hopefully, I could do that soon because I missed them all like crazy.

***

I was wiping down the tables at the end of my shift when Cassie burst through the door – literally. That wasn't good. She had on her *I'm on a mission* face as she stalked towards me.

Pointing her freshly manicured finger, she said, "Right, you and me are going to sit down and talk about why you're back to looking like you're not sleeping much or eating properly. *And* why you're avoiding us. If you think I believe you forgot about seeing Nell you're very mistaken."

"I'm working, Cass."

"Then give me a cloth and I'll wipe tables with you... while you talk."

So there was no way I was getting away with this. Cassie didn't give up when she set her mind on something and it would seem that operation *get Chloe to spill all* was her number one project right now.

But I really didn't want to tell her.

"I'm just worried about uni starting up again."

"Bull. Shit." Her eyes widened a fraction. "If you think I don't know what's going on you're stupid."

"Well, if you know then why are you asking?"

"Because I want you to come to me. I want you to tell me."

I can't, I can't, I can't. God, I wanted to. I wanted someone to talk to about it but Cassie was the wrong person for that. Jesus, *Nell* was the wrong person. My friends had the right to give me their opinion and I already knew that what I felt was wrong.

She couldn't know the real reason or she'd be pulling my hair out and telling me what a terrible person I was. There was nothing she could say to me that I didn't already know. It shouldn't be Logan.

"Come on, Chlo. We've been through so much, you can talk to me about *anything* and I'm not going to judge."

"Not going to judge?"

"No. I promise I won't."

I wasn't sure if she really did know. It sounded as if she did and she was clearly confident that she did but I couldn't help thinking she would hate me.

I dropped the cloth on the table and sat down. Cass joined me. I felt sick and the words got stuck in my throat. "I don't know what to do," I said.

She sat still, silent and patient, not giving me any help to get out something as big as what I was about to tell her.

Dropping my gaze to the table, not being able to maintain eye contact, I said, "I like Logan."

"I know, Chloe."

I swallowed a lump in my throat and looked up at her with tear-filled eyes. "I'm so sorry, Cass. I don't want to and I tried to stop myself. I can't help it."

"Hey, it's okay." She reached across the table and took my hand. "It's really okay." I could've cried I was so overwhelmed that she was supporting me rather than spitting on me. "I know you like him and it's nothing to get yourself this worked up over. We're all worried about you."

All including Logan?

"What kind of person am I?"

"One who lost so much and deserves every bit of happiness."

"You're not getting this, Cass."

"No, I think I am. You were going to fall for someone eventually, no one expected you to stay celibate for the rest of your life. If it was my choice I'd want it to be Logan."

Was I asleep?

"What?" I asked.

"You're like a sister to me and I know Logan cares about you, he's the one who gets through to you, he protects you and keeps you safe. I get it, I really do, but I also know that if Jace had the choice he would want the two people he loved most to be happy. He would want Logan, someone he trusted with his life, to be the one who looked after you for the rest of your life."

That all kind of sounded like better the devil you know. She wanted Logan because she knew he wouldn't hurt me. I wanted Logan because he turned my world upside down, he made me question everything, he made me see impossible love in my future, he just made everything better.

"I appreciate that, Cass, but how can you not be mad? Jace is your brother, too."

"And I love him just as much but Jace isn't here, Chloe, and there's nothing we can do about that. Logan's here and you two have the chance to be happy. You'd be an idiot to ignore it when you *know* Jace would want you to do what made you happy."

"See, I can't wrap my head around that. Surely it would be anyone but Logan?"

"Why?" she asked.

"I don't have to explain that."

Sighing, she leant her arms on the table, getting closer, more serious. "You can't help who you fall for, period. I know you and I know there is no way in hell you'd *want* Logan to be the one you fell for. I can see how hard this is on you and I hate that. You shouldn't feel bad. We all love you, Logan and Jace. No one wants either of you to be unhappy. Life is so short, Chloe. Please, don't make a mistake and push Logan away."

I felt like I had just been abducted by aliens and planted down on Mars.

"I feel horrible, like I'm betraying Jace. I wish I could've just liked Rhys."

"But you don't and you don't have to feel bad for something you can't control. If Jace was still here then I'd be shouting but if his death has taught me anything it's grab happiness whenever and wherever you can. No one wins if you don't give this thing with Logan a chance, there's just more loss and I'm so tired of loss."

She struggled to keep it together when she talked of loss. Three years ago she had both brothers, a husband and was starting to try for the baby they both wanted.

"Even if something could happen with Logan, if I can get over the guilt, I don't want to rush anything."

"I'm not saying you should run into his arms right away, just don't close yourself off. Nothing has to change now, Chlo. Logan knows something is up but he doesn't know what, which is half of the reason why I'm here right now. I won't tell him though, of course."

Great, he knew something was up.

I groaned. "I don't want him to be suspicious. I want to keep everything normal until I know if I can act on these stupid feelings."

"If you want to keep things normal then you need to act normal. Logan doesn't know so there's no need for you to avoid him, and he deserves better than that." Yes, he did. "Go do your ridiculous exercises, hang out, and do all of the things you usually do. Let it happen naturally or not, but keep an open mind."

"Ugh, you're right. Just because I feel like this doesn't mean I have to act on it." I hadn't given myself any time before I condemned myself to going to hell. I could control it long enough to figure out what I wanted to do and until I, hopefully, stopped feeling like the evilest bitch on the planet.

"Exactly. Be what you are now and if it's meant to be, which I believe it is, then it will happen when you're both ready for it."

I didn't know how Logan felt about me, that was not a conversation that I planned on having, but the way she was talking was as if the ball was entirely in my court and one word from me would see us as a couple. I wasn't sure how I felt about that so I had to ignore it. That was way too much pressure on an already fragile situation.

CHAPTER TWENTY

Logan

Something was definitely going on with Chloe. She'd been distant and cancelled two of our workouts already. It was unlike her and it bothered me way too much. The last time I'd seen her she was weird and not just in the *I'm female, try and guess how I'm gonna react* weird way.

I didn't want to hope because I'd thought she had feelings for me before, right until she got with Jace but she'd avoided physical contact and barely looked at me. That *might* mean something.

I was between clients at work so used the half an hour to try getting hold of her, again. The last few days had been, well, shit without her around. Like the big pussy I was, I didn't function that well without contact with her.

Her phone rang off and went through to voicemail, again, and I tried not to think too much into it, again. She could be busy or sleeping. It was the summer holidays in uni world and she might be sleeping. Or at work. She was probably at work.

"Sian," I called. "If anyone asks I'll be back in thirty."

She nodded and went back to whatever it was she did behind that desk, browse clothes online probably.

Driving to the pub in the hope that I'd catch her was

slightly too clingy and psychotic for my liking but she didn't leave me much choice. Something was going on and we just didn't let the other deal with shit alone, not anymore.

I parked in the only empty space and noticed her tiny, baby blue car immediately. That was why she didn't answer. Not that she could use that excuse for the other million missed calls she had on her phone from me over the last few days, unless Sam had taken to kidnapping his staff now.

I walked through the doors and they were in the middle of the lunchtime rush. Chloe and the R named guy she had a brief thing with were behind the bar while the rest of the staff were running food to full tables.

She broke it off, they weren't together and I still wanted to punch the guy. I had it bad. I watched her for a second as she smiled at the customers she'd just served. Her hair was sexy messy and I could see her running around having woke up late, shoving mousse in it and saying *that'll do*.

She looked up, eyes locking with mine, and stilled. She looked wild and panicked. Then she straightened her back, gave me a smile and stepped closer to the bar.

What the fuck?

I stopped on the other side and sat on a stool. *Don't get ahead of yourself.* I wanted so bad to believe that her avoidance of me was because she wanted more but I couldn't let myself run with it. That was a fall I didn't ever want to experience again.

"Did you contract a highly contagious disease?"

She frowned. "No…"

"Murder someone?"

"No."

"Get amnesia?"

"What're you doing, Logan?"

"Just listing the only reasons I'll accept for you avoiding me."

"Murder is a reason I can avoid you?"

"Hey, if you've snapped I don't wanna be next."

She rolled her eyes, fighting a smile. "Can I get you something, Scott?"

"Yeah, Holland, you can get me you." Now there was a sentence with a double meaning. "What's going on?"

"Nothing," she replied, her eyes darting around the room, avoiding me, again. "I've just been working, planning my parents' trip, and tired."

"So you're not avoiding me on purpose? I haven't done anything?"

"Of course not." She looked back at me all soft eyed. "I'm sorry. I should have called you back, I just needed a couple days to catch up on some sleep."

"You're not doing that thing where you barely exist again?"

"No," she said, her fierce eyes begging me to believe her. I did. "Just needed a bit of me time, that's all."

"Alright, I'll accept that reason too." She smiled. Fuck, I'd missed that smile. "You up for a run tomorrow?"

Her lip was pulled between her teeth and I had a hard time breathing evenly. R guy watched us carefully between serving drinks. I wasn't sure if he wanted her or not but he was far too interested in us to be completely fine with their just friends status. Welcome to my world, buddy.

"Tomorrow sounds good. Not early though, I'm not working and would love to have a lay in on a Saturday, can't remember the last time I got one."

"I'll drop by at midday. Or better still, you come to mine, Cass misses you, too."

"I'll be there at twelve."

"Good, now I have twenty minutes before I need to be back at work and I'm starving."

She leant forwards on the bar. "You want me to get you a grilled chicken sandwich and chips?"

"You're the best, sweetheart."

Pushing away, she gave me a wink over her shoulder and headed out the back.

"Can I get you a drink, Logan?" R asked. Tension was dripping off him. If I wasn't sure about him liking Chloe before I was now.

"Bottle of water, please," I replied.

His grin was false and a little sarcastic. Thank God I ordered a bottle and not glass, he'd probably spit in it if he could. It was pretty damn clear that he knew I wanted Chloe. I just had to count on things being too awkward between them for him to mention it to her.

Between serving customers, Chloe hung out with me. She gave nothing away today but that could've been because we had a bar separating us so there was no danger of any real contact. There was a lot of eye contact, if that fucking meant anything.

God, I used to tease Cassie for obsessing over someone and here I was doing the same damn thing.

While I ate I watched her work, tilting her head when laughing and chatting to the customers. "Stalker," Ollie said, sitting on the stool beside mine.

"What? What're you doing here?"

"Lunch," he replied. "And you're stalking her."

"I'm not stalking her." No way was I admitting that today I kind of was. I pointed to my half eaten sandwich. "Lunch."

"Mmm hmm."

"I hate you, man."

He chuckled. "No, you don't. What's going on then?"

"Nothing."

"One day you'll tell me straight away and we won't have to have an argument before you spit it out."

I looked up to make sure Chloe and R were nowhere around. "She's been avoiding me." *What does that mean?*

"Why?"

"If I knew that…"

"Alright. Well, I can't help you, I don't speak woman. Hey, maybe she's on?"

I rolled my eyes. "This is the first time in ten months she's avoided me, I'm fairly sure that's not it."

"Got any theories?" he asked, taking a swig of *my* water and picking up a menu.

One that I didn't want to share and make it real, you know, in case I'm left crying like a girl again. "Nope, she said she's tired and helping her parents but I don't buy it."

He looked as out of his depth as I was. "Sorry, bud, can't help you," he said.

"Don't worry," I replied, looking up at Chloe pulling a pint of beer. "I think there's only one person that can."

CHAPTER TWENTY-ONE

Chloe

"So what have you got in store for us today? Just a run?" I asked Logan as I walked up the path, praying that I looked and sounded normal when I felt like everything I did screamed *I want you*.

He was outside the house, stretching on the lawn. I bet the female neighbours had their blinds pulled back. He looked so painfully perfect I wanted to slap myself or gouge my eyes out.

Since he came into the pub yesterday I hadn't been able to stop thinking about him, not that I'd thought of much else recently, and I knew that I had to ignore what I was feeling so we could have our friendship back the way it was.

Looking up, he smiled. My heart beat that little bit faster.

Not good.

"Hey, Chlo. Run, push ups, run."

The first and last sounded okay. Push ups I hated, but Logan was the personal trainer so I trusted that he knew what he was doing.

"Don't make that face, I won't get you to do many," he said, smiling.

"Our definitions of *not many* differ greatly, Logan."

With a devilish smile, he replied, "You're right, you're going to hate me after today. Bingo wings'll be gone, though."

My mouth hit the floor. Did I have flabby arms?

Unable to keep a straight face any longer, he laughed and shook his head. "I'm kidding! There is no excess fat on you anywhere, sweetheart."

"I'm still going to kill you."

Rolling his eyes, he nodded to the front door. "Cass made me promise to send you in before we left, she said she wants to say hi but I'm assuming that's girl code for *I need to talk to you but don't want the ones with penises to know*."

"Nicely put," I muttered as I walked past him.

Of course, he couldn't have waited until I was inside to start stretching, he raised his arms up over his head. His t-shirt lifted and I caught a glimpse of the toned muscle of the top of his arse and over the hips. I took a deep breath, forcing myself to stay behind him and not run round the front for a look at that V.

Lord, help me!

It took literally every ounce of self-control to get myself inside the house but I managed it.

"Cass," I called.

"Kitchen!"

She was sitting at the table with her hands around a mug of tea. I sat opposite her. "What's up?"

An envelope was pushed towards me. This didn't look good. She didn't look at me as I opened it. Divorce papers. "I'm sorry, Cass."

"I knew it was coming so I don't know why I feel like this."

"It's the legal end of your marriage, you're allowed to feel however you feel." I shoved the papers back in and put it down. "This isn't just the end of one chapter in your life, Cass, it's the start of another. This new chapter will be better."

She sighed. "Well, it couldn't get much worse."

"Stop it. Cassie, you're only twenty-five, you're still a baby. Rick is the biggest idiot on the planet but that's over. You have a chance to start again and build a new life. You're not past it just yet. When you're ready we'll have a night out and celebrate your single status."

"Okay, and get me good and laid!"

"Oh God!" Logan groaned in disgust behind me. "I was checking if your arse is ready yet but I'll give you two a couple more minutes while I go shove my head in the oven."

Cassie laughed. "A little dramatic, Logan. You're on though, Chloe. I could do with a night out and a man in."

Groaning louder, Logan swivelled around and left the room, throwing his hands up in the air and letting out a string of swear words.

"Now we know what we have to do to get rid of him," I said, standing up. "I've gotta go run a lot but I'll talk to you later, okay."

"Thank you," she replied, pushing the mug away.

"Anytime," I called over my shoulder as I went in search of the grossed out one. "You ready?" I asked, finding him leaning against his car, shuddering.

"I need warnings for shit like that," he said, waving his hand in the direction of the kitchen where I'd left Cass.

"Hey, we thought you were outside. That's what you get for walking in on a private conversation."

"Very private in the middle of the kitchen. I don't wanna think about my sister sleeping with some random guy she met in a bar."

"Then don't think about it. Which route? Left or right?"

"Right," he replied. "I'm coming when you go out."

"Sorry. It'll be a girls' night."

We started off on a light jog. "You two are out to score and fuck knows what sleazy fuckers are around." Could he fit anymore swears into that sentence?

"We'll be careful."

"Chloe, how many times have you and my sister been out on the pull?"

I didn't want to answer because we both knew that was a big fat zero. "We're adults, Logan."

"That's not what I asked."

I glared at him as we turned the corner, picking up the pace. "Fine. None."

"Exactly. If she goes home with someone how do you know he's not a murderer? How do you get home?"

"Well, she'll just have to do him in the bathroom then." He flinched, turning his nose up. "Lighten up. She's older than you for Christ sake!"

"I don't want to know *anything*."

"Do you think she wanted to see and hear the women that passed through your revolving door?"

He stopped and frowned, eyes darkening. *Shit*.

I cringed. I hadn't meant to say that and make him feel worse, I knew he regretted the way he was after Jace died. "Logan, I'm sorry."

"You don't have to be. You're right. I literally have no idea how many women I've slept with, not even ballpark. I'd barely remember them if I bumped into them in the street I was so wasted." He'd probably bumped into many of them. "Almost two and a half years of my life is a blur of alcohol. That's it. That's all I have to show for that time – one long hangover."

"I know." Ugh, why did I have to bring it up?

Gulping, he ran his hands over his face. "I'd give anything to go back and change those first couple years."

"Yeah, me too." I was worse than pathetic, barely leaving the house or taking care of myself.

"We're a bundle of fun today," he said.

"No more past talk." I held my hand out and he laughed, gripping it in his own. I thought he'd shake but he yanked me to his chest and wrapped his arms around my shoulders.

With my chest pressed firmly against his, my heart rate trebled. I hugged him back, feeling his taught, muscular back. This was a bad, bad position. Not only was there no space between us but I suddenly realised how well he fit around me, how well I fit tucked into his body. And I could smell him. There wasn't even anything I could compare the smell to, it was uniquely Logan, and it was the most comforting smell in the world.

He pulled back far too soon and let me go. I wanted him to hold me again. I wanted so bad to feel that complete and content as I did just seconds ago.

Although Logan had let me go he didn't let me go far. I was just inches away, not close enough to be touching but too close for a normal, considerate of personal space distance.

His eyes, now deeper, brighter and bluer than I'd ever seen captured me. I knew I should look away and continue the run but I couldn't move. The horrible, selfish part of me wanted him to kiss me. I wanted to physically feel the connection between us.

My lips parted and I took in a small, shaky breath. He was it. He was the one I could see myself with. He was the worst person I could be with but he was the one I wanted.

Logan broke the moment first. His back straightened and nodded ahead. "We should get going if you want to be back at a reasonable time to get ready to pimp my sister out," he said. There was a joke in there but he couldn't quite make himself smile.

I stepped back, half turning. "Yeah, we should. Push ups at the park?"

With a quick nod, he started the run again.

CHAPTER TWENTY-TWO

Logan

I couldn't concentrate, which sucked because I had a two-hour session with one of the gym's most valued customers. Vivian Braithwaite was a fuck off rich trophy wife that had been my client three times a week since I started years ago.

She was beautiful in that older woman cougar way but the fact that she sold out for money made her almost ugly to me. She was fun and flirty and could've had one of those 'epic' loves that everyone fucking rabbited on about. Instead she was with a wealthy man that she 'cared' about.

The reason I sucked at my job today: Chloe Holland. Bloody girl. She was the only one that was able to make me forget everything but what she was doing to me. Our almost kiss was on repeat in my head. Now she was ignoring me. Yesterday she bailed out of our session with some crappy excuse about a headache. Today she hadn't answered my calls. I knew I had to give her some time but it was driving me fucking crazy.

"Good," I said to Vivian. "Five more and then we'll move to the cross trainer."

She nodded, lifting the light weights above her head and pursing her lips. "Is there something wrong, darling?" she asked, tightening her manicured fingers around the weight as it began to take its toll on her.

"Everything's fine, Viv."

"You're usually able to hold a conversation and you've lost that devilish look in your eye." With a huff, she lowered her arms and handed me the weights. "I'm a good listener. What's her name?"

I took the weights to clean them off before putting them away. "Why do you assume there's a girl involved?"

"There is always a girl involved."

Of course.

"Her name's Chloe."

"Pretty name."

"You should see the rest then."

Viv smiled. "What's the problem? You like her but she doesn't like you?"

"I'm starting to think that maybe she does like me."

With a throaty laugh, she playfully swatted my arm. "Then I don't see a reason for that look on your face."

You wouldn't from the outside but as soon as you learnt one massively important piece of information all of a sudden things changed. Viv would go from charming smile to judgemental frown in an instant. Not that I gave a fuck about what other people thought but I was pretty sure Chloe did.

"Things are complicated," I replied. That was a fairly accurate description of the situation. Fairly understated but accurate nonetheless.

"I understand complicated, darling. You have to work it out if she's worth the trouble."

"She is. I worked that one out a long time ago."

"You're not sure if she thinks you're worth the trouble."

"Bingo."

"If she believes that she's crazy. If she's the one nothing will prevent you being together."

I'd thought of about ten different comebacks before she'd even finished her sentence. I was shocked that she could say the words and keep a straight face. Viv was hypocrite. She could give the best advice but never listened to it herself.

"Yeah, perhaps. Why don't you get started on the cross trainer and I'll bring you a bottle of water over."

***

If I checked my phone again I was going to punch myself. I wasn't a teenage girl waiting and hoping her crush would text back. I was a twenty-two year old guy doing that. I was so absorbed I didn't notice Cassie walking into the room until she sat down beside me.

"How was work?" she asked.

"Alright. You?"

She shrugged. "Same shit, different day."

Sounded like we both needed a strong drink, only I couldn't because I was determined to deal with stuff in a way that didn't end up with my having a raging hangover.

"Has Chlo been round?"

"I don't think so, I've not been in long. Is everything okay?"

"Yeah, why wouldn't it be?"

"She didn't come over yesterday and that's one of your crazy arse exercise days."

"She wasn't feeling well."

Lie. She was avoiding me, again. If it wouldn't push her further away I'd go over to her house and demand she either forgot about it or, even better, we just fucking got together!

"Oh, okay." She yawned.

"You not sleeping well?"

"Not really. I have a lot on my mind. The house sold."

"Yeah? That's awesome, Cass."

She didn't look convinced. "I guess. I mean, it is. It really is. I can't wait to get my own place and feel like an adult again." Ouch. "But I hate the idea of having to start over. If I find someone else I like what's the odds that they're going to be okay with never having a child of their own?"

"Not every guy is going to let you go because you can't carry a child, Cass. Rick's a twat, it has nothing to do with you."

"Oh, of course, it did, Logan. I don't blame him for wanting a child and I don't blame him for that being a deal breaker. He's to blame for how he went about it but that's it."

"Not your fault either. You got the shit end, too."

"I know. He's off with his pregnant girlfriend now so he's fine."

"You'll be fine too. Some guy will love you no matter what, Rick wasn't that guy so thank fuck it's over before you wasted any more years with the little prick."

She sighed sharply. "Yeah. In six to eight weeks I should have the money left over from the house, we'll get about fourteen thousand each so I can start looking for another place to buy. I guess I should get my new start head on and plan something positive for the future."

"Glad to hear it. You're only twenty-five, you've got time to do whatever you want."

"I think I'm going to buy somewhere closer to town. Rick wanted a more rural location. This time it's all my way."

"Sounds good, Cass. If you need someone to go house hunting with let me know. Don't take Mum."

"Oh God, I wouldn't! She's the worst."

Mum gushed about how *fabulous* everything was so the sales man knew he could get a few more quid out of her. Dad would never let her buy a car by herself anymore; she'd never get anything knocked off the price.

"Thanks, Logan. I'll start looking when the buyers have had the surveys on ours done so I know they're serious and hopefully won't pull out of the sale. How's your situation going?"

My *situation* was what people mostly used to refer to my dire financial state. I wasn't in debt but I was so close to being there when I was drinking.

"Better now. Ten months of not drinking and pissing away everything I had and earned is doing wonders for my savings. Got about five thousand saved so only another seven and I can afford a deposit. I'll be moved out by spring next year."

Should've been three years ago but I was in a dark place and could just about haul my arse off to work, then to a bar or club for booze and a shag almost every day. I lost my drive and ambition and although I was a couple years behind where I wanted to be I was fucking proud of what I'd achieved in the last ten months.

Cass gave me her proud smile; it was much like Mum's. "I'm so happy for you, Logan. God, I feel like, although we all still have a little way to go, things are finally looking up for all of us."

Minus my woman troubles things were.

"So what's really the deal with you and Chloe?" she asked with a stupid smile.

Fucking reading between the lines sister.

"I'm an idiot, that's what the deal is."

"What did you do?"

"I almost kissed her."

There was no shouting, which no matter how supportive I knew my sister would be I still expected. She didn't even give me a disapproving glare.

"She was right there, too. There was no screaming at me to get the hell away from her. Chloe wanted it, too, and that's the problem. You know I've had a hard time accepting how I feel about her and trying not to hate myself too much. Chlo is going to be much worse at that than I am. If I was anyone else…"

"But you're not and that's fine, Logan. Yes, Chloe will be beating herself up about it but I honestly don't think it'll stop you two getting together in the long run. She's ready to date now but she's not quite ready to date you yet. Give her time to deal with whatever demons she's battling over wanting to kiss you."

"Why does everything have to take time?"

"Instant gratification doesn't leave you happy for long. If you do everything right away what do you have to look forward to?"

The rest of my life with her. Cass made sense, though.

"Yeah, I guess you're right."

"Of course, I'm right. You should talk to her. When she's hurt or confused or stressed she pulls back and tries to deal with it all on her own."

"I think talking to her will push her away. What if she's not ready for that conversation yet?"

"Then don't have it yet."

I nodded, tapping my leg. "Yeah. I'm gonna call her house, hopefully she'll answer that, and act normal." I ignored Cass snorting at me acting *normal* and stood up. "Thanks for the chat, loser. House hunting offer stands, just let me know."

"Thanks yourself, poo poo head."

Looking over my shoulder, I laughed. "It was Jace you used to call that."

"Still do," she replied, "but I get a reaction from you."

"You'll be getting a reaction from him, too."

"Yeah, I bet it's him that keeps moving my hairbrush, little shit."

I walked out of the kitchen feeling lighter. Cass was going to be okay, I was going to be okay, Chloe was going to be okay and Jace was a hairbrush moving ghost. All of those things made me grin like an idiot.

CHAPTER TWENTY-THREE

Chloe

The sharp morning air felt good as Logan and I jogged one of our routes. It was easier now and I felt incredible again. I loved exercising, although that could be because of the company. Working out was never boring with Logan. It definitely didn't hurt that he was nice to look at. Or that my insides turned to mush when he smiled at me.

I'd missed it, missed him over the last few days. My illness excuses were running thin and I knew I couldn't keep it up. I didn't want to avoid him but I didn't want to feel so guilty whenever I was around him.

"I wish summer was over," I said. "I prefer running in winter." The clouds were grey and it looked like it would rain soon but it was still bloody hot.

"So do I," he replied, stealing a lot of not so subtle looks at me.

Logan loved running as the sun started to rise. It was one of my favourite times too, but there was no way I was getting up at five in the morning to do it. I couldn't wait until late mornings.

Logan gripped the bottom of his t-shirt and pulled it over his head, never faltering his steps. I did. I almost fell over. I'd seen him shirtless too many times to count before but it always took my breath away. Flawless, soft skin covered defined muscles in a way that made almost every woman do a double take. And he had the V. The one that sent girls into a frenzy. He worked hard for that body and the female race was grateful – myself included.

I looked away, feeling a deep stab of guilt. I shouldn't look at Jace's brother at all, but it wasn't completely wrong to appreciate a physique so bloody spectacular it made my heart go a little crazy, right?

Stupid, bloody moment last week. I hated that a couple of seconds where nothing actually happened could change things so much.

Logan was too important for me to let things change. I didn't want awkwardness between us. We'd been through too much to let staring at each other a fraction of a second too long do any damage.

I stopped dead just as the sky started to drizzle. This needed to be addressed so it wasn't in my head, driving me crazy. I had to know nothing was going to change or get too weird. Logan halted and spun around. "You okay?" he asked.

We'll see in a minute.

"I think so. Are *we* okay?"

He shrugged. "Yeah, why wouldn't we be?"

I knew he'd pretend he didn't know what I was talking about.

"Come on, Logan. Last week we…"

"We?"

If he bloody makes me say it!

"Chlo, forget it if you want. I don't want you feeling shitty for something that never happened. That's pointless."

Forget it if you want to? What did that mean?

"Have you forgotten it?" I asked.

"It doesn't matter."

"It does."

"I'm not the one stressing over it, Chlo, so it doesn't."

And what did that mean?

"Logan, you're doing the head fuck thing right now. I don't like it."

Frowning deeply, he took a step closer and we were almost chest to chest. "What? How am I doing the head fuck thing?"

He is actually going to make me say it.

"You basically just admitted that you haven't forgotten it and now you're trying to brush it under the carpet. I don't want there to be something hanging over us. Not us, Logan." I couldn't let anything happen that resulted in me losing him. Any other friend I could just about handle but not Logan or Cassie or Nell

His topaz eyes clouded. "Nothing will ever come between us, Chloe. There is nothing that could happen that would ever make me leave you."

His words hit me like a sodding tsunami. He took my breath away. "Promise."

He took that tiny step closer and our chests touched. Brushing a lock of my hair behind my ear, he very slowly swept his fingers down my jaw. I couldn't look away, I stared at him like an idiot as my heart tried to escape out of my chest.

What was he doing?

Why wasn't I running?

"I promise you will never lose me. I will be here forever."

"Just forever?"

"Alright." He smiled, brushing his thumb under my bottom lip. "Forever and a day."

My body burst to life. Blood scorched in my veins. Longing pooled between my legs. I was going to kiss him. I wanted him. I was going to fucking kiss my dead boyfriend's brother and as his eyes rooted me to the spot I didn't even want to attempt to stop it.

Logan lowered his head a fraction. This was it. I shouldn't want this. My body shouldn't be screaming for his lips on mine and hands all over my body. I knew it was wrong but it didn't feel wrong. It felt like coming home, like we should have been doing this all along.

He didn't look torn, not at all. He was one hundred per cent in this. I wanted him even more.

The rain came down harder, not enough to soak us but enough that we should probably move. We didn't. Logan's other hand pulled me closer, fingers slightly digging into the small of my back while his maddening fingers trailed down my neck.

I thought he was taking it slow so when his lips landed on mine the next second I was a little shocked. It was like he literally couldn't wait any longer, not that I was complaining.

His lips, soft but hard at the same time, moulded against mine. I sank into the kiss, gripping his hips as he took control of everything, of the kiss, of my heart, of my body.

He moaned and it sounded more like a growl. Walking us back, he pushed me against something and pressed his body flush with mine. My hands left his hips and tangled around his hair, gripping and pulling him closer.

He bit my bottom lip, tugging and then his tongue found mine. I shuddered, nails grazing his scalp. I thought I'd hurt him when he groaned but his assault on my mouth turned wild. I was pinned between him and whatever he'd pushed me against. His desperate kiss made me feel faint. His knee nudged my legs apart and then we were the closest we'd ever been but it still wasn't enough.

I moaned or whimpered, I couldn't hear properly over the thudding of my pulse, and he arched his lower body between my legs. Gasping, I bit down on his lip as heat surged through my body. I clawed at him when he arched his lower body against mine. I was painfully turned on and so was he. The kiss was frantic and made me feel alive.

We finally broke apart, gasping for breath, now soaking wet from the rain. I was scared, scared to fall for him, scared to lose him, scared of what people would think, scared that if I didn't give us a chance I would never find someone I wanted badly again.

"I'm soaking," I said, pulling my head back a fraction to speak. He didn't let me go far, I was still moulded to his body, still gripping his hair.

"Yeah, it's hot," he replied. His voice was rough and sent a shiver of desire straight down south.

"I bet I look like a drowned rat."

He brushed my dripping wet hair from my face. "That's the last thing you look like, sweetheart."

His use of sweetheart was swoon-worthy but now it was the sexiest thing in the world and made me melt.

"What happens now?"

"Now we go back to mine and get you dry before you get ill," he said. That was a good start.

I nodded and he moved back, unpinning me from the…tree and his body, and for the first time ever we *walked* back hand in hand. It was nice – more than nice. "You know what I mean, what happens with us?"

"I want this, a lot actually, and I know things will probably get hard and complicated but I want us to try. No pressure, Chlo, let's just take it one day at a time."

"Okay." That was exactly what I needed to hear. We neared the road and I pulled my hand free. Logan stopped. Biting my lip nervously, I said, "I'm sorry. I just…"

"Don't want anyone to know?"

"That's not it." Not completely. "Look, if we're trying this I want to do it right. That includes telling your family – Jace's family – before some busy body calls them as we walk home. You know what this place is like, how you can't do anything without someone knowing. We owe your family and Jace's memory better than that."

Logan took a minute to take that in and the rain started

pouring harder.

Finally, after long, agonising minutes, he replied, "Yeah, you're right." He looked angry with himself and I suddenly understood why he still felt guilty over Jace every day – me. It was because of me. I bloody knew there was more to it than a stupid argument that Jace would have had a second thought about.

Shit, this just got a lot more complicated. I felt our potential happy ending slip that little bit further away.

"One day at a time," I said.

"I'm going to take you back to mine, then I need to do something."

We started walking again, not hand in hand. I missed the contact, it warmed my entire body. "What do you need to do?"

He didn't reply but he didn't really need to. He was going to Jace's grave. To tell him about us? Jace would probably already know. To apologise and ask for forgiveness? To plead for Jace's understanding and blessing? None of those things he'd be able to get from visiting the place where he slept. Jace already gave us that because it was who he was. But I didn't speak up because if it helped Logan to feel better and forgive himself, then it would be worth it.

"Do you want to tell my parents and Cass or do you want to wait?" he asked.

"I'm not sure." I wished we were in the situation where we could shout it out but things were complicated and we had to be sensitive about his family's feelings.

"We can wait, Chloe, see how things go."

It sounded like he wanted to wait and that hurt a little. But it was for the best.

CHAPTER TWENTY-FOUR

Logan

Chlo sat on my bed and flicked through the endless house brochures Cassie had. I was under strict instruction to have a look through them and see which ones were the good ones she should consider. She was out on a much-needed night out with two friends she'd met back in uni so it was up to me and Chlo to pick her some good ones to view.

Cass wasn't good at seeing a place's potential so would likely pass up something perfect because she couldn't look past ugly decoration or a wall that could easily come down to create a bigger room.

Me and Chloe together was everything I'd hoped it would be but there was something not quite right. I wasn't sure if it was the rate that we'd jumped into it – not that I wanted to go slow – or the fact that it was a secret. I tried not to dwell on the why though, because she was all I wanted and I was happy.

"I want a house," Chlo said, pouting at the one she'd just put on the 'view' pile.

My in love with her mind went straight to a house that was *ours*. It was very early days and we were still together in secret so I was getting way ahead of myself but I'd wanted her forever and I couldn't help planning for the future.

"Yeah, me too. I love my parents but I can't wait to get my own space where there are no glass figurines anywhere."

She laughed. "You really don't like those, do you?"

"I do not."

"Think we'll end up doing this?" she asked, holding one of the brochures up.

It was hard not to cheer. She was on the same page. Her page was about the possibility of it happening in the future whereas mine already had us living together but I'd take it. Being with her was about a million times better than I'd imagined and I'd imagined it a lot.

"I was just thinking about that," I replied.

Her shy smile was so endearing. "You were? Do you think about that stuff a lot?"

Only most days for the last seven years.

"I guess."

"You guess? You're trying to play this so cool, Logan, but I can see in your eyes you do."

Cocky little girl. I fucking loved her.

"Fine, I think about it a lot. I've wanted this for a while now. Didn't really think I'd get to the stage where I'd want to live with another person, have their stuff mixed with my stuff and have to factor someone else in whenever I wanted to do something." Once I thought I could never have Chlo I was convinced there wouldn't be anyone else that I wouldn't mind sharing everything with.

"You didn't want to spend your life with someone? That sounds quite lonely."

"I used to think it was all a load of shit. Why would you settle for one person when there were so many out there? Then I met that one person."

"Me?"

I grinned. "You know it's you. You crashed in my life; actually, you crashed into me into my life and changed everything. I liked you back then, I've liked you for a really long time, Chlo."

"Oh…" She blinked a full five times before continuing, "Wow. Okay, I had no idea it was right back then, too. You gave nothing away, you were always so smug and cocky."

"Of course, I was. I was a teenager and teenagers are smug little fuckers that know everything."

"That's true. I thought everything was going to be different back then."

"You couldn't help or predict him dying, sweetheart."

"I know. That's not what I mean. Just that I was so sure and so naïve. My life was mapped out and that was exactly how it was going to be. Me and Jace planned so much that we left no room for change or to grow. I don't think we would have made it, Logan. Looking back now on how we were I think we would have found it really hard when we actually moved out and life started getting real. We expected all of our differences to just work out magically because we'd planned it that way."

"Doesn't mean it wouldn't have worked."

"Yeah. I'd like to think that we could have made it. Or I think I want to believe that." She looked away, twiddling her fingers. "Either I wish me and Jace were still together and that means we… Or I don't and I'm just a bitch."

"Hey," I said, lifting her chin. "You're not a bitch. I wish he was still here and if that meant I'd have to continue loving you from a distance I'd do it. As long as you're happy, sweetheart, I can live with whatever."

I heard a little intake of breath and then she was on top of me. I lay slightly shocked beneath her on the bed, the brochures now crumpled up under us.

As surprised as I was by her attack it took just seconds for me to catch up and I did so just as her eager mouth slammed against mine. I made a mental note to say things like that more often if this was the treatment it got me. I reached for her top that as great as it made her breasts look, was just plain in my way.

***

Chloe was a lot less exhausted at the end of our run and I was proud of how far she'd come. It wasn't just fitness, it was her returning almost completely to the person she was before Jace died. The things she used to care about mattered again.

Her bright, all's right with the world smile was back and I was taking credit for some of that. In private, things between us were hot and pretty fucking full on. In public we were friends. I didn't like public time. I wasn't, however, too stupid to know it was the right thing to do. Chloe cared what people thought and I cared about her.

"That was good," she said, downing the last of her smoothie.

"Yeah, you did great. It's easier, isn't it?"

"So much easier now. I don't want to curl up in a ball or stab you anymore."

I took a step back, holding up my hands. "Alright then. Hey, you want to do something tonight?"

Dates were a bit of a no no to her. We'd been out but it wasn't date stuff. I was kinda looking forward to getting my romance on, or just feeling her up at the back of the cinema.

That was another thing that I *really* hoped would change soon. Sex. If I dry humped her anymore I was sure my dick was gonna rub off. I'd be seconds from tearing her clothes off with my teeth and she'd stop us. I got the impression it was because of Jace. As far as I was aware she'd only been with him.

"Sure, like what?"
Date. Date. Date.

I shrugged, playing it cool when all I really wanted to do was get on my knees and beg her to let me take her out properly.

"Comedy Club?" she asked. "Cass and Nell mentioned going after I told them about my date with Rhys. So did you, actually."

Rhys got a date. Rhys got a fucking few.

"I was thinking more just me and you."

She tapped the side of her glass. "Yeah, we can go there together, if you want."

"As friends."

"Logan," she whispered, looking anywhere but at me. "You know it's not that easy for me to be out in the open like that. I don't want your family finding out from strangers."

"Then let's tell them. Come on, Chlo, what are you waiting for?"

"I'm waiting to not care like you!"

"I do care." I really did but I knew my parents and Cass would be cool with it. What I was mildly terrified of was admitting how much I fucking loved Jace's ex girl. I shouldn't and I felt weak for not being able to turn it off the second they got together but that love shit was a bitch.

"Sorry," she said, shaking her head. "I know you do but it's not as hard for you, for whatever reason. I love your family so much but we're not related, they don't have to forgive me for wanting who I shouldn't want. I don't want to lose them."

Oh, I was such a prick. I didn't think about it like that. Of course, she was scared, she thought they could wash their hands of her and that'd be it. We weren't related – thank fuck – but she was part of the family.

"Okay. I get it, Chlo, and I can wait. For the record though, they could never hate you."

She took a deep, shaky breath. "I just want to wait until I feel ready to tell them. Please, just give me a few months."

"You want to wait a few months."

"Yes," she whispered.

"Okay," I replied. "I can wait a few months."

"Thank you. God, this is hard. I wish I could stop missing him."

I ran my hand through her long hair. "Yeah, me too."

I still had to make allowances for the fact that my girlfriend – if I could call her that – was going to get upset over another guy here and there.

"Is there anything else?" I asked, sensing her hesitation.

"I worry that they'll react badly at first, even if they come around quickly. I don't know how I'd handle them getting upset about it, even if it wasn't for long." Frowning, she ran her hands over her face. "I'm not trying to lead you on or mess you around, Logan."

I walked around the counter and wrapped her in my arms. That was exactly where she was supposed to be. "I know you're not, sweetheart. We're both trying to figure this out as we go. It's not a normal situation. Let's rewind a bit, okay? There's no rush, so tonight let's go out and just have a good time, no pressure."

She looked up at me, resting her chin on my chest. "I'd really like that. Could do with some chilled out Logan time. Plus, my parents are at my aunt's, helping paint the new rooms in the extension."

"I don't want to get all excited over here so can you be really, *really* clear on what that means?"

Laughing softly, she placed a kiss just below my Adam's apple and replied, "Not going out. You. Me. Home. Alone. Naked."

My fingers sprouted a life of their own and dug into her back and I momentarily lost the ability to speak. "Yeah, let's skip going out. Who wants to hear amateur stand up comedians anyway? I'd much rather spend the entire night inside you."

I grinned at the tinge of pink in her cheeks.

"All night, Logan? No guy can even keep it up all night let alone go for it the whole time."

"Viagra, sweetheart." I'd fucking order a truckload.

"You've done Viagra?" she asked, her voice so high pitched it almost broke glass.

I shook my head. "There's no one I've wanted to take it for before."

"Um… Thanks?"

Fuck, I loved this girl.

"Maybe we can just have normal people sex until you're too old to get it up, then we'll get you that little pill."

"Sounds like you're giving yourself to me indefinitely."

"Hey, *you* said forever and a day, mister!"

"Wasn't complaining. I'll take it. You're mine until we die and decompose, then you'll be mine in wherever we'll be after that."

She snorted. "Hell, probably."

Ouch.

"I don't think what we're doing is quite on the same level as rapists and murderers." Although, I couldn't quite believe there wouldn't be some sort of consequence for it. Karma and all that.

CHAPTER TWENTY-FIVE

Chloe

I was in the kitchen dancing around to Justin Timberlake and cooking dinner while Logan watched me from the other side of the counter. I'd banished him from the cooking side because he was far too distracting and we'd never get to eat if I kept letting him kiss me.

Since we'd got to my house I'd started to have nerves added to the excitement of being with him for the first time. So I suggested dinner as soon as we walked through the door. He'd immediately agreed, I think he was nervous as well. The idea of Logan being nervous about sex was pretty outrageous but I took it as a good thing, obviously it meant a hell of a lot more with me than the women he couldn't even remember.

"I really can't do anything?" he asked, watching me with the breathtaking smile he seemed to have tattooed on his face recently.

"Nope, you just sit there and look pretty."

He tried to look mad but he was grinning too much to pull it off. I bloody loved seeing him happy.

"How long's it going to be?"

"About twenty minutes. You hungry?"

His eyes were suddenly on fire. "Very," he growled. Whoa, I could see that in his head I was already naked and beneath him. I was momentarily planted to the spot. Naked and under him sounded exactly where I wanted to be and I was no longer hungry for food.

"Well," I said, trying desperately to keep my voice even. "Soon—"

"Fuck, Chloe, turn the oven off."

"Sorry?"

He walked around the counter with purpose – that purpose being getting me in bed.

"I couldn't care less about dinner right now. You've got that look in your eye."

"What look in my eye?"

"The *I want him now* look. I promised myself that if I ever saw that look for me I would never deny it. So you might want to be careful where you think of us getting naked and sweaty."

My throat went dry.

"So we're just going to turn dinner off?" Why the hell was I still talking about the stupid food?

He reached around me to turn the oven off and as he pressed his body flush with mine I felt how much he wanted this. "That's exactly what we're going to do."

I took his outstretched hand and he led us upstairs. His thumb brushed across my knuckles. I held onto him a touch too tight but my body was buzzing. He hadn't even kissed me and I felt like I was going to burst into flames. His words were sexy; the look in his eye was sexy. "Logan," I whispered. I thought that since he turned dinner off he'd waste no time but he seemed to revel in torturing me.

He closed the door behind us and the sexual tension became almost unbearable. I wanted him so bad I could barely think straight.

I closed my eyes as he very slowly and very seductively walked us back towards my bed. His lips, soft and warm, grazed over my skin so gently it made my toes curl. Lightly nipping my jaw, he lifted me off my feet and I shuddered. *Kiss me!*

"Logan," I whispered again, wrapping my legs around his waist, again feeling how equally ready he was.

He laid me on the bed, lowering himself with me so we never broke apart. He chuckled deeper than usual; his voice was as lust-filled as those gorgeous blue eyes were smouldering. "I'm going to need to take your clothes off really soon and you're not being very cooperative." His hand slid along my thigh, accentuating his point.

"Right," I replied and pressed my lips together, releasing the death grip my legs had on him. His hands went straight to the bottom of my t-shirt and I pushed myself up, allowing him to get it over my head.

Lying beneath anyone in my bra and jeans would usually make me self-conscious but Logan made me feel beautiful. I hadn't felt like that in a very long time and I tried not to think too much about how Logan's brother was the last person to do that.

"That's better," he said as he pinged my bra open and pulled it off, discarding it on the floor somewhere. "Now…" His fingers glided between my breasts down to the button of my jeans. "…these need to go. Are you on the pill?"

Right, contraception. I'd never forgot that before. "Um, no, I have the injection."

Smiling, he replied, "Good, because I want to feel every inch of you." I shuddered and I wasn't sure if that was what made him groan or having his hands on me.

My breathing was rough and loud and borderline embarrassing. Every touch was designed to drive me wild and he succeeded. I felt it everywhere. "Logan," I breathed, aching for him already.

"I've got you, sweetheart." He popped my button undone and my jeans came off pretty quickly. "You're so beautiful, Chlo. I could spend every second of every day kissing every inch of your body."

"Do it then," I replied, panting as his lips circled around my nipple. Moaning softly, I arched my back.

He chuckled and the sound vibrated thorough my body.

"I love how you react to me," he said.

"You're not the only one." I had never wanted anything or anyone so much, as bad as that sounded. I ached, throbbed. Biting down on my lip, I tried to

Logan was it for me. I couldn't even make myself consider the possibility that this might not work out. We fit in every way possible.

"I think I hate foreplay," he groaned into my skin, kissing down dangerously close to where I wanted his mouth the most.

I wasn't that crazy about it right now. As much as I wanted his hands and mouth everywhere I wanted to feel him inside me more. I wanted, needed, that connection. "Let's skip it then," I replied.

He shook his head, lips brushing my hipbone. That felt *really* good. "Oh no, I've wanted to do this for a while, too."

My throat went dry as he hooked his fingers over my lace thong. His lips parted and I heard the sharp intake of his breath as my underwear slid down my thighs. I heard the soft thud as my thong hit the floor but I couldn't look away from his hungry eyes.

Slowly, too, too slowly, he lowered himself and his mouth between my legs and I almost jumped up. It was too much already. I gripped the sheets, crying out to try to deal with the sensations he was creating in my body.

I didn't want to think about how he'd come to be so talented with his tongue. I was jealous and grateful for all those women in equal measures.

He rolled his tongue around the sensitive ball of nerves and I clawed at the sheets. I was so turned on, so ready to burst I wasn't sure how long I was going to last.

His tongue left my skin and his mouth clamped over my

opening. I gasped, fisting my hand in his hair, pulling him deeper into me. I heard him briefly chuckle before his tongue entered me.

"Logan!" My body jerked and arched. That made him flick his tongue harder, faster.

When the soft pad of his thumb rubbed the most sensitive part of me I fell apart, gripping his hair and tugging what was probably a little too hard. My eyes closed involuntary as I convulsed around his tongue.

I don't think I pulled too hard for Logan because as soon as my eyes flicked open he got up, removed his clothes in a second flat, and buried himself inside me in one very quick, very swift movement. I hadn't had enough time to recover before I was building again and he hadn't even started moving yet.

He kissed me and I'd never had someone do that before, kiss right after they'd been down there but I was too caught up in how he felt, how I felt, to worry about that.

"What're you doing?" I asked when he still hadn't moved.

His lips were swollen and red and his heavy lidded eyes were on fire. "Nothing has ever felt this good before, Chlo, I can't..." Closing his eyes, he kissed me again and I felt what he was trying to say. He was savouring the feeling, the moment of our first time. Or he was close and wanted to hold off.

He stopped kissing me and I felt a gentle pressure as his forehead touched mine. His breath, shallow and twice as fast as normal, blew across my face. This was just as big of a deal to him as it was to me and that made my heart ache.

He finally started to move but his eyes stayed closed and he groaned, low and deep in his throat. It was the most erotic sound I'd ever heard and did nothing to slow down the race my body seemed to be in to finish, again.

His eyes finally opened and his hand tangled in my long hair. Moaning again, he bent his head and kissed me. I got my legs back around his waist and the slight change in position sent him deeper. I gripped his toned shoulders, feeling the muscles ripple beneath my fingers. I felt every inch of him, felt myself tighten around him and thought I was going to go crazy with how intense it felt.

"Chloe," he breathed into our kiss and slipped his tongue in my mouth, winding it around mine. Everything became more frantic. My nails cut into his skin and he grabbed my hip roughly, holding me in place and kissing me harder. My lips felt like they were going to be twice the thickness when we stopped but I could not have cared less.

My heart was flying in my chest. I clawed his flesh, writhing under his unrelenting pace. He was too much, too good, too everything and I didn't know how to cope. My back arched and toes curled. Scrunching my eyes so tight it almost hurt, I cried out against his mouth, his tongue, and fell over the edge, taking him with me. With one last guttural groan he thrust hard and held himself deep inside me.

We clung to each other, slick with sweat. No doubt the skin we'd attacked would bruise.

Logan was panting hard when he finally let me up for air but then I was too. He didn't say anything, just stared into my eyes as if I was the answer to every question he'd ever had. He pulled out slowly, sucking air in sharply, and lay beside me, bringing me with him so we were still face to face but on our side.

We were still silent; there weren't any words for how amazing that was, so neither of us tried. All we did was watch each other for a long time and occasionally he leant forward and gave me a soft kiss that was so far away from the passionate *I need to bruise your lips* kiss we'd shared just minutes ago. Both were perfect.

I worried that it might feel weird after but it wasn't, at all. We were supposed to do this. When we were together I wasn't Jace's ex and he wasn't Jace's brother, we were just us and nothing had ever felt so good or so right before.

"Well, that was considerably better than my right hand," he said, being the first one to break the quiet. He smiled in amusement

"I could've lived without knowing that, Logan." I hadn't expected the moment to last long but had hoped I'd get at least ten more minutes of Sweet Logan before he went back to Logan Logan. Still, I was pretty much crazy about all versions of him.

"Sorry," he replied, chuckling. "It is, though. I've thought about how this would be many, *many* times and it was never anywhere near that good."

"You thought of it a lot, huh?"

"Every damn day." He tightened his arms, holding me closer.

"Well, now you can have me every damn day."

"Hmm, can I get that in writing?"

Laughing, I slapped his chest playfully and he rolled on top of me. Every inch of him was perfect and I had a hard time looking into those gorgeous eyes when I got to see the rest.

Putting his weight on one arm he trailed the other down my side. My skin broke out in goose bumps. "Logan… What're you doing?" I closed my eyes as his hand worked its way across the bottom of my stomach.

"What do you think?"

"My parents will be home soon," I said, making a feeble attempt to push him away.

"What time did they say they'd be back?"

"Twelve."

He looked at the clock on my bedside table and brushed his thumb over my bottom lip. "That gives me twenty minutes. I'm pretty confident I can make you come a handful times in twenty minutes."

I bit my lip, squirming underneath him. "I bet you can't," I whispered.

He gave me a devilish smile. "Game on, sweetheart."

CHAPTER TWENTY-SIX

Chloe

Being in Logan's room and not Jace's had only been strange for that first night, now it felt so natural I knew for sure that giving us a chance was right.

Logan stirred beside me and rolled over, wrapping me in his arms. "Not yet, Chlo," he mumbled into my back, his sexy voice filled with sleep.

The sun had just risen and soft light drifted in through the gap between the curtains. Julia was an early riser and I didn't want anyone to learn me and Logan were me and Logan before we sat them down and told them.

I didn't want to leave. Since our first time four nights ago it had been a lot harder to leave his room in the mornings. Plus, he was a fan of replaying our twenty-minute bet and I was happy to report that he won every time.

"You know I have to."

He sighed and I felt his hot breath cascade down my back. It did nothing to help me stay strong and get out of bed. In the last four days we'd barely been able to keep our hands off each other. If we were alone we were going to end up naked and sweaty.

"Chloe, I don't want you sneaking out of the house." He

let go and sat up. I rolled onto my back. "Let's tell them now."

Was I ready for them to know?

"Come on," he said. "I don't want to wait. I don't want to pretend we're not together. My family loves you so what are you scared of?"

"They love me because I was Jace's girlfriend."

"You're more to them than that and you know it. Why're you holding back?"

"That is why? You're intelligent, Logan, surely you can understand."

"I do. I loved Jace as much as you." He stopped and frowned. "But in a completely different way. We're not going to get egged for being together though, you know that."

"Please, just give me a little more time?"

He held his hands up. "Fine. I'll speak to you later."

There was no point in talking to him anymore, especially when he'd gone brooding, moody male so I got dressed as fast as I could and left his room without another word.

I reached the living room when Logan grabbed my wrist. I was too lost in thought and hadn't heard him creeping down the stairs behind me. "Don't leave," he said, turning me around. "I'm sorry, okay. I was a dick. Please… just don't leave, Chlo."

Julia stepped out of the kitchen and I stopped breathing. She was up earlier than usual and she was staring at us. With both of us having a mini-domestic at half past five in the morning and Logan just in a pair of jeans it was more than obvious what had been going on.

Please, don't hate me.

"Good morning," she said.

Good morning? That was it? I didn't know what to do, where to look or what to say. Was that all she had to say about the fact that I was now with Logan? I almost felt like crying with happiness. She wasn't ordering me out of her house, screaming at me that I'd betrayed Jace. Either that or she really didn't have a clue what was going on under her nose.

"Hey," Logan said, letting go of my wrist. "You're up early, even for you."

"So are you two."

He smiled. "Touché, Mother."

Frowning, she said, "Don't call me mother, you make me sound old. Is everything okay? Chloe?"

I opened my mouth to say speak but not a word came out. She was going to hate me, of course, she was. Even if she was glad Logan was happy she couldn't think very highly of me, surely. I'd promised her I'd love Jace forever and while I still did that love had changed.

"Why don't you two come in the kitchen for coffee and a chat?"

Oh, she was going to do the speech calmly. I wanted to run. *Shit, shit, shit!*

Logan agreed and walked past his mum. I wasn't quite sure why he was so calm when I was full on panicking.

Silently, I sat at the table, listening to the thudding of my heart. Logan was beside me, watching me so intently I felt naked. "At least breathe, sweetheart," he said.

Julia turned around. "Are you okay, Chloe?"

"I..." Licking my dry lips, I sat up straighter. How was I going to convince anyone that me and Logan were meant to be together when I looked ashamed of us? "I'm okay," I replied.

"How long?" she asked, speaking softly.

"Not long," I replied. "Just over three weeks. Are you mad?"

Cocking her head to the side, her eyes softened and she replied, "No. Of course I'm not mad. I love you both and I want you both to be happy."

"What about Jace?"

"Jace is my baby, always has been and always will be. Nothing will change that, but he's gone and nothing will change that either. If you and Logan have a chance at happiness then you take it because you never know what's around the corner. I don't believe everything happens for a reason, there's far too much suffering for that to be true. I believe that if you want something you work for it. Little satisfaction comes from what just falls into your lap. You and Logan have worked damn hard at rebuilding your lives and through all the pain you've found each other. I could never be angry at that. Besides, who else is going to put up with him?"

I laughed and wiped a tear away. My emotions were all over the place recently. Logan was a complete head fuck and I was pretty sure he felt the same about me.

"Thank you," I whispered, too choked up to speak properly.

Logan was quiet beside me but I took that as a good sign. Rather than crying he went quiet.

"No more sneaking around, okay. I don't want you to have to hide what makes you both happy."

"Yeah," Logan said. "Chloe?"

"I never *wanted* to hide anything."

He hesitated for a second too long before nodding. Did he not believe me? If the situation wasn't complicated I wouldn't have waited. It wasn't something I wanted to do it was more something I needed to do.

"I know." He said the words but didn't look at all convinced.

"Thank you for understanding, Julia," I said. "You don't know how much it means to not have you throw me out of your house."

She laughed and hugged me. "That would never happen. You'll get no judgement from me. I can see it's not been easy and I know that neither of you would risk creating a rift in the family over nothing. I won't lie, when I first started suspecting I was surprised but I never felt angry, I guess that was my clue that I'm okay with it. And I can't see Jace hating either of you."

Shit. I swallowed hard, almost on the verge of tears again. I didn't think he'd hate us, not really, but to hear his mum say it meant a lot and made it real. And when did she suspect?

"I am right that this is something serious, aren't I?"

We hadn't had that conversation about where we were going but we didn't need to. We were in this for the long haul.

Logan looked at me, right into me, into every part it seemed. "It's serious."

Oh, it was definitely serious.

CHAPTER TWENTY- SEVEN

Logan

"I think we should have a party," Chloe said. She was currently curled up on my lap as we were spending the afternoon lounging on the sofa at my house. I loved having her here as my girlfriend and I loved that it was totally normal, even to my family.

"Where is this coming from?"

"Suck it up, you're having a party to celebrate your birthday."

"You didn't have one." It was a child's argument but an argument nonetheless.

"I had a night out."

"Hmm, that's right, you had a *girls'* night out. I might have a *boys'* night." I didn't really want a night out now we were getting down to it at every opportunity, I'd rather spend my birthday naked and nasty but a piss up with Ollie could be a laugh, too. We'd not really spent much time together since he was working long hours as a lorry driver while he tried to think of a business he wanted to start up himself.

"Absolutely. Your birthday is on a Tuesday this year so have a boys' night then. The party will be the Saturday before." She smiled triumphantly. I was a little surprised, and slightly overjoyed, that she knew what day my birthday was on. I didn't know what day it was on.

I wasn't really opposed to a party, it made no difference to me, but I really liked the banter when she disagreed or tried to get me to do something.

"Fine, I'll have a party," I replied, pulling her closer. Little things like chilling on the sofa with her were the things that I looked forward to the most. That and getting her naked at every opportunity.

It was easier now we were out in the open, I could be with her properly at her house and mine. We still hadn't done the *tell the world* thing yet but that didn't matter. One step at a time.

She laid her head on my shoulder. "Good. Who do you want to invite?"

"You and Ollie."

"Really, Logan!" she said.

"What're you two doing?" Mum asked, walking in the front door, dropping her bag down and slipping off her shoes. I wanted to frown. Chloe being off uni for the summer and early shifts this week meant we got the house to ourselves for a couple hours before everyone got home. I preferred having her to myself.

"Planning Logan's birthday party," Chloe replied. She went to sit up but I held her in place, keeping her body flush against mine. She often pulled back that little bit and I knew she was only trying to be respectful but Mum pretty much had a huge smile on her face every time she saw us together, as did Dad and Cass.

"Oh, you're having a party?" Mum asked, her eyes lighting up. I didn't really have parties so she would be all over this.

"Apparently."

Chloe nudged me. "We're working on the guest list."

"Family will be there, right?" Mum asked.

"Sure." I shrugged. "Ask whoever you want."

Mum sat down, grabbing a note pad and pen from the

side. "When were you thinking, Chloe?"

"The Saturday before his birthday."

"Good idea."

So I wasn't even needed anymore. Maybe they wouldn't need me to be there either.

It was decided – not by me – that all my family, Chloe's parents, Ollie and Nell were invited. We were having it at home and Dad would do a barbecue.

I sat there quietly as Cassie came home and got involved, too, volunteering herself to bake me a cake and make vodka jelly. When Dad, my saviour, got home, I kissed the top of Chloe's head and followed him into the kitchen.

"What're those three cooking up?" he asked.

"My birthday party. You're doing a barbecue by the way."

He opened the fridge, grabbing two beers. "Right." He opened the bottles and handed me one. "You want a party?"

"Nope. Clearly doesn't mean I'm not getting one, though."

"Ah, just go along with it. Much easier that way."

That was Dad's motto. He liked the quiet life so he said at least a hundred times a day *yes, Julia*.

"How is everything going? We've not had a chance to talk in a while."

He meant since he found out, when Mum went dancing upstairs to tell him, that I was with Chlo now.

"Going good. She does tend to step back when people are around, though."

"Give it time, it's a change for everyone."

"Yeah, I know." I took a swig of beer. "Good change or...?"

"My son is happy. As a parent that's all you want."

"That simple?"

"Yes," he replied. "It was more of a shock to me than your mum and apparently, that's because I'm a clueless man but the bottom line is, you could love a girl that used to be with your brother, love a man, or even a goat and as long as you're happy, I'm happy."

Alright, I wasn't great with father/son moments but that meant a fucking lot to me. "Thanks," I replied. "If I fall for a goat though, I'd like you to try talking me out of it."

"Okay, I came into this conversation at the wrong time," Chloe said, standing at the door, raising her eyebrow. "Something I should know?"

I held my arm out and she hesitated for less than a second before curling her body into mine. I loved the way she always put her hand on my chest whenever we stood like that, there was no reason for that arm to do anything, the other one was around my back, but that one always had to touch me.

"I was just telling Logan that if he wanted to have sex with a goat I wouldn't think any less of him," Dad said, smiling around the top of the bottle.

She looked up at me, eyebrow rising higher. "Well, your dad might not…"

"Don't worry, you're better looking than a goat." It was impossible to keep a straight face.

"Wow, thanks." She took the beer out of my hand and stared up at me, smiling.

"So, Logan's having a party, hey?" Dad said.

"Yes, we've organised everything."

"Why a party?"

Good question, Dad.

She bit her lip before replying, "Because everything's good now. We've made it through losing Jace. Me and Logan are back to normal… Well, I use the term normal pretty loosely but you get what I mean."

I raised my eyebrow, she didn't look at me but she did fight a smile.

"Logan hasn't celebrated a birthday in years and even before Jace died he never really did much."

I got it, this year I was happy so why not go all out?

Dad nodded. "I think it's a great idea. My son turning twenty-three is definitely something to celebrate and you're right, Chloe, we could all do with a good ol' celebration."

Chloe beamed. "See, this is a good idea."

I kissed the top of her head. For once, having a party for me didn't seem like the most terrible idea in the world.

CHAPTER TWENTY-EIGHT

Chloe

To say I was nervous was an understatement. "I should've stayed at home and pretended I was ill," I said to Cass as noise from both sets of Logan's grandparents, uncles, aunts and cousins buzzed around the room.

Logan's slightly early birthday celebration with family was in full swing and he was determined not to hide away. I was all for being together out in the open, finally, but I wasn't sure how confident I was that doing it at his party was a great idea. Surely it would be more considerate to everyone to sit down and tell people individually? Everyone in this room loved Jace, and loved me and Jace together.

Cassie laughed. "Calm down, it'll be fine."

"Hey," Nell snapped, appearing in front of us all of a sudden and snapping her fingers in my face. "Will you stop looking so bloody guilty. You're here to tell your bloke's family that you're happy together and you look like you're doing something wrong. Enough!"

Her eyes looked a darker green that I'd ever seen them, she was mad and/or pissed off and rightly so. I had a horrible feeling in the pit of my stomach but clearly I looked like they'd already condemned me.

"Anyway, I'm going to get another one of those mini burgers, they're so cute."

She was gone as quickly as she appeared like the little whirlwind she was.

"Nell's got a point," Cassie said. "Relax."

Nodding, I took a deep breath. "Where is Logan anyway?" I asked, trying to look over the crowd of their teenaged cousins playing on the Wii. They were blocking the view from the living room to the kitchen.

"Kitchen making some concoction he calls a cocktail for mum and my aunts."

"They're letting him do that?"

She shrugged. "Clearly they're too trusting. I bet he sneaks at least three extra types of liquor in that aren't in the recipe."

"Right, I'll be avoiding that then."

"I dunno, I might have some after this week."

"Oh?"

"Not bad, just very long. I was ready for Friday evening by Tuesday morning. Reception work is exhausting. Receptionist seems to cover general slave duties too."

"Yeah, I bet. Plus, you can't sleep with your boss to get ahead."

Her boss was a stuffy old man that tried to fire a woman for asking him out for coffee before she realised he was engaged. He was claiming sexual harassment. The miserable old fucker should've just been flattered.

She lifted one shoulder and let it drop. "I could try but it'd be my last day."

"Problem solved."

"Yeah, but then I'd have to become a stripper to pay the bills."

Logan stopped abruptly in front of us, looking appalled. "Wow, that was bad timing," he said. "Anyway, Chlo, you ready to be introduced to my family?"

"I've known your family for years, Logan."

"You know what I mean, smart arse."

My heart was in my stomach. I was so not ready to be introduced as Logan's girlfriend but I did want everything out in the open. It would make my day if me and Logan could just be a normal couple.

He held his hand out and I felt like I was going to throw up as I took it. Being with him, holding his hand, felt so natural. He tugged me closer, letting go of my hand and tucking me under his arm. It wasn't particularly intimate so no one batted an eyelid.

"Why're you considering stripping, Cass?"

She stopped looking at us like she was cooing over a litter of puppies and rolled her eyes. "I'm not, just had a rough week at work. I'll stick with answering phones, filing and being a slave for now."

Logan seemed satisfied with her answer so he turned us away from the safety of conversation with his sister. His grandparents, his mum's side so I was more worried because they were closer to the family, were right in front of us talking to Julia.

They smiled as if nothing was going on until Logan kissed my temple. We'd moved from friendly arm around the shoulders to something coupley and their smiles faded.

"Logan?" Ann said.

He stood proud when I wanted to climb inside his hoodie and hide. Why did I care so much what everyone else thought?

"Yes, Nan?"

"What's going on?"

He faltered a little but it was a slight tense so I was the only one to catch it.

"Me and Chloe are... Well, we're me and Chloe."

"Together?" Ann squeaked.

Shit.

"Mum, calm down," Julia said.

"You knew about this?"

Alan, Logan's grandad, put his hand on Ann's shoulder. "Julia's right, calm down, love. The least we can do is allow our grandson explain what's going on."

"I just did explain, Grandad, I'm with Chloe."

By this point everyone in the room had stopped what they were doing and we were the main attraction. Nell shot daggers at Logan's grandparents from across the room.

"But she's Jace's girlfriend," Ann said.

And that was exactly what I feared. Jace died three years ago and I'd moved on but when it came to me being with his brother I was still Jace's and probably always would be.

Logan tensed to the point where it couldn't have been just me that noticed. It was now my time to say something. I closed my eyes and felt Logan's body stiffen more and more the longer the silence went on.

"I'm not Jace's anymore, Ann. When I felt ready to move on I *never* thought I'd want it to be with Logan but it is and there's nothing I can do to control that. There's nothing either of us can do."

And with that short speech all the tension left Logan's body.

"There's always something you could do," Shona, Julia's sister, said. "You didn't have to act upon it. Logan, Jace is your brother for crying out loud!"

"Julia, are you supporting this?" Ann asked.

Julia, bless her, stood her ground. "Yes, I am. Logan is my son. They're happy and I won't ever stand in the way of that."

"Jace is your son, too," Shona said.

"He is, and I know for a damn fact that he would react with more grace, dignity and understanding than you are right now. Jace loved his brother and Chloe and I don't care what any of you think but he would *never* want either of them to be unhappy. If anyone dare says otherwise you clearly did not know my son at all."

"Jace isn't here so we can't ask him," Ann said.

"Get out," Julia said. Her voice was so icy calm it sent a shiver down my spine. "Anyone that doesn't understand can leave now."

Most left, although a few of Logan's aunts and uncles did say they were supportive but felt it was best if they left. Logan's paternal grandparents hugged us both and said they'd rather leave as it was getting late anyway but that we had their blessing.

I watched people filter out in a daze. It took less than five minutes from them finding out to leaving. It didn't look good. I wanted to throw up. Nell did her staring dagger bit to everyone that walked out of the door and Ollie soon joined in.

What happened was exactly what I was afraid of.

CHAPTER TWENTY-NINE

Chloe

When the front door finally closed there were only three guests left, Julia's brother, Marcel, his wife, Clarissa, and their daughter, Stacey. And Nell and Ollie of course.

I wanted to cry. That was actually much worse than I could have ever imagined. I didn't want to break apart a family. Julia was close with her mum and sister and I'd never seen them argue before.

Clarissa hugged Julia. "Don't worry, it'll blow over soon enough."

"I won't apologise to anyone for supporting my child," Julia said.

"And you never should have to. I'm sure it was the shock. It was very unexpected. Leave them to cool off and they'll see how wrong they were to react that way."

"Are you okay?" Logan whispered in my ear.

I shook my head. "No, I feel awful."

"None of that," Daryl said, pointing at me. "You have nothing to be ashamed of."

"Dad's right," Cass said. "I'm so sorry for how they reacted. Family shouldn't do that. Clarissa's also right though, they will realise what they've done."

What if they didn't?

I leant against Logan, trying to hold it together. It didn't look good for us. We couldn't break up his family. *I* couldn't do that. They treated me like their own, all of them, and I couldn't betray them.

Shortly after they left and Ollie took a reluctant Nell home, we were alone. Julia, Daryl and Cassie made an excuse to go to the kitchen, obviously feeling awkward around us. The atmosphere was tense and I could tell they were eager to give us some space.

Without saying a word, I walked up to Logan's room and he followed like I knew he would. I felt cold.

I couldn't get their words out of my head, the way they looked at me, like I was some evil bitch that was out to hurt them in any way I could. They looked at me like I wanted to stomp all over Jace's memory, like I'd moved on so easily and didn't care anymore.

Sitting on the bed, I tried to figure out what I was going to do. Logan tiptoed around me, straightening his room up in complete silence. I hated tension between us and right now it was palpable.

Faces of Logan's horrified relatives flashed through my head on a loop. I couldn't stop seeing the disgust. I couldn't stop seeing the hurt in Julia's eyes when she argued with her family and defended both sons. She shouldn't ever have to do that; everyone knew she loved them both equally, or they should.

"Logan?" I said, unable to watch him tidy any longer. He was quite a tidy person but whenever he cleaned he made noise, whistled, sang or messed around.

"Don't, Chlo. I know exactly what you're about to do." He closed his eyes, clenched his jaw and sighed. "Please, just don't."

Everything inside me turned to stone.

"Your family is falling apart."

"They've had no time to process it. This was my fault. I

thought they'd be cool right from the start but they need time. I was an idiot but I'll talk to them."

"And what if they still don't like it? What if it's something they can't get past?"

"Then that's their problem."

"No, it's not just their problem though, is it? It'll never just be their problem. It's ours, too. Hell, it's your parents'! I can't be the reason your mum doesn't talk to her sister or parents, not after everything she's done for me. Please, understand that."

He threw the t-shirt he was holding back down on the bed. "I can't lose you. Please, understand that."

"You won't lose me."

"It sounds that way. You want to bail again. Fuck sake, Chloe, why is your instinct always to run?"

"That's not fair. This isn't about me."

"Yeah, actually, it is. This is hard, I get that, but it's always going to be hard at first. How are we ever going to make it when you keep hurling us back to the start?"

Groaning, I stood up. "Logan, I want us to work but maybe we can't. Maybe there's just too much for us to ever have a real shot. We're not just trying to work through differences in opinion or lifestyle here."

I heard the air leave his lungs sharply. "You're talking like we're already done."

Emotion, deep and painful, slammed into my chest and I found it hard to breathe.

"I don't know what else to do. I won't come between you and your family, not ever."

"Wow," he said, turning around. "That's fucking great, Chloe. You've decided this for *us* yet again. I never get a choice."

"Logan."

I saw tears in his eyes before he turned his head. "Don't. You've made your decision, so you should go."

"Logan..."

"Please go, Chloe."

I didn't want to leave. He made no sound but I could see how cut up he was. I could tell he was crying. I'd never felt so low or so awful in my whole life.

"Go," he whispered so quietly I almost couldn't hear it.

I left his room and his house as quickly as I could. Cassie saw me leave but I'd slammed the door behind me before she got off the sofa. From the tears that poured down my face she would understand what had just happened between me and Logan and be on her way up to him. I needed her to go take care of him.

Getting to my house seemed to take forever and no time at all. I didn't remember the journey, just the searing pain of losing him and the knowledge that I needed to not be driving soon because I couldn't hold off breaking down for much longer.

The feeling of complete loss was something I'd felt before but this time it took my breath away. It hurt so much. I felt sick it physically hurt that much.

Logan was one of the best things – if not the best thing – to happen to me and I'd thrown it away, again.

***

I missed him so much I felt like I was going insane. Every time something happened, even if it was nothing important, my first instinct was to go tell Logan. It had been just one day but I already knew I couldn't be without him for much longer.

As messy as everything was at the minute I had to have him in my life. I had to make it up to him and his family. Hopefully, Julia and her family would have made up by now. I wanted nothing more than to be with Logan but I wasn't prepared to split his family up. Julia had already been through enough, she lost a son, I wouldn't be the reason she wasn't talking to her parents and sister.

Mum peeked her head around the door. "How're you doing, love?"

I smiled or at least I tried to. "I'm alright. Think I'm going to text Logan in a bit."

She stepped into my room. "In a bit? Why not now?"

"I'm a big chicken."

"Come on, I'm sure he's dying to hear from you. Text him and get this put right. You were happy again and I can't even begin to tell you how much of a relief that was."

Was happy, but now I couldn't have Logan. Unless his family would be okay we couldn't be together. Girlfriends and boyfriends come and go but this was family.

CHAPTER THIRTY

Logan

I'd never been that big on birthdays. Every year I'd get asked how it felt to be a whole year older when in reality I was just a day older than before. I didn't feel anything; it was just another day.

This year was worse than any other. Everyone tried to be cheerful and positive around me when I just wanted to smash things, shout and drink. I wanted something to make it stop feeling like I was freefalling into a bottomless black hole.

Walking downstairs, I plastered on a probably too obvious fake smile so Cass wouldn't be able to call me the Miserable Birthday Bastard this year.

"Happy Birthday!" Mum, Dad and Cassie sang in unison.

"Thanks," I replied, really trying to sound happy about the fact that I was now twenty-three, living at home, and missing Chloe so much I could barely think straight.

"Breakfast or presents first?" Mum asked.

"You didn't have to get me anything."

Cassie rolled her eyes. "Of course, we did, it's your birthday."

Well, hurray for me.

"Breakfast sounds good then."

There was no Chloe, of course. It was also the first birthday in years that she hadn't joined us for breakfast. I was dying to ask if she was coming, even though I knew she wouldn't. A simple, casual *no Chloe?* would do but I couldn't force the words out of my mouth.

Mum and Dad went to the kitchen to cook and as soon as Cass sat down on the sofa and looked up at me, I knew I should've gone with them. She was going to ask questions.

"How's being twenty-three?"

"Same as twenty-two."

"Heard from Chloe this morning?"

There we go; that was what she really wanted to talk about.

"Nope," I replied, sitting down.

She smiled sympathetically. "I'm sure she'll call or stop by at some point." I didn't reply because there wasn't really a lot to say. "How're you doing? I mean *really* doing?"

I wasn't a *spill his feelings* guy, unless I was wasted, so I didn't want to get into it with Cass but she was like a dog with a bone when she was on something and I knew she wouldn't drop it. Fucking interfering woman.

"It sucks," I said.

"Yeah, it does. It won't be forever, though. You two will sort it out."

Alright, I definitely didn't want to talk about this. "Yeah," I said. "What's going on with you anyway?"

"Nice divert. I can take a hint, Logan, consider the subject changed. For now. Nothing's going on with me. What're you doing tonight?"

"Charlie's with Ollie and the guys."

She gave me her mirror image of Mum's disapproving face. "You sure that's a good idea?"

"To go out on my birthday?"

"To go out when you're fragile."

"I'm not one of Mum's hideous figurines, Cassie."

"I just worry that what's happened with Chloe is going to set you back. You've done so well to get everything together this last year."

"It won't *set me back*. I don't want to piss away all of my money, Cass. Stop worrying so much, will you. I'm fine and I'm gonna continue to be fine. What's happened with Chlo..." *hurts like a bitch,* "is shitty but I'm not gonna fall back into my old habits. Okay?"

"Yeah, alright. Can't blame me for being concerned. You're my brother and I care about you. I don't like seeing you unhappy."

"I'm not unhappy."

Her eyebrow rose much higher than seemed humanly possible.

I laughed. "Not *not* unhappy but not quite ready to pickle my internal organs yet."

Yet. I was fairly close to giving in to the craving to make it all go away. We had a bottle of Jim Beam in the cupboard. I'd wanted to reach for it about a million times since she called it off.

"Good. Please, don't give up yet."

Unless she knew something I didn't, which was unlikely since Chloe probably wouldn't tell my sister if she was having second thoughts about ripping my chest open and stomping on my heart.

After breakfast and presents my grandparents and aunt stopped by. I didn't want to see them, not after what they said to me and Chlo, but I knew I couldn't avoid them forever. It needed sorting out if I was going to have any chance at having Chloe back as a friend.

"Happy Birthday," Nan said, smiling shyly.

Shona sat on the sofa along with Nan and Grandad. "Logan, we are so sorry. We reacted badly and the things we said were unforgiveable."

"Yeah, it was."

"We feel awful," Nan added. "Please, accept our

apology and know that we support you one hundred per cent. It was a shock and while that doesn't excuse how we behaved I hope that you can understand."

"Do you still think it's wrong?" I asked.

"No," Grandad replied. "No one thinks you and Chloe are wrong. It took us too long to realise that but your mother's right, as long as you're happy we're happy."

"Chloe now thinks we're wrong."

"No," Nan said. "Oh, Logan."

"Don't. Can't blame it all on you, I didn't handle the situation well. Should've spoken to you all individually."

"Is there something we can do?" Shona asked.

"No. Just tell Chloe you don't think she's the devil, that's what she's thinking right now and I don't want that."

"Of course," she replied. "We had every intention of apologising to Chloe and asking for her forgiveness, too." I smiled tightly. It was a bit too little too late but what could I do? "Can we give you your presents now?"

I faked a smiled and nodded. Honestly, I could've skipped the present and just had them call Chloe now so she wouldn't be at home feeling like shit. But I didn't want to be the one who runs to her, not yet, she had to come to me when she was ready to.

***

My phone dinged with a text and I almost didn't pick it up. Chloe's name sat on my screen. I opened the message. 'Happy Birthday! I hope you have a great day. I miss you. Xxx'

I miss you.

I miss you.

What the fuck was she trying to do to me? We couldn't ever be together but I miss you. The girl, like most women it would seem, was a total head fuck. But like the pussy I was I replied, 'Thanks. I miss you too.' No X. I was pissed off still.

'Can we meet? X' she texted back.

I couldn't stand the slow texts or messing around any longer, I called her.

"Hey," she said, answering on the first ring. "Happy birthday, Logan."

A smartarse reply of *you said that already* almost slipped out of my mouth but she'd made the first move and I really wanted to know what was going through her head.

"Thank you."

"Are you going out tonight?"

"Yeah, Ollie and the lads are dragging me to Charlie's."

"Right."

That was it?

"You wanted to meet up?"

"I do. I hate how things are at the minute. We've never been distant. I miss you like crazy. I've got about a hundred things I've thought to myself *I'll need to tell Logan that* and then I realise I can't."

"That was all you, Chlo."

"I know. I get that it's my fault and I hate myself for how things ended, I never wanted that. Everything is just *so* messed up and I can't really make sense of it myself. My head is spinning and although I have no clue what to do about anything right now, one thing I know for sure is that I want you in my life."

"In your life how?"

"I want to go back to how it was before things got complicated."

"You want to be friends?" Fuck, I hated that word.

"Yes. I want to take a step back and be friends."

This birthday was definitely the worst one I'd had.

"Can you do friends?" she asked.

What fucking choice did I have?

I closed my eyes and took a deep breath. "Yeah, sweetheart, I can do friends." It was all I was going to get. It was probably all I should have ever had. You didn't get to screw your dead brother over and not have it bite you on the arse. My throat felt way too tight.

"Thank you," she whispered. "Can we do something soon?"

"Really have missed me, huh?" I said, trying to keep it light. I didn't want to talk about feelings or have an awkward conversation about how horrendous it was going to be to go back to being her friend.

"I really have. I felt like I did before...back when Jace died. You need to be in my life in some way, Logan."

"Yeah, I know what you mean." Not being with her was awful but never seeing her at all would be unbearable.

"So…?"

"Right. Tomorrow I'll be sleeping off tonight so why don't you come over Thursday?"

"Okay," she said, her voice suddenly low, husky and full of emotion and I realised it was because I'd said I'd be recovering. Chloe assumed because I was getting drunk that I would also be getting laid, which wasn't difficult to understand how she got there, that was what used to happen. Everything was different now. I'd dodged the sexual infection bullet about a hundred times so my turn was surely coming up and there was the fact that I was so in love with her the thought of being with someone else made my stomach turn. But I was a wounded man with a hugely dented ego so I didn't tell her that.

"I better go and have a shower before Ollie gets here. I'll speak to you later."

"Have a good night," she said. "Bye." The phone was cut off quickly and I wished I'd told her I wasn't going to sleep around. I shouldn't have to, we were *friends* so I owed her no explanation but she was upset and I fucking hated when she was upset.

I threw my phone down on the bed and stalked off to the bathroom. My chest ached. Everything *ached*. I needed to get drunk. I needed to forget. I needed to make it stop hurting so damn much.

CHAPTER THIRTY-ONE

Logan

It was a choice between friendship and nothing. There was no fucking way in hell I was choosing nothing. So again I was left feeling like my heart had been through a shredder because of this girl I couldn't get over, no matter how hard I tried.

She was due here any second and I didn't want things to be awkward. Shit, I shouldn't be so nervous to see her.

"Stop tapping your foot, Logan," Cass said. "Things are gonna be alright, you know. You both just need more time."

"I don't think she's interested in anything with me, even if we waited fifty years." Yep, felt like swallowing razor blades.

"Oh, please! You're smart, Logan, so stop playing dumb. Some people that Chloe cares about, some of our *family*, have been less than supportive so it's understandable that she's pulled back. She cares what people think a hell of a lot more than what you do so you need to be understanding of that. Don't give up on her, just give her the time she needs."

Giving up on her wasn't even an option. I'd wanted her for the last seven years so I could handle waiting. I was so good at waiting for that girl it was unreal.

"I'm not giving up. It just sucks, royally fucking sucks."

"Language! I know it does but I have total faith in you both. You're meant to be together, you two make more sense than her and Jace did."

I smiled. "Yeah, that little gamer geek really was punching well above his weight." Fuck, I missed him. "Not that I'm not."

"She wants you, Logan. Don't screw this up by doing what you do best in times of complete shit."

"You put that so lovely. But you don't have to worry, I'm not going to drink or screw this away." I'd compare them all to her anyway. It wouldn't be worth it.

"Good, because that's not the best way to show her you've got everything together."

"I don't think me having my shit together is the issue."

She raised her eyebrow. "No? I don't think the main concern was necessarily that she was Jace's girlfriend, it's that you're both replacing something you lost in each other – which wouldn't be healthy and probably destroy each other. You need to show everyone that it's not like that and you love *Chloe* not the idea of keeping hold of something so precious to Jace."

"Our family is fucked up."

She shrugged. "Not saying they're not but that's how it is. You can't blame them, they've not seen much of her because she hid away for so long and you drank yourself stupid. They haven't had a chance to see how far you've both come. They also don't know how much you guys struggled with wanting to be together."

Maybe she was right.

"You'll get there and you know you have my support and Mum and Dad's. We're all team Cogan."

She what? "Never say that again."

Laughing, she got up. "I hear a car so I'll get going."

"You're scared of cars now?"

She rolled her eyes. "Just remember what I said and

don't put any pressure on her."

Barely ten seconds after Cass left, Chloe appeared at the door. I stopped breathing for a second. Why did she only get more beautiful? She couldn't have stuck her face in a blender and made this easier on me?

"Hi," she said, biting that full bottom lip nervously.

My jeans got tighter. I sighed. Here we go. "Hey, sweetheart. You okay?"

Releasing her lip, she walked into the room and sat down. "I'm alright. You?"

Nope, not at all.

"I'm fine. We missed you last night. Mexican isn't the same without you getting your taco everywhere."

"Hey, it's messy food, you're not supposed to be clean at the end of it."

Okay, I could do this. We'd just gone back to the start where we were friends. We could pick up from here and work our way back to each other, now knowing what we needed to work on.

"I know," I said. "What did you do last night? I called your house but…"

"I read and went to bed early. Mum told me you'd called but I figured I was coming over anyway…"

"It's cool, I figured you'd probably be locked in your room."

"I didn't lock myself in."

"As long as you're not moving backwards, Chlo."

She shook her head, playing with her fingers "I'm not. Well, *we* are. I don't like it but I don't know what to do about it."

"Don't stress about it. No pressure, no expectations. We can do the friends thing – we did it well before we got horizontal." I paused to smile at her light blush. "I get why you want to cool things, I don't like it, but I get it. We were moving too quickly when there are people, and I hate to admit this, that we have to be sensitive around. This isn't a normal situation where girl and guy can sail off into the sunset right away."

She smiled sadly. "No sunset for us, huh?"

"Oh, there'll be a sunset, sweetheart, we just have a longer journey."

Groaning, she slammed her head down on the table. I wasn't too sure what to do with that.

"Err, you okay over there?" I lived with two women so I was used to crying, shouting, screaming, throwing things and all that other fun womanly hormonal crap but I was lost right now.

"When you say things like that, Logan, it makes it ten times harder."

"Oh. Right… Sorry. Do you want me to make a joke about how it'll never happen because you turned me gay?"

She peeked up over her hands. "You're ridiculous, you know."

"Wanna go for a run?"

"A run? Now?"

"Yeah. Well, I was gonna offer you a bedroom workout but I figured that's a no no… right?"

Picking up a wooden coaster, she threw it at me. I caught it and laughed.

"Thought so."

We'd work on that one later.

"Fine. A run it is."

"You know where some spare clothes are." Would she wear mine or go back to borrowing Jace's? *Mine, wear mine.*

With one last bitey lip smile, she left to go get changed. *Wear. My. Fucking. Clothes.*

CHAPTER THIRTY-TWO

Chloe

I went straight to Logan's room to change and wondered if I should be helping myself to his clothes anymore. But the fact that I'd mindlessly gone to his room told me everything. I wasn't Jace's anymore, I was completely Logan's, no matter if we could eventually make a relationship work or not.

After quickly changing into some of his old clothes and ignoring the urge to climb in his bed and call him up, I went downstairs to meet Mr Motivator.

Logan stood by the front door, leaning against the wall, texting on his phone. He looked painfully perfect. While he was distracted I took a minute to really take him in and as I raked my eyes over every inch of his body my heart hurt in the best way.

Finally, I cleared my throat and he looked up. "I'm ready."

He smiled a lot and nodded towards the door. "After you then."

We started at a gentle jog, both careful to keep a safe distance. I could feel the pull. I wanted the contact. Having him in my life was all that mattered and right now we could only do that as friends.

"How're things at home?" I asked.

"Fine. Mum and Cass have talked to them so things are alright, like I thought."

There was definitely a dig in there; a little *if you'd have stayed rather than ran again things would be fine by now*.

"Yeah, your nan and aunt called me and apologised. It was an awkward conversation at first but they explained how they felt and the reasons behind the reaction, and I did too. That meant a lot to me, and I'm glad you sorted it out with them as well. I hated the idea that I'd driven a wedge between you and your family."

"You didn't, we didn't, they did."

We were never going to agree on this one. He would only see my side if he was in my shoes. I knew he would step back if he thought it was hurting me. As much as he wanted us to happen I knew his family hurt him and I knew he wouldn't want to go through life without their support. I knew they were getting their heads around it but if that was how Logan's own family reacted then how would other people? I didn't want to be *that* girl in people's eyes.

I pursed my lips, not wanting to continue the conversation and have it turn into an argument. We were walking on ice and I was scared to say the wrong thing in case he decided he was done with me completely.

"Work okay?"

"Oh, for fuck sake!" he shouted, stopping suddenly, grabbing my arms and pushing me against the nearest tree. I gasped as my back made contact with a thud and his chest pressed against mine.

His eyes were on fire.

I was against a tree, again.

"What're you doing?" I whispered, swallowing sand.

I could feel what he was doing. I could see it.

He was making it impossible.

Against everything my body was screaming for, I put my hands on his chest and pushed him away. My fingers gripped his shirt as I put some distance between us, not really wanting to let go. I wanted to cry. He could crush me in a second. Not even Jace could do that.

He looked devastated as he let go of my arms.

Fear gripped me by the throat. I wasn't just scared of how I felt about Logan; I was outright terrified. "I need… time. I don't know." Not time, that wouldn't help. I didn't know what I needed, but I definitely needed something.

He stroked my cheek and my heart stuttered. "No more time."

"Why are you doing this, Logan?"

"Why?" His eyes lost their tenderness. "Seriously, why? How blind can you be? I fucking love you, Chloe!"

The floor fell away. I froze. He loved me. Shit. I felt two very big, very conflicting emotions at the same time. I wanted to hear that so bad but I also didn't.

Yeah, I definitely couldn't do this. I wanted to be with Logan but I couldn't stop the crippling guilt. He couldn't love me. There were things I couldn't get past and we'd only end up hurting each other. He looked like he was in pain now so what would he be like if things didn't work out six months or a year down the line?

Logan was perfect and since I'd walked through his door right up to a minute ago he'd been a perfect gentleman, but it was already getting harder for us both to ignore what we wanted. When we were around each other everything was right but the line between friends and lovers was fading faster than I could have ever imagine and I was panicking. And he *loved* me.

He looked up and the sunlight hitting his topaz eyes made them shine. I gulped. Something was going to happen between us soon, it was inevitable… unless I put a stop to it.

"Logan, I can't see you anymore." I wanted to hit myself.

His perfect face fell, even though he didn't look surprised. "What?"

"The guilt is…" I rubbed my chest and swallowed. "I can't do this to Jace."

"You're not doing anything to Jace. We're not doing anything."

"Come on, Logan. You don't believe that, we just almost… I don't know, kissed!"

"So I can't touch you anymore? Chloe, I've done nothing more than smile at you since you called it off, excluding that moment but you were being ridiculous. What do you want from me?"

"I'm sorry." God, my head was everywhere and nothing made sense. "We're getting closer again already and we can't do that but I want you *so* badly."

He groaned. "Come on, don't tell me that."

We'd never given us a real shot but I was completely caught up in him. He was in every thought. He was everything I wanted. Why couldn't it just be easy? Why couldn't I stop stressing or worrying?

"Look, Chlo, I'm sorry. Don't run. We'll try harder. You said yourself that we have to be in each other's lives and you're right. You know we do." He took a step back away from me and I wanted to bring him closer again.

How were we supposed to be friends if we could barely keep our hands off each other? Battling the need for that contact was exhausting and it'd only been an hour. But we did need to do it. Not seeing or speaking to him for a few days drove me insane.

I took a few deep breaths before I responded, "Okay. Let's just cool things down. You're right, I'm right, that we have to make this work. Run, then lunch at Pizza Hut?"

He nodded, holding his hands behind his back as if he had to physically restrain himself. It didn't help with the wanting him badly thing at all. "Sure."

"Good. I'm paying."

"I don't think so," he said, both of us now trying to brush what just happened under the carpet. I could smile and joke but inside my head I was replaying everything and obsessing. I wanted him to push me against that tree again.

"Oh, stop the macho man thing, Logan. I missed your birthday and I want to make it up to you."

"There's nothing to make up, it was just another day."

"Ah, the Miserable Birthday Bastard strikes again."

He laughed and I felt some of the tension between us melt away. "I almost got through this year without hearing that."

"It wouldn't be your birthday if you didn't have one of us talking crap at you. Plus, you really are grumpy on your birthday."

We started to run again. "I'm not grumpy, I just don't get all the fuss."

He never would. I wasn't exactly huge on birthdays either but I at least enjoyed mine a little.

***

"This pizza is so good," I said. My heart still hadn't calmed down since he'd told me how he felt and I wasn't sure if it would anytime soon. "How mad would you be if I got the waitress to put a candle in your dessert so I can sing happy birthday."

His eyebrow arched and he stopped chewing.

"Right, really mad then."

Swallowing his food, he replied, "Yeah. Don't do that."

"Are you back at work on Monday?"

"Tuesday," he replied. "Had Monday off anyway. Thought I should take a birthday week off work." He turned his nose up. "No idea why, though."

I rolled my eyes. You took time off work to enjoy your birthday, or normal people did. "What's going on this weekend then?" I asked, still grinning at his reaction to my singing question.

He shrugged. "No plans other than running and a gym

session with you."

"Ugh," I groaned. "Nothing too heavy."

"You can do it now. I'd never push you beyond what you can take."

Physically, he wouldn't.

"I know that. So, really? We're working out and not having a chilled weekend eating junk food?" I was hoping to tempt him but I didn't expect to get that far.

"We can do both. If we're junk fooding it you'll want a big work out, stop the chocolate going to your thighs."

My mouth dropped open. He'd already put his hands up, laughing and shaking his head.

"I'm kidding, Chlo, every time! You know I'm kidding."

"Oh, I am so bloody getting a candle for your dessert and singing on the table, you bastard." Then I started laughing too. God, I really had missed him.

CHAPTER THIRTY-THREE

Logan

She was entirely too close and entirely too far. I could see the faint freckles she got from the sun and the darker, almost black ring around her amber eyes. Fighting to stay away from her was getting harder by the day. Hell, by the second.

I wanted her so much. I was going to fuck up really soon and do the one thing I promised her I wouldn't. Soon I was going to give in to what my body screamed for. I was going to kiss her.

She did nothing but stare into my eyes, breathing a touch heavier than normal. She was gravity and I couldn't help myself.

"I don't know how much longer I can not kiss you," I whispered.

I unconsciously inched closer to her, my desperate body working independently to get what it needed. She was all I wanted and it fucking hurt to be around her and pretend that just being her friend was fine.

She gulped audibly and licked her bottom lip. I knew she didn't mean to but she just made things ten times harder – literally. "Logan, we can't."

"We shouldn't, not we can't."

"Does it matter?"

"He would want us to be happy."

I couldn't believe I'd said it. I wasn't going to, I really wasn't going to go there but she was driving me crazy. And it was the truth. Jace *would* want us to be happy.

I was going to hell.

Chloe sat back, taking a deep breath. "I know that but it's how *I* will feel if we do this."

"How's that?" Fucking hell, I probably didn't want to know.

"Guilty. Who gets with their dead ex's brother? It's just… wrong."

Yeah, I definitely didn't want to hear that. Groaning, I rubbed my forehead where I was starting to get a headache. What the fuck was I supposed to do? Being around her was too hard but not having her in my life was worse. Could I stay away from her to give us both some space?

"I'm sorry, Logan. You know I want this, too, but we can't do that to Jace or your family."

"Is that what you're really worried about, what other people will think?"

I felt a glimmer of hope. If that was what it was I could talk to my family, who I already knew would support us. She kept her eyes on her quilt cover. If she didn't want me I would back down and never mention it again, but she did.

"That and me. I can't get past the guilty feeling. I feel like I'm betraying Jace just by having feelings for you so I can't imagine how much worse I'll feel if we acted on this, again."

"What do you want?"

"Now or in an ideal world?"

I frowned. "Both."

"Ideal: you. I think that's pretty obvious." Her cheeks turned the lightest shade of pink as she gave me a shy smile.

"And now?" I asked.

"Now: I don't know. What if I can't get past this feeling that I'm the worst person in the world? I can't ask or expect you to wait for something I can't guarantee you."

"Time? Is that it? You need more time?"

"Stop, Logan, don't look at me like that, it makes me feel worse." Look at her like what? I frowned, and she sighed. "You look hopeful."

"I am. Look, Chloe, I want this, but I want you to be happy more. If you don't want to do this, for whatever reason, then I'll back off. I swear. But if there's a chance that giving you time and space will make you stop judging yourself, then I'll do it. I want us to be together but only if you're one hundred per cent happy with it. No doubts."

"You can't wait, Logan."

"Why not?"

"Because it's not fair to you."

"None of this is fair to either of us but it is what it is. I've had longer to accept how I feel about you. I was where you are, too, and I understand. There's no pressure, Chloe, I promise you that. Let's take a step back and just be us again."

"Us again."

I rolled my eyes. "You know what I mean, smart arse."

She smiled faintly. "Thank you."

Standing up, I held my hand out. "Doesn't mean you're getting out of running today. Up."

We left the house and started to run.

"Are we just pretending that conversation didn't happen?" she asked.

"For now, yeah. We're friends until you can put your hand on your heart and say you truly believe Jace would be okay with us and you don't feel bad for feeling how you feel."

It wasn't like waiting for her was a new concept to me and I wouldn't want her to jump back into this if she had even the slightest doubt. We would work out, I *knew* that, but I wanted the little runner to be right there with me when we got back together.

We upped the pace, running out of town, towards the endless fields of the countryside. "You ready to go back to uni?" I asked. Next month was the start of her final year.

"Yes and no. I want this year to be over already but then I'll have to think about the after."

"The after being?"

"Exactly! I'm still undecided. Weddings or general."

"Why not both?"

"I've not found a both. Places have a separate wedding planner to other events."

"So do it yourself."

"Come on, Logan, I'm so not ready to start up my own business."

That was shit. "You are. Chloe, you run shifts at work and parties like a military operation."

"I'm confident that I can organise any event but a business would be a part of me and in case you haven't noticed, I've not been that great at organising myself."

"You always wanted weddings."

"I did. That was part of the plan. Move in with Jace, he goes off to be a fancy architect and I find a job at a nearby grand hotel and plan couples' fairytale weddings all day. I hate that I'm questioning what I want to do when it used to be so clear."

She wasn't great at relinquishing control over anything, especially what she thought she should be in control of.

"You've got time to figure it out."

"That's not been at the top of my list but I'm going to have to figure it out soon."

"Right. Us."

"Yeah, us. When I started having feelings for you I could feel everything slipping out of my control."

Good.

"Maybe that's not a bad thing, sweetheart."

"Maybe not but I'd just finally felt like I was getting everything straight again and then…" Then I fucked it up.

"It's okay though, I have a year to slot back into my plan what kind of event organiser I want to be."

If her plan was written down on something I could physically destroy I would have burned it by now. She drove me crazy with all this planning shit. And the most frustrating part was she didn't *want* to plan quite so thoroughly.

I didn't think it was a bad thing that she was questioning everything. I wanted her to do more of it until she reached the point where none of it made sense and she threw her fucking plan away.

CHAPTER THIRTY-FOUR

Chloe

"Alright, what the piss is going on, Chloe?" Nell snapped, pulling a chair out and sitting down.

What the piss?

I put my fork down; I wasn't at all hungry anyway.

"Logan called. He tells you he *loves* you and you leave him hanging, again. What're you doing, girl? Stop being scared, stop running, and stop hurting the both of you. Seriously, I'm seconds from whacking both of you!"

I almost choked on the lump in my throat. "What am I doing, Nell? I don't... I don't know anything anymore. Every time I think it's going to be okay I feel like I can't breathe again. It's so fucking overwhelming, I feel like I'm losing it."

"You're starting to sound like him, you know."

I managed a small laugh.

"Lucky for you though, I've figured out what's really wrong."

"I was with his brother."

"Nope," she replied. "You said before that you were past that. So is everyone else. That's old news but it's easier for your confused little mind to focus on. This isn't about

Jace, it's about Logan."

"You've stopped making sense again, Nell."

"You and Jace loved each other but it was young and sweet and fairytale-like. Logan's the real deal. You're older now, you fell in love with him as a stronger, more passionate, ambitious *woman.* You're in love with him and it's so much more and so much deeper than you've felt before and it scares you."

She should be a shrink.

I glared. "I kind of hate you right now." She laughed and hooked my plate with her finger, drawing it over to her side of the table. I shoved it the rest of the way. "Have it, I'm not hungry."

"I wonder why," she sang in the most annoying voice I'd ever heard. "You going to class or to see Logan?"

I should go to class since it was the start of my final year but I wouldn't be able to concentrate anyway. I grabbed my bag. "I'll see you tomorrow."

"Good girl."

***

I rang the doorbell and prayed he wouldn't slam the door in my face. Things were still tense and it was what I deserved for being such a stupid idiot.

The first thing I saw when he opened the door was how tired he looked. "Chlo," he whispered.

"Hi."

He gave a small nod. Well, this was getting awkward pretty fast. Neither of us knew exactly how to act as friends, especially since we both wanted more.

"Can I come in?"

He opened the door a little more. "You know you can."

I walked past, ignoring the flutter of excitement as my arm brushed his. Shit, I *really* loved him. Nell was right; it was so much deeper. It was painfully intense and all consuming.

I stopped by the sofa and turned around. "I realised something earlier and while I was coming over here I thought about it so much I haven't really had time to actually work out what I'm going to say so I'll just get it out there... I want to be with you, Logan. I'm ready and I promise nothing is going to hold me back or make me run from you again." *Why can't I say I love you?*

He stood still, slowly taking in my words in but he didn't move. I expected more than a statue but I was probably getting what I deserved.

"Aren't you going to say anything?" I said when silence had stretched to almost a minute.

He took a deep breath and the pain was back in his eyes. Fuck, he was going to tell me to leave. My stomach turned.

"I don't know what to say, Chloe. You've done this before, you've been in and then ran so many times I kinda feel like I need to go into protective mode around you. I can't let you run from me again."

My eyes stung. "So that means you're not going to let me back in." Nope, couldn't blame him. I'd been so back and forth lately that I wouldn't trust me either. Funny, or not really funny, thing was, *I* did now trust myself where he was concerned.

"It means I need to know for sure, sweetheart," he said, walking closer. I felt my tears roll over the edge when he called me sweetheart again.

He was close enough for me to reach him now so I did. I stretched my arms out and placed my hands on his stomach. He closed his eyes and I heard a sharp intake of breath. I ran my hands up his chest and stepped closer.

"I'm right here, Logan. I'm ready to be yours, to deal with whatever we have to deal with *together*. I want this more than anything and I swear I will never run again. Please, give me a second chance."

His eyes flicked open as I took the final step, bringing

us flush with each other. My arms continued up until they were around his neck. I could smell him and it was doing nothing to help me stay calm until I knew if he even could give me another chance.

"No more running."

I shook my head. "I *promise* I will never run from you again."

He groaned and pressed his forehead to mine. "This is going to work, Chloe."

"I know it is." I was damn determined, no matter what happened. "I've missed you so much."

With closed eyes and a boyish grin, he replied, "Back atcha."

Pressing his lips against mine in a much needed hot and heavy kiss that had me clinging to him and wrapping my legs around his waist, he carried us to what I assumed was the sofa.

I was suddenly on my back and Logan was devouring my mouth and tangling his hands in my hair. I returned the kiss with as much enthusiasm and emotion, loving the feeling of having his weight pressing me into the cushions below us.

This was where I was supposed to be. Not being around him was hard but at least it taught me that I never wanted us to be apart again. I was ready for our sunset.

He let us up for air right when I was feeling lightheaded and laid beside me. I curled into him, laying my head on his shoulder.

"I really am sorry, Logan, I've been the biggest idiot."

"You were scared," he replied.

"I was. I didn't even really realise how much and that it I could get past it until Nell said."

"Remind me to buy her a drink."

I smiled and burrowed closer. "How dumb could I be to not know why I was running?" He still didn't know the real reason I was running because I couldn't say those three, terrifying little words.

"There's been a lot, Chlo. Your emotions were all over the place, everything got blurred and the easiest thing to focus on was guilt, but the important thing is that you found your way back to me. I'd rather it happened like this than you forcing yourself to stay and it causing more problems. You had to know why you were running before we could move forward."

"You're so understanding."

"It's understandable. Over the last seven years I've wanted to run a few times and I did leave for a while when I took those three weeks off. No one can force you to realise something."

"Nell did."

"She just told you what you couldn't get your head around. Wanting you messed me up for a while, too. It's hard to understand the problem when you're that close and painfully easy for others to see."

"I guess."

"Seriously, don't beat yourself up over this. We're good now. If you ever feel like it's too much again—"

"I won't," I said, cutting him off. "I'm in this one hundred per cent, Logan." But telling him I loved him was still stuck in my throat and I think it was because I wanted to say it when everything had calmed down. I didn't want him to think I was only saying it to convince him I wasn't going anywhere. When I told him how I felt I wanted him to know that it was because he was everything and that I wasn't afraid anymore. Or I was just a big baby and hoping he'd say it again first.

He smiled, rolling half on top of me.

"I promise you, I want this."

"You don't have to convince me, I believe you, Chlo."

"But I want you to be sure that I—"

He shook his head, eyes gleaming. "Just kiss me, sweetheart."

Gripping the back of his head, I pulled him down all the way and for pretty much the first time I took full control over the kiss.

CHAPTER THIRTY-FIVE

Chloe

I met Nell in the local coffee house and we ordered subs for lunch. She was overly happy about me and Logan – mostly me – finally getting our shit together, as Nell had put it. I kind of was too. It felt nice to be happy without the misplaced guilt weighing me down.

The terrorists that killed Jace were sentenced four days ago. We didn't go. I went to Logan's where we waited for a call. They both got life, it still wasn't enough. Even though it was a hard day we got through it knowing they'd never hurt anyone again. The day was quiet and we stuck together but once it was over it was like a weight had been lifted. Jace had justice.

Everything had clicked into place and I'd realised that I didn't need to be scared of how I felt about Logan, he wanted me and he wasn't going anywhere.

"Alright, I can't *not* ask this," she said, green eyes gleaming. Her hair was down and stylishly messy. She never really did anything but she had the type of hair that played along and looked great when she just washed it and left it.

"Go on," I replied, narrowing my eyes cautiously.

"Who's better in the sack?"

"Oh, fuck no!" I said. Did those words seriously just leave her mouth?

"Come on, Chlo. You've slept with brothers. Dish the dirt. My money's on Logan, all that exercise and plenty of practice."

I was so close to throwing my coffee in her face.

"You've got to be kidding me, Nell!"

She sighed, rolling her eyes. "Alright. Just know that if the roles were reversed I would totally tell you."

"You just asked me who's better in bed my boyfriend or my dead ex."

"So? This is girl talk. I seem to remember you telling me once that no subject was off limits in girl talk."

"Well, now there's a limit. Comparing Jace and Logan is officially one of them."

My mind was screaming *Logan, Logan, Logan*. But that was probably because the love I had for him was different, more grown up. I suppose it didn't hurt that he'd had *a lot* of practice too.

"Ugh, you're no fun today."

"How's your love life?" I asked, earning me a flip of her middle finger. "Ah, now you're all for girl talk limits, huh?"

"Screw you, Chlo."

I grinned. "Seriously though, nothing happening there?"

"Nope. I think if I don't get laid in the next couple days I'm going to become a nun."

The idea of Nell being a nun was hilarious. She wasn't a slut but the girl liked sex. I blamed her and her on/off sorta boyfriend, Damon, for both of their unhappy situations.

I rolled my eyes. "You and Damon need your heads banging together."

"I don't want Damon," she said, frowning stubbornly.

Of course, you don't!

"Well, what do you want, Nell?"

"Before I wanted good sex with a man that respected

me. It didn't have to be anything serious or life changing, just good sex while I focused on my degree."

"Before what?" Was she actually about to admit that she wanted a relationship? Her and Damon had been together a few hundred times in high school but they were both as stubborn as each other so neither would admit what they wanted – a real, meaningful relationship with each other – first so they went around in circles, both claiming it was just a bit of fun.

She narrowed her eyes. "Before you and Logan."

I wasn't expecting that. I wasn't really expecting her to admit she wanted something real with Damon either, though. "What do we have to do with it?"

"You two are all happy. It makes me sick."

I popped a chip in my mouth and muttered, "Thanks."

"Seriously, you two are the reason I'm unhappy right now. I hope you feel bad about it." I laughed. "I met this guy."

Of course.

"He's on my course and he's so sweet."

"The problem is…?"

"He doesn't do casual."

I almost choked on nothing. "You *asked* him that? You want that? With him?"

"No," she replied, looking horrified. "He's mentioned it in passing before."

"Damon?"

She growled. "I told you I don't want him. I like Aaron."

"Right, okay." My head was spinning but then I never could keep up with her. "I'm failing to see the problem here then. You just said you want something more than casual."

"I do."

Now I completely understood why men thought women were confusing.

She sighed. "I can't jump in like that."

"Why not?"

"What if it doesn't work out and I'm left with a broken heart?"

"Nell, if you get your heart broken you get it broken. You'll survive. I did. But you can't go through your life never taking any risks. Love is a risk, a chance, and if you never jump you'll never find happiness."

"That was deep, Chlo."

"Plus, Aaron can't break your heart, only Damon can do that."

I was rewarded with a glare and then she brushed right over my comment, "I understand where you're coming from but as much as I want something meaningful I'm not ready to jump yet."

"That's fine." I understood full well that she wasn't ready. Sometimes jumping before you could handle it only hurt everyone involved. "But if you really think this something could happen with this guy, then don't let being afraid interfere with—"

"Okay!" she said. "I get it. I won't let him go if he's *the one*. Can we please change the subject now?" I wasn't sure if she was referring to Aaron or Damon but I moved on like she'd asked.

"I love Logan."

"Yeah, I know."

"I can't tell him."

"Why? I thought you were past that running shit."

"I am and I don't know why I can't. There's been so many times I've wanted to but I open my mouth and nothing comes out."

She waved her hand at me. "You really have to get over this being a baby thing, Chlo."

"Pot. Kettle. Black," I said.

"You. Fuck. Off."

I laughed, shaking my head. "It's a big thing to tell someone you're in love with them."

"He's told you. Seriously, I hate you sometimes! You've got this perfect guy who is totally in love with you, you're safe with him, Chloe, he'll never not say it back. What are you still scared of?"

"Saying it and losing him." If I hadn't loved Jace I wouldn't have ended up with a broken heart, not that I regretted it, loving him was worth it but it already scared me how much I loved Logan. If he died on me, too, I don't know what I'd do. I wouldn't just be lost or stuck. I'd be nothing. I'd just exist.

"You won't lose him. Not everyone dies young, sweetie. You've got to allow yourself to think of the future with Logan because you two are going to have a great one. Please, stop letting your fear keep you from being even more deliriously happy. Tell him."

"Yeah, I will. Thanks, Nell, you always put things into perspective. Shame you can't take your own advice, huh?"

"If you still want a lift to the garage you're going the wrong way about it. Plus, I was just reciting what you said to me. You can't take your own advice either."

I held my hand up, surrendering. "Alright, sorry. No more Damon talk this week."

"Promise?"

I crossed my heart and then smiled because it reminded me of Logan.

"Ugh," she scoffed. "You're disgusting when you're all loved up."

I was the happiest I could ever remember being, so I could definitely handle that.

CHAPTER THIRTY-SIX

Chloe

The words were stuck in my throat, still. I felt it – I loved him so bloody much – so why was it so hard to say? Well, maybe because I'd said *I love you* to eyes almost the same bright topaz as that before and look how that ended. Losing Jace was horrific. Even the thought of anything happening to Logan was torture.

And it was also hard because it had been two weeks since we got together and he hadn't said it again yet. I should've just said it back then. He'd said it to me before though, and I didn't want us to not have that connection.

I'd just wrapped a towel around myself when Logan – or I hoped Logan – knocked on the door. "Yeah?" I called.

He laughed. "It's me, Chlo, no one else is here. Even the cleaner's left for the night." We'd just finished a pretty intense work out and it was Logan's turn to lock up the gym.

I relaxed a little. "I'm just getting dressed."

The door opened. "Why didn't you say you were naked sooner?"

I flushed and shooed him. "Get out! This is the ladies' changing room."

"I know that," he replied.

"Then get out. What if someone comes back in?"

"I locked the doors. No one's here but us." He stalked closer, breathing heavier, eyes on fire. "Drop the towel, sweetheart."

I wasn't quite sure if I was more turned on or more shocked. Probably equal measures of both.

"Sorry?" I spluttered. He wanted us to have sex in the changing room where he worked. Logan had *that* look in his eye again and my bones turned to mush. Gulping, I said, "Logan, we—"

With one little flick of his hand my towel dropped to the floor. A rush of cold air did nothing to cool me down under Logan's hungry gaze. His breath blew across my face, covering my skin in goose bumps.

Oh, we are so having sex in the changing room where he works!

His eyes dropped, raking over every inch of my skin. I didn't feel the urge to cover up. I wasn't embarrassed. With Jace I had always changed quickly if it was in front of him. I was never this comfortable.

"You are so fucking beautiful, Chloe."

"Do you always have to swear?"

"What can I say, you bring it out in me." Enveloping me in his arms, he feathered kisses across my shoulder. "I've never felt every single emotion as strongly as I do with you. Whatever I feel, if it involves you, I feel it a thousand times over. I can't get enough." He worked his way up; kissing my skin so softly I barely felt it.

I arched my back and gripped his hips with trembling hands. "This really isn't a time to go slow," I said.

He flicked his tongue out, dipping into the crevice of my shoulder bone. *Fuck!* "Turned on, are we?"

"Don't tease."

He added his hands, gliding them over my hip and the back of my thighs. I reached for his jeans and managed to get them down in record time. I half expected him to stop me and really make me suffer before he gave us both what we needed.

His erection sprang free and I gripped it with my hand. Two could play his horrible, teasing game. Logan's fingertips bit into my skin as I squeezed, rubbing my thumb over his sensitive tip.

"Shit," he hissed, arching into my hand and slammed his mouth against mine in a rough, desperate kiss that made me forget my own sodding name.

My back hit the painted brick wall and I moaned into the kiss. Logan positioned himself between my legs and the friction was enough to send me to the place I loved most – the place where nothing else but me and him existed. Clawing his back, I nipped his bottom lip, earning a deep growl.

He sank inside me in one sharp thrust, causing us both to gasp. I loved when he first entered me; it was stimulation overload and almost drove me to madness.

"Logan," I breathed against his lips as he picked up his relentless pace. It wasn't slow and tender but it was exactly what we both needed and when we came together I thought I would pass out from the physical feeling and the emotion that went into it.

I placed my hand above his heart, feeling the thumping beat. He stared at me, those topaz eyes shining with love, pulling me under. I tightened my legs around his waist, scared that he was going to pull away soon. I needed him to hold me. My heart matched his, wild.

"I love you, Logan."

He closed his eyes, mouth opened and he sucked in a shaky breath. It felt like an eternity before he opened his eyes again but when he did they were blistering. "Shit... You have no fucking idea, sweetheart."

That was the oddest *I love you, too* but I'd take it. After all, it was so completely Logan.

Laughing quietly, I stroked my fingers through his hair.

He looked as overwhelmed as I felt. I'd seen Logan struggle to control his emotions before but this time was different. This was happy. This time made my heart ache for him in a completely different way.

"We should probably go soon," I said after we'd held each other for a while.

He didn't say anything but very gently pulled out and set me on my feet. My legs were still boneless and if I wasn't still floating I would've collapsed to the floor.

Logan zipped up his jeans and then helped me get dressed. He still hadn't said anything and I was getting a little concerned. "Are you okay?" I asked, slipping on my shoes.

"Yeah," he replied.

"Really? You've not said anything in a long time and that's sort of not like you. At all."

"It's just…" He took a deep breath and looked up at the ceiling. "Sometimes it's too much and I don't know how to deal with it."

"Oh," I said in utter shock. *Too much.* I could identify with that. The way I felt about him was so consuming it took my breath away.

"Oh?" he asked, now smirking. *Logan's back.* "You do have interesting reactions to me spilling my guts."

"I told you I love you and your reply included *two* swear words and no mention of love."

"Hmm, maybe we're perfect for each other."

We were.

"Yeah, maybe we are," I said. "Want to go to dinner now? I'm starving."

"Sure," he replied, kissing my forehead, letting his lips linger on my skin long enough to make the ache I felt for him burst back to life.

He took my hand and led me through the empty gym, setting the alarm and locking the door behind us.

"Chloe," he said once we reached his car.

"Uh huh?"

He bent his head, looking into my eyes. I knew what was coming next but nothing could prepare me for how amazing it felt. "I love you."

"Logan, you have no fucking idea."

He laughed and then pressed me against his car, kissing me until we could barely breathe.

CHAPTER THIRTY-SEVEN

Logan

I woke with my arms wrapped around a naked Chloe. I'd literally never felt so fucking happy before. I'd dreamt of her telling me she loved me back a million times over but I wasn't prepared for how incredible it would feel. I thought I understood how much I loved her but I was wrong. Hearing her say those words – *I love you, Logan* – filled a void, made me believe I could be something, gave me hope. She just made everything better, made me better.

We could do it together. We'd build a new life. We'd take Jace with us, he was a part of us both and that was how it was supposed to be, but we could be happy together, too.

I'd preached to her about moving on and that made me a hypocrite. Until now there wasn't one moment since Jace died that I felt truly happy. My last words to him haunted me. *Just get the fuck out of my life, Jace.* I didn't mean it. Jace knew I didn't mean it. I still hated myself for it. My last words should have been *I love you, brother*.

The night before I'd overheard Jace telling Chloe he'd marry her one day and I lost it. When I saw him the next morning I picked a fight. I loved her long before Jace died, hell, I loved her long before he did. She stumbled into my life – literally – as my brother's friend and I fell for her quick wit, those amber eyes and her love of junk food and keeping her body fit in equal measures. She was my other half. And then she fell for my little brother.

Now she was finally lying in my arms, I was harder than I'd ever been in my fucking life and it was taking every ounce of self-control I had not to push inside her and start the day right now with a handful of orgasms.

Stirring in my arms, Chloe let out a deep sigh and snuggled closer. Her naked back to my naked chest. One little movement sent my already lust filled body on high alert. I wanted in her as much as I wanted to lay with her.

Keeping myself as still as I could while my hips willed me to move and give the friction I screamed for, I decided to let her sleep and prolong the conversation we'd have as soon as she woke. I wasn't ready for more guilt over Jace just yet. I wanted a few more moments to just be Chloe and Logan with no drama.

Admitting she loved me wasn't easy for her; she still battled with the moral dilemma we faced. It was hard for us both.

Showing no sign of waking soon, I watched her for a few more minutes, then I really needed to take a piss. Chlo rolled over and settled back under my quilt as I got out of bed. I loved that I'd worn her out last night. I vowed to do it again tonight and pretty much every fucking night for the rest of our lives.

I went to the toilet and as I came out of the bathroom I heard the unmistakable sound of my mum crying. I didn't like it. She'd shed too many tears over the last three years and I hated to see her upset.

Ducking back in my room I slipped my jeans over my boxers and headed downstairs. My heart weighed of lead as I approached the kitchen, where her muffled sobbing was coming from. It had been a while since she'd cried openly like that.

"I-I can't believe…" Mum muttered. Her voice was low

and hoarse, like she'd been crying for weeks. I gulped down a deep breath.

Shit, what's going on?

I pushed the kitchen door open and froze. My eyes popped out of my head and my heart stopped beating.

"Hi, bro," Jace whispered, smiling over Mum's head as she clung to him.

CHAPTER THIRTY-EIGHT

Logan

My brain rejected what I was seeing. Jace was dead; he couldn't be standing in the fucking kitchen. Only he was, and I didn't know what to say or what to think. I could hear my heart thumping.

Jace peeled Mum off him and Dad took over. He stepped closer and smiled that full smile I would've sold my soul to see.

"Fuck," I breathed, stumbling forwards and enveloping him in my arms.

What the fucking fuck is going on?

I didn't care that it was impossible or it didn't make sense. My brother was back – somehow – and that was all that mattered.

Jace clung to me as hard as I clung to him. He was smaller. For someone that sat around playing computer games he still had muscle but that had mostly disappeared. What the hell had happened to him? "Jace?"

Was I dreaming?

"Yeah, man," he said, pulling back. "God, you have no idea how good it is to see you."

I fucking did.

Every day I wished I could see him again, even if it was just for a second so I could tell him how sorry I was and that I didn't mean the words I'd said. Now he was here and I had a chance to make it up to him, to be his brother again.

"How? I don't…" I rubbed my eyes, checking I wasn't asleep or seeing things that weren't there. I wasn't. Thank God.

I blew out a deep breath to control the urge to cry like a little girl. My brother was back.

"I survived the bombing. Me and another girl, she was with another school but we all walked together. We were taken to a hospital after the explosion. When the police learned that we'd seen the bastards that had done it we suddenly had other people around us, people in suits that looked like James bloody Bond. I've been in Witness Protection ever since."

Shit.

"I wanted to come back the second the sentences were given but we had to stay and make sure there was no backlash, no one wanting revenge. We couldn't risk it."

Three fucking years and we'd thought he was dead and he was hiding out somewhere. I wanted to be angry. I *was* angry but it was completely eclipsed by the fact that my little brother was alive. I would get my chance to put things right.

"I can't believe this," I said, my smile stretching. I hugged him again because I was so grateful he was here. "Never thought I'd see you again."

"Don't get all sappy on me," he said, fighting tears too. "I pissed you off more than anyone else in the world."

"Yeah, you did and I'm so fucking happy you're back to do it all over again. You're not going anywhere again, right?" Screw Witness Protection, he was my bloody brother and they weren't getting him back.

"I'm here to stay."

Mum sniffed from while being in Dad's arms and said, "I need a strong cup of tea."

Me and Jace laughed. She was a Brit through and through.

"I'll put the kettle on and we can all sit down," Dad said, still unable to take his eyes off his returning son.

"I could do with something a bit stronger," I said and instantly regretted it as Mum looked to the floor. Right, no drinking. I looked back at Jace to make sure he was still really there. He was. I gulped. "Tea is good, Dad."

I heard a gasp behind me and knew it was Chloe. *Shit.* Turning around, I watched her face drop and her mouth fall open. She looked terrified, as if she'd just seen a ghost. I guess she kind of had.

"Hi, Chloe," Jace said.

She took a step back and it was then I noticed that her hands were shaking. "No. What is…?" she whispered, taking a few ragged breaths as she continued to stare at Jace in complete shock.

I couldn't speak and the longer her eyes stayed attached to his I started to feel sick. What did that mean? I was so glad, happy, and relieved that Jace was back, I would never want the alternative, but where did that leave me and her?

"W-What?" she whispered again and gulped.

"Chloe, honey," my mum said, holding her hands out for her. Chlo looked at her and then back to Jace. "It's okay. The bombings… Jace saw who it was. He's been in Witness Protection this whole time, until the trials were over."

Her eyes widened and then flicked to me. I felt like she had just stabbed a knife into my chest. If she knew that would she have waited for him? Did she now regret us? Out of the corner of my eye, I saw Jace look her up and down. She was wearing my t-shirt from yesterday with her leggings. She looked guilty as she stared at me through tear stained eyes.

I didn't need to see my brother to know he was looking between us, figuring out what had happened.

"What's going on?" Jace asked and turned to me.

I couldn't take my eyes off her. She looked like she had stopped breathing. I stepped forward. A part of me needed to explain to Jace right this second but a bigger part needed to make sure the woman I was hopelessly in love with was alright. She certainly didn't look alright.

"Chlo," I whispered "Hey, you okay?"

She flinched and took a step back, shaking her head. I clenched my jaw as she stabbed me for the second time in as many minutes.

"I... I can't." She turned around and ran from the room.

Shit!

I bolted after her. "No! Chloe, wait."

The daily workouts had really done their job; Chloe was back to running like Usain Bolt. She was up the stairs in two seconds flat.

"Chloe, stop!" I said, grabbing her hand as I finally caught up with her in my room. "Please, don't leave. We need to sort this out."

Her horror and shock filled tears tore me apart. "He's back," she whispered. Her hand tightened around mine. "How? Why didn't he tell us? I can't... I don't..."

"Shh, calm down. I know." I closed my bedroom door, giving us some privacy. Stepping closer, I looked into her eyes for permission. When she didn't push me away, I wrapped my arms around her. "It's a huge shock for all of us but please, don't run. We need to deal with this. You need to talk to him and understand." She shook her head. "You know we do. Jace is *here*, Chloe." This wasn't going away. I didn't want this to go away. "He's alive."

She pressed her fingers to her temple as if she was getting a headache. "Is this real? I don't get..."

My bedroom door burst open, making us both jump. "Alright, what the hell is going on?" Jace said. "What is this? Why is she in here?"

Shit.

"Oh, Jesus. You're *together*? While I was away missing

my family and *girlfriend,* waiting for the fucking trial of terrorists who murdered my classmates to be over, my brother and girlfriend were screwing each other."

"It wasn't like that, Jace, and you know it," I said calmly.

Chloe stepped away from me, closer to him. "Why didn't you tell me, Jace?"

"That's not the fucking point!"

"Yes, it is! *Three years,* Jace! We all thought you were dead. We *buried* you! Shit!" She ran her hand through her hair roughly. "You have any idea how hard it was to watch your coffin being lowered into the ground? The whole time you were alive. You must have known what it would do to us but you still didn't say a bloody thing."

She still loves him.

"I couldn't tell you."

"Yes, you could."

"How long did it take to fall into my brother's bed? Have you been seeing each other behind my back before I left or did you at least wait a week after?"

"Screw you!" she snapped and shoved past him, sprinting down the stairs. I let her go because I knew she needed some time alone to process everything. If I followed her I would push her away and she already had a thing for running from me, I didn't want to give her an excuse to bolt for good. And her car was at her house so she wouldn't be driving in a state.

Jace knew she needed time too; he didn't try following her. He turned to me. "How could you?"

"Neither of us planned it, Jace."

"How long?"

"We've been together a couple months."

And last night was the first time she said I love you.

He closed his eyes and took a deep breath. When he opened them again I could see how much he hated me. "Why her?"

"I didn't plan it to be her."

"And everyone knows?" he asked. I nodded. "Wow, that's just…"

"I'm sorry. Shit, we had no idea this was going to happen. How could we?"

"Seeing my family and my girlfriend again kept me going. You have no idea how lonely it is living a lie and being cut off from the people you love. I thought about my reunion with Chloe a thousand times and not once was she ever with my fucking brother!"

"Did you ever consider that she would've moved on? Three years is a long time."

"I know how long it is, Logan. Of course, I thought about it, but I was confident I could win her back."

Was confident or is confident?

I didn't want to hurt Jace. He was my brother for Christ sake; he was one of the last people in the world I wanted to hurt but he couldn't expect me to hand her over like she was a toy. What happened between me and Chlo was real and as long as she wasn't letting go I wasn't.

"You thought you could come strolling back into her life and expect her to drop everything? Do you have any idea how hard she's fought to get back on track? You didn't see how cut up she was, you didn't have to watch her cry every single day or hold her hair while she threw up after sobbing for hours straight. You didn't hold her up through your *funeral* and pray that the light would come back in her eyes. You didn't worry about her because she stopped leaving the house or coming over. You didn't pick her up and force her to get out of bed again. You didn't start to see her breathing easier again and hearing her laugh. You have no right to expect anything from her."

Jace wanted to punch me, that much was obvious but my words hit him hard. It was the truth. One phone call could have ended all of our suffering and I got that he couldn't but that didn't mean we weren't damaged by it.

We'd all been through something that changed us and as much as I was over the fucking moon that he was back he couldn't expect things to magically go back to how they were before.

CHAPTER THIRTY-NINE

Chloe

I slammed the front door and my legs gave out. "Chloe!" Mum said, rushing to my side. She dropped to her knees. "What's wrong?" Lifting my chin, she checked every inch of my face.

"Jace," I whispered, staring off into the distance. My mind hadn't caught up and I was still struggling to accept that he wasn't dead. He was in Logan's sodding kitchen!

"Oh, honey," she said.

She thought I was just upset. I shook my head. "No. No, it's not that. It's not guilt or I don't... He's not... Jace isn't dead."

"What? No, Chloe, are you okay? Has something happened?"

Why wasn't she believing me?

"Mum, he's *back*. He's... God, he's there now. In the kitchen. Jace never died. He didn't die and I..." I fell in love with his brother.

"I don't understand, Chloe. How is he back? Love, he died."

She thought I was crazy. I could see the way she looked at me that she was terrified I was going insane.

"Witness Protection," I whispered. "He saw the bombers." I said the words but they still didn't make complete sense to me.

Mum's mouth popped open audibly. "I don't... I can't believe it. Oh, honey."

Wrapped in her arms, I closed my eyes and tried to wrap my head around what was going on. I wasn't dreaming. I'd dreamt that he walked back through the door millions of times and this was nothing like that. For one, we leapt into each other's arms. There was no leaping. There was just shock and more shock.

"I need to go to bed, Mum," I said.

"What?"

Breaking out of her grip, I pushed myself to my feet with trembling hands. I felt cold and exhausted. All I wanted to do was curl up in a ball and sleep. Not that I'd be able to sleep. I wasn't that lucky.

"Okay," she said, momentarily stunned. Rising to her feet too, she brushed my tears away. I was crying? "What do you need? I should call Julia."

Julia was in a worse state than me; there was no way she'd be able to hold a phone call.

"I need to go to bed," I repeated and walked off.

How I made it upstairs I had no clue. But I was tucked up in bed, staring at nothing in particular. Jace was alive. This whole time I'd been heartbroken and fighting to get through the day he'd been alive. How could he stay away and let us think he was dead?

How could he not love me enough to stop me suffering?

I heard the front door open and the hushed voices of my parents as my mum undoubtedly told Dad all about Jace. I didn't know if she'd spoken to Julia or Daryl. She checked in often but left with a sigh when I didn't respond. I just needed to not think or do anything until I knew what to think or do.

My phone rang until I switched it off. Logan would

know to stay away for a little while but I wasn't sure how long he'd give me. I wasn't really sure how long I'd need. Maybe there wasn't enough time. Yesterday everything was perfect and I was looking forward to my future with Logan and now everything was a mess again.

I curled up tighter and sobbed into my pillow until my throat was raw.

***

"Chloe!" Nell said as she burst through my bedroom door. When I'd heard thudding up the stairs I was worried and hopeful at the same time. "Your mum called. I don't even know what to say. Jace is back? He's not…?"

"Not dead, that's right," I replied.

"You okay?" she asked, sitting down on the bed.

"Not at all. I don't know what to do. Last night I finally told Logan I love him and I wake up to Jace standing in the kitchen. This whole time, Nell. He's been alive while I was dying and never once thought to let us know he was okay. I fell in love with his *brother* for fuck sake!"

"Jesus. So he was in witness protection?"

"Until sentencing was over." I rubbed the bridge of my nose. I had a headache just thinking about everything. "I don't know if I want to hug him or kill him. Burying Jace and getting over him was the hardest thing I've ever done and I didn't need to do any of it."

"What did Logan say?"

I shrugged. "I couldn't really focus on anything other than my dead boyfriend standing beside my current boyfriend. The Scott's will be thrilled to have him back though, of course."

She frowned. "You're not?"

"No, I am. Shit, of course I'm glad he's alive. It's all I've wanted since the second I thought he died but he let me think he was gone for over three years."

"I doubt he wanted that Chloe."

"He still did it. I would've called or done something."

"Would you have waited for him if you knew?"

"Yes."

"And Logan wouldn't have happened."

"I guess not." Of course not.

"Do you still want Jace?"

"No," I whispered. "I will always love Jace but I'm not in love with him anymore. I moved on…to Logan. God, this is such a mess, Nell, I don't know what to do. Tell me what I should do."

She opened and closed her mouth a few times before shrugging. "I don't know, girl. This shit only happens in soaps. I keep trying to think what would happen on *EastEnders* but you probably shouldn't use those as—"

"Okay," I said, cutting her ramble off. "Shit. He's not dead." I put my hands over my face and sobbed.

"Shh, don't cry," Nell said. "We'll figure this out."

"How?" I wiped my eyes, even though it was useless, they were replaced straight away. "Jace is back, he hates me and Logan, and Logan probably thinks I've done one again. Why did I have to fall for him, Nell?"

"You can't help that," she replied, her eyes distant, "no one can."

"There something you want to talk about?"

"Right now I think we should concentrate on you, hun."

"But if you're going through something…"

"Nothing I can't handle, I swear. We'll talk about it as soon as we get this…"

"Mess?" I offered.

She grimaced. "Well, yeah, as soon as we get this mess sorted out. Talk me through what happened, you told Logan you love him and the next morning Jace is back."

"Yeah, that pretty much sums it up. Jace knows about us. I thought he was going to punch Logan."

"I don't think that'd get him anywhere."

"Logan wouldn't retaliate. Anyway that's not the point. Jace is *alive* and I love his brother. He left three years ago thinking he was protecting us and planning for the day he got to come back and what does he walk into?"

"Wow, that's rough."

"Yes, thanks for stating the obvious." I groaned and squeezed her hand. "Sorry, I don't mean to take it out on you."

"It's okay. What're you going to do now?"

"I have no idea. Talk to Jace, I guess, but what do I say? I'm still so angry with him for letting us all believe he was dead. Every night I cried myself to sleep because I missed him. I didn't have to go through any of that."

"I can't believe he did that. He must have known how heartbroken you and his whole family would've been. His parents buried their son for Christ sake!"

I shrugged. "He was doing the *right thing*." One phone call could have saved so much pain but he chose to let us suffer.

CHAPTER FORTY

Chloe

Again, I expected Logan to be the one walking through my door. It was Jace. I wasn't at all prepared to see him. His eyes were a few shades darker than Logan's but just as striking. He'd never had stubble before, his face was always smooth but now he had short hairs around his jaw, meeting his sideburns.

I licked my lips. Seeing him in the flesh again made my heart ache. I wasn't supposed to be able to talk to him again. I'd accepted that a long time ago but here he was, standing just outside my bedroom door wanting to talk.

"Can I come in?" he asked, looking at me the way he used to when we were each other's everything.

I wanted to say no. It hurt to look at him. It hurt to think that everything I went through was all his fault. I didn't have to feel like I'd lost a sodding limb. He let me go through that. But this was Jace and he was here so I sat up and gave a short nod.

"I don't know where to start, Chloe," he said, closing the door. I watched as he awkwardly walked to my bed and sat down. It kind of reminded me of when we first got together, before we were comfortable with each other.

Well, I knew where I wanted to start. "How could you? How could you allow us to think you were dead?"

"I didn't have a choice."

"Yes, you did." There was *always* a choice. It just might not always be a good one.

"Do you have any idea what would have happened to you all if anyone found out where I was and why I was in hiding? They're *terrorists*, Chloe, they'd have no problem killing you as well, they wouldn't think twice about ending your life."

"I used to wish I'd died, too. I used to lay in bed, close my eyes and pray I wouldn't wake up." His jaw tightened, eyes tensed. "It was horrendous at first. I could barely get out of bed. Your mum sat on the sofa all day and night until your dad made her go to bed. Logan drank his bodyweight in whatever booze he could get his hands on. Eventually I stopped going over or really going out at all. I didn't know what to do. We were inseparable and I suddenly had to be without you. I felt like I was walking around in complete darkness."

"Stop," he whispered. "Please, I can't…"

"Painful, is it?" I spat through clenched teeth. I started crying again at the memories. It hurt just as much thinking about it as it did when I was going through it.

"You were safe, that was all that mattered. I couldn't let anything happen to you or my family. You have to understand that, Chloe. There wasn't another choice. You had to believe I was gone."

I shook my head. "No. You could have found a way to tell us the truth but you didn't. You sat back."

"I'm sorry."

"We had to *bury* you so don't you dare try justifying it. I would have never let you go through that."

"I don't know what you want me to say. I've told you my reasons and I'll never apologise for keeping you safe."

"You just apologised!"

"For hurting you, not for protecting you."

It was the same thing to me but I couldn't have that pointless fight with him. He didn't even seem to realise what his 'death' had done to us.

Sniffing, I wiped my nose with my sleeve. I wanted to leap into his arms and breathe him in but I was still too angry. I missed him. As much as I knew I was beyond lucky that I got to have him back in my life, I was pissed that he didn't end our suffering.

"Where have you been?"

"Wales. A remote little village in the middle of nowhere." He was just a few hours drive away. "I lived with the other survivor. I finished college and then we went to university together, using a student flat share as our cover."

"God." I stood up and ran my hands over my face. This was too much to take in.

Jace didn't seem to think so; he didn't stop his story.

"We helped each other. She missed home as much as I did but she dealt with the new identity a lot easier than me. Alyssa was having a hard time coming out but being April gave her the opportunity to be who she is. She picked me up and reminded me why I was torturing myself by staying away. The men that planted the bomb and killed all those people deserved to go down for it, Chloe. I didn't want them walking the streets with you."

I almost snipped that I didn't walk the streets but I understood what he meant, and I knew it wasn't easy for him either.

He stood up slowly, cautious of my reaction.

"You and my family are the last people in the world I want to hurt but I couldn't risk it. Please, understand that. I just needed you to be okay… and you are." His voice faltered, and I think part of him wanted to come back to me being a total mess still.

"It took a long time for me to be okay, Jace."

"Logan helped," he said, his voice cold, hard and

detached.

It was obvious where this was going and I knew we'd need to have several conversations about me and Logan but right now I just wanted to make sense of my ex being alive.

"I don't want to talk about Logan right now."

"I think it's a pretty important subject, Chloe."

"So is you coming back from the..." I couldn't say *dead*.

"You know what happened there. I did what I had to do to help put two dangerous men behind bars. Now I want to know how the hell you fell for my brother."

"I don't know what to tell you, Jace, I just did. We got closer and it happened."

"It happened?"

"Yes. What else do you want me to say? We've been over this."

"Well, maybe I can't get my head around it."

"Well, maybe I can't get my head around what you did." I was shouting now. I wanted to have a calm conversation but that wasn't going to happen, there were too many fucked up, mixed feelings for this conversation to be anywhere near civil.

"Where does that leave us?" he asked.

I shrugged. It was too soon to decide that.

"Are you going to keep seeing Logan?"

"I don't know," I replied. I wanted to but I had to find out how he felt about everything. He loved me, that much I was sure of, but I didn't know if he'd be able to stay with me now that Jace was back. Brother came before girl.

"Right," he snapped. "I'll see you, Chloe."

Without another world or glance back in my direction he left as quickly as he could. My door was slammed behind me and I fell to my knees as soon as it was closed, winded by the situation and our argument. It was all way too much. I collapsed back against the bed and cried.

***

Again, Nell burst through my door as if she owned the place. I really needed to get my parents to start announcing her arrival, or getting her to call first.

"You're still in bed," she said as if she'd expected me to be doing anything else.

I rolled onto my back, looking up at the ceiling and groaned. "Jace stopped by a while ago."

"Oh." She was sitting beside me in a flash. "How did that go?"

"We argued. Big shock there."

"Have you spoken to Logan?"

"Not yet. I figured he'll have a lot on at home at the minute. His family needs to deal with Jace being back rather than the Chloe/Logan/Jace drama right now. We've waited long enough, I don't think a few more days are going to hurt."

She sighed. "Chloe, Chloe, Chloe, you're running again."

"No." She didn't look convinced. "I mean it, Nell. I promised him no more running and I meant it. This is just time and space so we can both deal with something that's..." Yeah, there really wasn't a word for what we were dealing with right now.

"You mean it? This isn't you bolting for the hills?"

"I mean it." I couldn't leave him again but I could stay away long enough to let him and his brother, hopefully, sort things out.

"Okay," she replied, nodding, her long, hair falling in her face. "Do yourself a favour though, don't leave it too long before you talk to him again."

"I won't. Anyway, tell me about what's going on in your life."

"You want to talk about me when all of this is going on?" she asked.

I looked over at my best friend and nodded. "Of course. I kind of need to think about something that's not my screwed up love life or my ex who's not lying below a grave I've cried over more times than I can count."

Nell's leafy green eyes shone with mischief. She shoved her long, pitch-black hair behind her ears. "Wow, my problems seem so small compared to yours."

"Thanks, sweetie," I said sarcastically. "Spill."

With a pissed off sigh, she launched into her rant, "Damon, the prick, has stepped up said prickiness. You know he had the cheek to ask me on a date. A *date*! Did the four thousand conversations we had about me not wanting a boyfriend not make him understand that I don't want a boyfriend?"

I held my hand up. "Hold on, not so long ago you were telling me you wanted something real."

"I changed my mind, Chlo, keep up!" *Right.* "Men are too much hassle. I mean, look at what you're going through. I told him I understand that he wants in my pants so we're just keeping it casual."

"Yeah, your problems are tiny," I muttered.

She slapped my arm. "Okay, I say we use the next few days to get your head around Jace being back and mega pissed off that his girl is shagging his brother and maybe get a little drunk too."

"Sounds good and thanks for being so sensitive there."

"How do we get your head around this?"

I shrugged. "Don't know. I don't even know if Jace will ever forgive us. If he doesn't what does that mean for me and Logan?"

"You and Logan continue without his blessing. The guy let you believe he was dead for over three years, what right does he have to walk back in and have an opinion on anything?"

"Well, he left knowing I loved him so I understand why he's hurt."

"No, I get it, but he needs to get over it. You're definitely staying with Logan, right? Oh God, this isn't going to be one of those messy love triangles, is it?"

"No. I told you I'm with Logan and not even Jace can change that. No *love triangles* and no confusion."

"Good, because Logan is way hotter. Those muscles." She wolf whistled and wiggled her eyebrows.

This was going somewhere I did not want to be.

"Think maybe we can go back to talking about anything else for a while?"

"Sure. Would you rather have your arms cut off or give birth to a twenty pound baby?"

Well, I asked for something else.

CHAPTER FORTY-ONE

Chloe

I'd passed being nervous to see Logan about an hour ago, now I was just plain scared. After a week I couldn't stay away any longer, even though my head was still seriously messed up from Jace walking back into our lives like he hadn't pretended to be dead. Me and Logan hadn't spoke once, not even a text. He was giving me time and I was doing the same. But I was starting to go a little crazy.

"Hey, Chlo," Ralf said, pinning a fitness poster to the wall. He looked at me a little longer than usual; it wasn't hard to understand why with all that's been going on.

"Hi," I replied as I walked past. Usually, I'd stop for a minute and chat but I was too anxious for small talk and I had a feeling he'd be lost for words, wanting to ask about Logan and Jace but not wanting to at the same time.

The main gym was pretty big, one side was cardio equipment and the other side was for weight lifting. Men with ridiculous muscles and no necks grunted as they lifted weights that were probably heavier than me.

Logan wasn't in here. He wasn't working out or training anyone. If he wasn't in the juice bar then I had no idea where I could find him, and I had to see him. It'd been too long. I was a huge idiot and I needed to put things right between us.

"Ralf," I said as I made my way back down the hall. "Do you know where Logan is?" Could he be in the staff room? He said he didn't really like it in there and preferred to be out with everyone else.

"Sorry," he replied over his shoulder. "Check the bar if he's not in the gym."

"Yeah, was going there now. Thanks."

My heart was going like a train as I approached the open double doors to the bar. *Please, be in here.*

Stepping through, I stopped dead. He was sitting at a table with Jace. Logan was facing me and looked up the second I stepped through the doorway as if he sensed I was there.

Eyes solely on me, he stood up. That was when Jace craned his neck around. Seeing them both was like a kick in the gut. I would always love Jace and I hated that I hurt him by being with Logan but we didn't know he was coming back. I moved on with the one person that made me happy. Unfortunately, I couldn't choose who was in my heart. It was Logan.

"Hi, Chloe," Jace said.

Smiling, I replied, "Hey."

Why was Logan just standing there looking at me? He didn't move, didn't talk, didn't bloody blink.

"You want to join us?"

Did I want to join my ex and my boyfriend? Awkward. And they were brothers. Double awkward. I had to do it, though. If we were all going to get through this we had to find a way of being in the same room together.

"Sure."

I sat on the spare chair at the table and Logan lowered himself down. Oh, I definitely would have preferred to do the trio thing *after* me and Logan sorted everything out.

Stealing a glance at him, I saw his eyes were still glued

to me as if he didn't think I'd ever come back. I just needed time.

"Hi," I said.

He smiled and looked so handsome my heart gave a squeeze. "Hi, sweetheart."

God, I had missed him saying that.

I was painfully aware that Jace was still sitting with us so I dragged my eyes away from Logan. "What're you two doing? Never thought I'd see you in a gym, Jace."

He grinned. I used to love the way he looked at me but now I hated it. I wish he wasn't still in love with me. "Very funny. I just came to see Logan."

I'm intruding.

"Oh. I can go if you're busy."

"No," Logan said, almost snapping. "You're not interrupting anything."

I was, but I understood that I had stayed away for a week so Logan probably felt like if I left he didn't know when I'd come back again. I was done running away and ready to face Logan and Jace and hopefully work through the issues we had.

"Okay." I sunk further into the seat.

"I'll get you a juice," Logan said, standing and heading to the bar.

"How are you getting on being back?" I asked Jace. There was just about a million other things I wanted to ask but I didn't know where to start and I didn't want to get into the heavy stuff in public.

He pursed his lips. "It's strange. Good strange but taking some adapting. I've had the same conversation with Mum, Dad, Logan and Cassie about a hundred times over."

"It's going to take everyone time to get over everything."

Everyone's lives were finally back on track. We were all starting to feel happy again. When someone died, as much as you wanted to, you never in a million years expected to find them standing in the kitchen again. You adjusted and found a way to go on without them there. Jace coming back flipped everything again, for the better, of course, but we still all had questions we needed answering. There was still anger and confusion and hurt that had to be addressed. As much as I understood he couldn't tell anyone he was alive I would never forgive him completely for breaking us so much.

"I know. I understand that you're pissed. I just wish you could be happier I'm not dead."

I gripped the edges of the chair. I wanted to swing for him. How fucking dare he say that?

Jace groaned. "I'm sorry."

"Chlo," Logan said, putting my juice on the table and crouching down. "Hey, you're whiter than Casper right now." He tilted my chin so I looked at him. "What's wrong?"

I looked back at Jace. "How could you say that?"

"Say what? What did he say?" Logan asked.

"I didn't mean it, Chloe. You know I didn't, it's just…"

"Just what?"

Logan watched us, still crouched on the floor. He put his hand on my thigh, claiming me. I hated that he felt the need to do it. I was his and nothing was going to change that.

"You ran away pretty much the second you saw me. I had to come to you and when I did you shouted. What else am I supposed to think?"

"You sound surprised. You don't get it, Jace. You have no idea what it's like to think the person you love is dead."

Logan tensed and I realised I'd used present tense. Damn it.

"I know I don't but–"

"I'm going to go," I said, standing up, forcing Logan to get up as well. He stared at the table, barely moving. Shit, I've done a real good job here. I wanted to fix things with Logan but I've had a pretty public almost fight with Jace, hurt Logan, and was on the verge of tears.

"Chloe, you don't have to leave," Jace said. "We'll change the subject."

"We can talk later. I'll come over tonight. Your mum's been asking when I'm coming back. I don't want to do this here. Logan, will you walk me to my car, please?"

He nodded robotically, still not making eye contact.

"See you later," Jace said. I smiled in return and walked away.

Why was nothing ever bloody simple?

Me and Logan walked in silence. He kept his focus ahead. He was far too tense and brooding. We stopped at my car and I leant back on the door. "Logan, I was talking about the past."

"Were you?"

Gripping his top, I pulled him closer. "Yes. I love him still, of course, I do, but it's not how it used to be. Logan, how I feel about you… What Jace and I had, it doesn't even come close. God, I'm rambling. I love *you*. I want *you*." I couldn't talk to Jace about us in front of Logan anymore. Of course he was going to feel insecure.

"Are you sure?" he asked, leaning forwards and pressing his forehead to mine. His eyes searched for the truth. "I don't know what I'd do if you went back to him and I know that's a shitty thing to say, you were his first and things only ended between you because you thought he was dead, but I can't help how I feel. I can't help loving you so much I feel like I can't fucking breathe."

I kissed him, pulling him closer, pouring everything into us, and praying that he felt how much I loved him, too. Logan squashed me against my car, one hand fisting my hair and the other gripping my hip desperately.

His tongue flicked my bottom lip and my knees almost gave way. It had been a week and I wanted nothing more than for him to take me home so we could make up properly.

"Logan," I said against his lips. "Logan?"

Groaning, he pulled back and frowned. "What? I was busy."

"I know but you have to go back in there to your brother. Not to mention we're in the middle of a car park."

"I don't care about any of that. It's been *ages*, Chlo."

"And later we'll make up for lost time. At mine. Stay over?"

"I'm there," he replied, grazing my neck with his fingertips. I closed my eyes and sucked in a sharp breath. I'd never get enough of him touching me, teasing me like that. "We could go now if you want." His voice was low and rough and seemed to have a hotline to my groin.

I pushed him back with one hand, needing to put some distance between us before I agreed. I *really* wanted that but we had things to do first.

"Tonight," I said.

"Fine, but I want you to know you've got five minutes of small talk with your parents and then I'm taking you to bed. I don't give a flying fuck if they're still up. And you're not getting any sleep."

I wanted to ask if I could have that in writing but the wild hunger in his eyes was enough.

"Deal," I said, claiming his lips in a soft, controlled kiss. "I'll see you at yours after work, then we'll go to mine."

"I love you, Chloe."

"I love you, too."

He smiled. "Forever and a day, sweetheart."

I melted.

Watching him walk back to the gym was hard. I forced myself to get in my car and lay back against the seat, trying to cool down. *Get a grip, Chloe.*

CHAPTER FORTY-TWO

Chloe

After going home and agonising about my whole screwed up situation, I texted Jace to ask if I could come over earlier and talk to him. I'd expected him to say no outright or at least make an excuse but he told me he'd just got home and I could come over whenever I was ready. I wasn't sure exactly how ready I was for another round but it had to be done so I got back in my little car and drove to his house.

I stopped in the drive and thankfully, I had the only car so hopefully no one else was in. Jace must have walked home, that or he wasn't really going to meet me.

He opened the front door as I walked up the path. "Hi," he said.

"Hey, Jace."

Stepping aside, he let me in and then closed the door. "Take a seat, Chloe."

I sat on the sofa and looked at him as if he'd called me round and should start.

"Logan's working until four," he said, breaking the silence that seemed to stretch into minutes.

That gave us an hour. "Okay. Actually, that's good."

"It's good?"

"We need to talk."

"And you can't do that in front of your *boyfriend*?"

"When you say it like that you prove exactly why I can't. This isn't about Logan anyway, it's about us."

"I didn't think there was an us anymore."

Oh my God, I'm going to hit him!

"Alright, sit the fuck down and grow the fuck up."

Jace blinked in shock and I kinda did a little too. But I was fed up of the animosity and bitching.

"Just sit, Jace. We need to sort this out. I don't want to lose you but if things keep going the way they are I don't know how I can have you in my life." *I will not cry.* "I lost you once, Jace, and I…"

He held his hands up. "Alright, I'm sitting." He flung himself down on the sofa next to me and then I was wrapped in his arms. "I don't want to lose you either."

I pulled back. It was too familiar. Being in Jace's arms used to be my favourite place to be and the first place I ran to if I was having a bad day. Now he was the cause of the bad day and the one I wanted for comfort was his brother. And just to fuck things up that little bit more I wanted to snuggle right back into Jace's arms.

The flood of emotion I felt was so overwhelming I didn't quite know how to handle it. I wanted to cry and scream and throw a party at the same time.

"You've got the floor, Chloe. I don't know where to start."

Neither do I.

"I don't want to talk about why you didn't contact us. We've been over that and I'll never be okay with it. I don't want to fight so let's just say I accept why you did it. I wouldn't want to put the people I love in danger either."

"Thank you."

I didn't expect that thank you so I just nodded. "When you… died I felt like I'd had the ground whipped out from under me and I was just falling. We made all these plans,

Christ, our whole future was mapped out. I knew what I was going to be doing for the rest of my life and it was all with you. Then I had nothing. Everything changed and I missed you so much I could barely breathe." I rubbed my aching chest.

Keep it together.

Talking about what a wreck I was brought it all back and I felt what I felt back then.

"I was a mess, Jace, and that's putting a positive spin on it. My whole future disappeared when you did. Saying goodbye to you was the hardest thing I've ever done. It was saying goodbye to the man I loved as well as a life I so desperately wanted. We'd never have chips on a bench by the sea when we were old and wrinkled."

"Chloe," he groaned.

"No, please. I need to do this. I missed so much school that I failed the year and had to repeat, which is why I'm not done with uni yet. I didn't go out, I barely ate or slept or spoke. I was trying to figure out what I should be doing but there was nothing but emptiness."

"Until?" he said, still reading me like a book.

"Until about a year ago when Logan pulled me out of bed, shoved me in the shower and forced me to leave the house. We went for a walk and he told me he wasn't going to let me live like a shadow anymore. And he didn't. Every bloody morning he called to make sure I got out of bed. He came over after work, sometimes before if I didn't answer. He made me eat and focus on something other than uni. He made me feel emotion again, rather than just emptiness. It was mostly anger when he wouldn't give me a break but it was still something."

I smiled as I remembered his sheer determination to piece me back together again.

"He let me cry over you and talk about you but he never let me wallow. That was the part I couldn't do. I couldn't let myself grieve without getting lost to it. Then he made me come to your house like I used to. I felt such comfort being with your family and being in your room again. It was like you were still there in some way."

Jace said nothing, he just watched me with tears in his eyes.

"I started to feel better and I looked forward to things again. It was all different, my future was nothing like the one I wanted, the one we created, but I knew that it could be good, too. Looking after me is the reason Logan hasn't killed his liver. He drank so much, Jace. Everyone was worried and I feel so bad that I wasn't there for him more at first. But the day he came over and quite literally pulled me out of bed was a turning point for us both. I had someone that was forcing me to get better and he had something other than his grief to focus on."

"Wow," he said. "Logan didn't tell me all of that."

"Did you ever give him the chance?"

"Not exactly."

Well, that's why.

"I'm so sorry, Chloe. I knew you'd be devastated but I had no idea. I thought you would all be okay because you had each other. You've always been close with my family."

"I was okay in the end. We all came together, I'm just sorry it took us so long."

"When did things change between you and Logan?"

"About five or six months ago. I started to feel more than friendship and it scared me. He was the last person in the world that I wanted to have feelings for. I went on a few dates with a guy from work but it never felt right. The only person I felt comfortable with was him. One day we almost kissed and then I tried to forget it, but I couldn't. Then I confronted him and we did kiss."

"Right."

"I ran away from him a few times. The guilt was crushing. But I could only stay away for so long. I realised that I wanted him and we ended up together."

"And that brings us to now."

"Yes."

"Okay." He took a deep breath. "Thank you for explaining. I think I get how you two got together."

Him understanding it doesn't mean he was okay with it. I wanted him to be okay. I couldn't ask for his blessing, it was too messed up, but I wanted it.

"You said you felt guilty."

"Of course, I did, Jace. I'm not that much of a terrible person."

Nodding once, he replied, "I know that. It's hard to get my head around the fact that you both went there. You felt guilty about it but you still did it."

How on earth was I supposed to explain that me and Logan were like opposite ends of magnets, that no matter how hard we tried to stay away we pulled back together. How was I supposed to tell Jace that Logan was on my mind constantly and that all I wanted was to be with him.

"It… We tried, Jace. We tried to ignore it and when we couldn't I tried to stay away. We didn't get a choice."

"Just like I didn't have a choice in staying away."

I bit my bottom lip. He was right. I screamed at him and blamed him for the pain he'd caused me and his family over the last three years but my choice to be with Logan was no more a choice than his not to call. There was still something there that blamed him, though. I didn't want to fight so I held my tongue.

"I'm sorry, Jace."

"So am I. Can't help thinking that if I'd done something, found some way of letting you know I was okay you would've jump into my arms the second I walked back through the door."

Was he fucking serious?

"*That* is what's making you question your decision not to call? Not the fact that your parents thought they'd outlived a child, or your siblings lost a brother? Me with Logan is why you wished you'd contacted us?"

He groaned. "Can you blame me? It's not like you're with some random guy, Chloe, he's my *brother*!"

"Yes, thank you. I'm well aware of who he is."

Could we ever get past that so we could have a conversation without it ending in arguing?

Ribbing his jaw, he slumped back in the sofa. "I love you."

No, no, no, don't say that!

I took a deep breath. "Jace…"

Turning sideways, he tucked my hair behind my ear the way he always had done. "I never stopped. I never even looked at another woman. I love you so much, Chloe, and I'll never stop wanting you."

I registered the front door being closed a little harder than necessary and knew it was Logan. Jace leant away, dropping his hand.

CHAPTER FORTY-THREE

Chloe

What was the protocol for situations like this? Logan couldn't exactly punch Jace when I'd been Jace's first. I didn't want them to fight over me or because of me. Behind Logan was Cassie, she muttered something and quickly scampered into the kitchen. I wished I could've gone with her.

"Got off half an hour early," Logan said. His voice was tight and I could see the confusion in his eyes. If Jace had been anyone else he would've kicked off by now.

I wanted longer with Jace because we had to sort this out.

"Me and Jace were talking," I said.

"I saw."

Shit, he really was mad.

Stalking his way over to the sofa, Logan never took his eyes off me, claiming me again. I was sure he was about to pee on me. Instead of peeing he sat on the sofa opposite mine and Jace's.

Finally looking at Jace, he said, "Maybe we should all talk."

That would've been a good idea if there still wasn't so

much animosity.

"Chloe wanted to talk to me," Jace said.

"Alright, stop! I'm walking out of that door in five seconds if you both don't cool it. We have to find a way to get past this. I won't be the reason you two aren't getting on, not after everything that we've been through. Sort it out or you both lose me."

Logan's eyes went wild in panic. I'd seen that look the first time I told him I couldn't be with him and walked away. I had to sit on my hands to stop myself from reaching out for him.

"You're expecting too much, Chloe," Jace said. "He crossed a line."

"So did I."

"He's blood, he shouldn't have touched you."

I didn't have to look at Logan to know he'd winced at Jace's words. He said that before, that he shouldn't touch me because he was the brother and you didn't do that.

I wanted to kiss Cassie when she walked back into the living room, scowling at both boys. "You've got to be kidding me? Three years you've been apart from us," she said to Jace, then turned to Logan, "and we thought we'd lost him forever. Chloe is right; you can't let this ruin your relationship. It means too much."

Jace shook his head.

"No," Cassie snapped, pointing at him. "I was there, Jace. You didn't see how hard they tried, how much they battled with their feelings and the guilt. You weren't the one grabbing the bottle off Logan when he was drinking over her for a change or bandaging his knuckles up because he'd punched yet another wall."

What? I gawped at Logan. I had no idea how bad it'd been for him. I wallowed in bed when I was hurt and he drank and punched things. Guess I should've known it'd be the same when he was hurting over me.

Logan's eyes tightened but he refused to look at me.

"We all thought you were dead, Jace. We knew you would want them both to find happiness again. We didn't think it would be with each other and neither did they. Everyone told them you would want them to be happy. You know you would, too."

"But I'm not dead, Cass."

"Thank God. But we didn't know that. What do you expect here, Jace? Do you think Chlo should jump back into your arms? She loves him."

Jace snapped his head round, looking at me appalled. Crap, he didn't know I was in love with Logan.

"Are you serious?" he asked. I looked away from the tears in his eyes. "Tell me you didn't fall for him, Chloe."

"Hey," Logan snapped. "Lay off."

"Lay off? You stole my girlfriend and you're telling *me* to lay off? How the hell could you have fallen in love with someone else, Chloe? Did you remember nothing we said?"

"That's not fair. I. Thought. You. Died."

"Well, maybe it would've been better if I had."

I slapped him. Hard. My hand stung. "Don't ever say that!" Standing up so fast that I almost fell back down again, I opened my mouth to shout but Jace surged to his feet and gripped my arms.

"I love you and I know you, Chloe, you can't just turn it off. You love me, too."

Shoving his chest, I replied, "Of course, I do but it's not the same anymore."

"Bollocks it's not."

"I want *him*, Jace." He took a step back as if I'd burned him. As the tears in my eyes freely rolled down my face, I added in a whisper, "I'm so sorry."

Without another look, he turned and walked away. Cassie gave me a sympathetic smile and went after him.

"You okay?" Logan asked once we were alone.

I was so not okay.

"No. I don't want to hurt him."

He took a cautious step closer. "Neither do I. Shit, you're my girlfriend but I feel like I should give you up. How fucked up is that?"

"You feel like we should break up?"

"No. I don't know. It's not happening if that's what you're thinking. When I said forever I meant it."

I smiled a little. "Actually, you said forever and a day."

He moved closer again, not worried that I was going to flip out anymore. "Right. Forever and a day, Chlo. I'm not giving you up, not for anyone. I will find a way to make things okay with Jace, I won't lose him again but there is no fucking way we're breaking up."

"You swear way too much."

"I tell you how much I want you and you chastise me for bad language."

"Sorry," I said, stepping into his arms. "I love you, Logan."

His grip was tighter than usual. He was scared about us. I was, too. I didn't know what would happen to us if Jace couldn't understand and accept we were together. His brother should come first, they were family but I didn't want to lose Logan. I didn't want to lose Jace either. I hoped we could find a way of being friends because I'd missed him so much.

"Where do we go from here?" I asked against his chest as I breathed him in. His Logan smell was enough to make everything better for now.

"To yours. You wanted me to stay, remember?"

"Don't you think you should speak to Jace?"

"I do, but I'm not sure right now is the best time. He just told you he wants you back. Don't think he'll appreciate me trying to tell him how sorry I am that's he's hurting over the fact that I fell in love with you again."

"Yeah, maybe we should leave it for today. Hey, why don't you two have a boys' night out."

"I'm probably the last person in the world he wants to

drink with, Chloe."

"I doubt that, you're his brother. You just need ground rules. Maybe a night out reconnecting will be good."

"I love how naïve you can be, sweetheart."

I pinched his bicep. "Not naïve, I'm just trying here."

Sighing, he pulled me closer into his chest. "Fine, I'll ask him. I'm not holding my breath though, think it's going to be a while before I get to go out with my little bro again."

Logan sounded regretful, and I knew he was hurting badly as well. He wanted to be a proper brother to Jace again, especially after the things that happened between them the day we thought Jace had died.

"He'll forgive us," I said, hoping I was right.

"I love you," he whispered and kissed me.

CHAPTER FORTY-FOUR

Logan

I stood in the kitchen at the arse crack of dawn, drinking a glass of water and picking at a slice of toast. I needed to exercise and clear my head so that meant putting something in my body to work off but I also felt sick as a dog.

Me and Chloe had agreed to see each other at her house until things cooled down and although I knew that was for the best it still sucked. I wanted her here right now, clinging to me with her head firmly on my chest, whining about how evil I was to make her get up so early.

Jace walked into the kitchen and I had to do a double take. What the fuck was he doing up at this hour?

His steps faltered as he saw me. Then I got the silent treatment. This was getting fucking stupid. He was my brother and we'd just been reunited after three years and the atmosphere was so shitty I'd actually contemplated moving out early.

"Jace, man, we need to sort this out."

His eyes were empty as he looked almost through me. "There's nothing to sort out, Logan, she's with you now."

"Nothing to sort out? You're my fucking brother."

"Funny, that didn't seem to stop you sleeping with my girlfriend."

I knew that one was coming. "You have *no* clue what you're talking about."

He made a big show of sitting down on a stool. "Well, why don't you explain it?"

Here's where I become a bigger dick to my little brother. I put my glass down and sat opposite him. "You remember when you brought Chloe back here for the first time with Kieran and Jessie?"

"Not really, was years ago," he replied.

"Well, I remember." That day was imprinted on my mind, every single detail but the clearest memory was Chloe's smile. I remember thinking she was the most beautiful girl I'd ever seen. "I liked her from the start. She was different and we had so much in common. The more time I spent around her the more I liked her. I was falling for her and then you two got together."

His jaw muscles clenched periodically. "You never said."

"I know. I'm a couple years older and she was only just fourteen. Looking back I knew I should've said something but I was trying to do the decent thing and wait until I couldn't get arrested for being with her. When you two got together it…" Fucking killed. I shook my head. "Well, I convinced myself it was nothing and my feelings for her would pass. I was sixteen and too young to have lost *the one* so I tried to ignore it. But it didn't stop, I couldn't ignore it and the more serious things got between you two the harder it was. We argued more and I hated that because it wasn't your fault but I just couldn't stop it hurting. The morning of your trip I was a dick because I'd heard you and her talking the night before about your future." Marriage. "I'm sorry for that."

He scratched the back of his neck. "You've loved her all along?"

"Yes."

"My *death* worked out real well for you then."

My hands fisted on my lap. "I am seconds from wrapping this chair around your fucking head, stop being such a little prick," I growled.

It was stupid of me not to expect that but I didn't think he'd go there.

"Every fight we had was because you resented me for having what you wanted?"

And now every fight he picked with me was because he resented and hated me for having what he wanted. Funny how life turned out sometimes.

"I didn't resent you. I resented me. You and Chlo weren't at fault, I was, and I didn't exactly deal with it that well. Anyway, no matter what crap you piss out of your mouth you know that I didn't plan anything to happen between us. I could've said something to you at any point in the time you were with her to make things hard, I could've told her how I felt and let that shit storm play out, but I didn't. You're my brother so I shoved it aside as best I could and kept my mouth closed. I would have never, *ever* said anything to her."

"But then I died."

"Then we thought you died. The first couple years were awful, we were both a mess, you know all this, and then I got her up. Of course, we became closer and I wanted her, just like I always had, but I wasn't going to act on it."

"So I was out of the picture but you were still going to lock it away?"

"Yeah. I waned to be the one she fell for but I wouldn't do anything to sway her. I supported her – sorta – dating this Rhys twat when all I wanted to do was rip his balls from his body."

"Huh," he said, laughing with no humour whatsoever, "that's exactly what I wanted to do to you when I realised you were together."

I deserved that.

"I started noticing things," I said, ignoring his jibe. "She was acting differently for a while, avoiding me whenever she could and looking at me a little longer than usual. At first I thought I was imagining it." I'd imagined it *a lot* over the last seven years. "But I wasn't. We kissed and then there was nothing we could do to stop it, not even taking a break or trying to be friends."

"That's lovely 'n' all, Logan, but you still went there."

We were never going to get anywhere. He knew we'd get his blessing if he'd been dead but he wasn't so we weren't getting it.

"Did you really expect her to drop everything when she saw you?" I asked.

"Not at all. I came back here fully prepared to be her friend. I imagined her with a boyfriend and as shitty as that made me feel I knew I couldn't blame her or interfere. What I found is her *boyfriend* is my *brother*. You don't go there, Logan, you just *don't*."

"But we did so now we've got to figure out a way that this doesn't rip the family apart."

"I don't know how to do that."

I held my hands up. "Neither do I. Do you want to try?"

"No idea. Right now I feel betrayed by both of you. I want to knock you out and shake her."

"You wouldn't be able to knock me out and touch her like that and you'll be in A&E." Plus, I was fairly certain that Chloe could take him. The girl could claw someone's eyes out if they pissed her off enough.

"Look at you playing the protective boyfriend."

"I love her."

His eyes narrowed. "So do I."

"Yeah, I know. What are we going to do about it?"

"I'm not sure, Logan. I can't just turn it off. You of all people should know that."

"Oh, I do. I really do get that. I'm sorry we hurt you, Jace, but we didn't know this would happen."

He nodded once, roughly. "I know."

"Come on, mate, do you want to figure this out?"

His hesitation wasn't a good sign. I wasn't willing to let this come between us. Now I wasn't a complete fucking idiot, I knew that it'd take time and probably a lot of shouting but I was determined to stay with Chloe and keep my brother in my life.

"Yeah, I want to figure it out. She thought I was dead and moved on. You thought I was dead and…"

"Couldn't fight wanting her anymore, not when I knew she felt the same. This isn't just some fling, Jace; I wouldn't put me or her through months of agonising over what to do and torturing ourselves for what we want over nothing. I love her and for some reason she loves me, too. I need you to know it wasn't easy."

He closed his eyes and breathed heavily for what felt like ages. "Alright," he said, opening his eyes. "I'm not promising anything and I don't like it but as pissed off as I am you're still my brother. No guarantees, Logan, but I guess I can try to not want to kill you every time I set eyes on you."

I smiled, pretending he hadn't basically just kicked me in the gut. "Good. It's a start."

"Why hasn't she been around much?" he asked.

"You don't really need me to answer that."

"God," he groaned. "I hate that nothing is going to be the same. I just wish that I hadn't gone on that stupid trip, then none of this would be happening."

"We all wish that."

He raised his eyebrow and smirked sarcastically. "I'm sure."

"I mean it. Loving Chloe from afar was nowhere near as bad than thinking my little brother was dead."

That shut the sarcastic little fucker up.

"Well, maybe you should tell her she doesn't have to hide away at her house. She's always hung out here."

There was about a two-year gap where that wasn't true

and she'd only visited a handful of times.

"Is that a good idea?"

"We're trying, aren't we?" I nodded. "Then she should be here, trying with us. I'm going back to bed, feeling tired again. Later."

I lifted my chin in a nod, head spinning from him saying he wanted Chloe back over here. Having that girl around me all day sounded like heaven but I wasn't quite convinced that it was a good idea.

It would be awkward if he saw us together and awkward if we had to implement a no touching rule. But the only way Jace would get used to us together was if he saw us together, subtly. Plus, her parents were going away next week and I was looking forward to having her all to myself.

I pinched the bridge of my nose and closed my eyes, feeling a banging headache coming on.

CHAPTER FORTY-FIVE

Logan

Having Chloe back at the house was, as I'd thought, monumentally awkward. Jace was being false nice and it was pissing me off. Chloe was being extra nice and understanding and that was kind of pissing me off, too. I didn't want her to feel like she had to apologise every five seconds.

Her parents were off on their two-week anniversary trip and we'd been making the most of having her house to ourselves. I wanted to be there right now but she insisted we come to mine because Jace had asked and that meant he was making an effort, and if he was making the effort we should, apparently. I knew she was right but it still felt too soon. Jace clearly didn't like how close we were. His face earlier when he saw me kiss her hello briefly told me that much.

I sat in the living room with her, Jace and thankfully Cassie. We needed that extra person or it was pretty unbearable. My parents were outside, avoiding the whole awkward thing. I was back to keeping my hands off her but this time I had every right to touch her as much as I wanted to. Chlo came over for lunch an hour ago but with Jace hanging around it felt like hours and hours had past.

"Oh," Cass said, finally thinking of something to say.

Hallelujah. "Comedy Club this weekend? Apparently, there's this old couple that go up together and talk about things that would make us gag if it was our parents. Could be fun."

"You want to go and watch a couple have an argument on stage?" I asked.

"Heck yeah!" Chloe replied. "We keep missing it."

Alright then. "I'll wait for you by the bar," I said.

Jace laughed but it was that sarcastic little laugh that made me want to punch him. "Why don't you just let her go out with Cassie if you don't want to go."

It wasn't a question. He was being a dick, accusing me of controlling her. If I wanted something to do what I said without argument I'd get a pet.

I clamped my mouth shut, refusing to retaliate. Technically, I was still an arsehole for being with her in the first place, I didn't have a lot of room to snap at him.

"Jace," Cassie said, her voice was a warning.

Things were going to, if possible, get a lot more awkward if he kept on like that. It was his idea for Chloe to come back to the house again so what the hell was he playing at?

"What?" he said. "I don't get why he'd want to go too, if he'd just stay by the bar. What's the point? Unless he's worried she'll replace him by the end of the set."

"Alright, that's e-fucking-nough, Jace!"

Chloe was on he feet, holding her hands up. "I'm out of here."

"Chloe," I said, leaping up with her. "Wait." If she left in a hurry I always panicked. Her first instinct was to run.

"I just need to leave, Logan, I'm not running."

I needed to hear that. I shouldn't need reassurance as much as I did, I wasn't a fucking child, but she drove me to insanity and I pure and simple didn't want to be without her.

"Don't go, Chloe, I'm sorry," Jace said.

It was a little too late; she was already out the door. I

was going to let her go. When she needed her space it was best to give it to her but Jace went after her so I followed them both to get him to leave it.

They were all the way down the path near the front gate by the time I got outside. "I said I was sorry," he shouted.

"I don't care what you said, just let me go, Jace."

Sighing, I made my way down the path. This was a fucking nightmare.

"Enough," I snapped.

"Go back in, Logan, I'm talking to her."

Amount of times I'd restrained myself from punching my brother today alone: seven.

"Oh, for fuck sake, Jace, stop being a little prick." I shouted. "Chloe, you really don't have to leave."

She swiped a tear from her face. "Yeah, I do. I'll call you when I get home but I think we all need to take a few minutes to calm down."

"Shit!" Jace growled. "No, Chloe, he's right, you don't have to leave. I just…" He looked up to the sky and exhaled hard. "This isn't easy."

"It's not easy for us either," she said.

His cocky one eyebrow raise had me more pissed off and no doubt that would only multiply when he said whatever he was about to say.

"I doubt that very much, Chloe. You seemed just fine when you had your fucking tongue down his throat."

"Oh my God," I said. "That's what this is really about. Christ, it was one little kiss and it's going to happen."

"I don't wanna see it."

"Then don't fucking look."

I was being a bit out of order but it literally was one peck while we were in the kitchen alone. We knew we had to make allowances and tone it down a lot but if I wanted to kiss my girlfriend in an empty room I shouldn't have to take a load of shit for it.

"I'm going," Chloe said, spinning around and running

along the path.

"Chlo, wait up."

I started opening the swinging gate to follow her when something happened that I couldn't quite process. Jace shouted about nine swear words almost simultaneously. A car revved and mounted the path. Chloe turned and gave a loud scream that was cut off as the bonnet slammed into her body.

I froze up for a second as my body turned to ice. Then I was sprinting towards her, passing Jace and dropping to my knees just after her petite body made a hideous *thud* on the concrete.

"No, no, no, no, no. Chloe!" She already looked like she was in a deep sleep. Her hair fanned out beside her head. "Fuck, Chloe, open your eyes." I was shaking. I could feel my body shaking and my heart thumping.

Cassie, once she'd stopped screaming, was on the phone, calling for help.

I wanted to pick her up and cradle her in my lap but I knew better than to move her. "What do I do?" I asked, leaning in to make sure she was breathing.

Jace crouched down, wide eyed. He gulped. "Her chest is moving, she's breathing, Logan." He sounded eerily calm. "Give her some room," he said, pushing me back a little with his forearm.

I fell back on my feet and watched Jace check her over. Mum came screaming out of the house, calling Chloe's name the whole way down the path. "What happened?" she asked, dropping down the other side of Chloe's head.

"A car hit her," Jace replied. "Cassie's called 999. She's breathing, she'll be fine."

"How the fuck do you know that?" I spat.

Mum put her hand on my arm, sobbing. "Calm down, Logan." She stroked Chloe's hair. "Hang in there, honey."

I was less than useless. Dad had taken over the phone, speaking to emergency services and Mum, Cass and Jace were speaking to Chloe, telling her everything was going to be fine. I sat back on my legs, still, hollow, watching my life fall apart.

***

"Dad said the Thornberrys have a camera that faces the front door and out on the road. They've probably caught it, he's told the police and they're checking it out," Jace said.

We were in the waiting room. Waiting. Chloe had been whisked off to surgery. She was also going to get scans and all sorts of shit that I couldn't remember because my ears were still ringing and my mind was still half rejecting reality.

"I hope so," Cass replied.

Right now the driver of the car was the least of my worries. My girl was in surgery. Chloe had fucking internal bleeding. Nothing else mattered other than her pulling through.

"Logan, are you okay? You've been staring at the floor for the last half hour," Mum said. "She's going to be fine. You know Chloe, she's a survivor."

She was, but just because she'd been through a lot of shit didn't mean she was immune to fucking hit and runs and internal bleeding.

"I need someone to tell me what's going on," I said. I'd never hated a place more than I hated this waiting room.

Nell bust through the door two minutes later. Mum had called Chloe's parents, who were out of the country, and Nell on the way to the hospital.

"I came as soon as I could. Where is she? What's going on?" she asked.

"She's still in surgery," Mum replied. "Take a seat, love."

Nell sat next to Cassie and looked at me with tears in her eyes. She avoided Jace, which meant she knew why we were outside in the first place. I wanted someone to blame but I knew it wasn't his fault. Jace could have not acted like a twat, I could have stopped her leaving, she could have not run. It was an accident.

"She's been through enough recently," Nell said.

Cassie squeezed her hand, telling her now was not the time. "She's going to be fine. Chlo isn't going anywhere." Cass nodded her head as if to convince herself.

I closed my eyes and lowered my head.

Please, don't leave me, sweetheart.

CHAPTER FORTY-SIX

Logan

"Why isn't she waking up?" I said for what must have been the thousandth time. She'd made it through surgery fine and was in a room that, thankfully, we were all allowed to be in until she woke up or it got too late. I wasn't leaving.

"The doctor said it could be a good few hours yet," Cass said.

Mum and Dad came back into the room with coffee and snacks from the café. "Bill and Bethany's flight leaves at six so they should be in England by midnight. We'll pick them up from the airport tonight," Mum told us.

Her parents must have been going crazy not being here when she was in hospital. I would be a mess if I were in a different country to her.

"Anything from the police?" Jace asked Dad.

"Nothing new. They're still questioning the driver," he replied. They'd caught him not long ago. Thankfully, the neighbours' CCTV showed a clear image of the car so they were able to get the plates and pick him up quickly. It was a kid that hadn't passed his test long so was probably showing off to his mates and lost control.

Jace leant back against the wall and closed his eyes. "I shouldn't have come back. If everyone still thought I was dead she'd be okay."

I gripped Chloe's hand and forced myself to ignore his stupid fucking comment. Mum, Dad and Cass didn't though, instantly telling him how idiotic his thinking was and that Chloe wouldn't want that either.

She wouldn't rather he stayed away and neither would I. He pissed me off and I wanted to strangle him but what happened to Chloe wasn't his fault.

I would deal with Jace's guilt over what happened later, right now all I could concentrate on was Chloe. She was going to be fine, the doctors had stopped the internal bleeding and her vitals were right where they needed to be, but I couldn't relax until she woke up. I needed those amber eyes looking at me as proof she was alright.

Jace and I had barely said two words to each other since she was hit and I knew full well that I was being a twat by ignoring him but I couldn't seem to help myself. Right now there was nothing I wanted to say to him.

"Logan, why don't you take five minutes and get some fresh air?" Mum said. Nell looked up, she hadn't left the room either and I had a feeling that, like me, she wasn't going to.

Tearing my eyes away from Chlo, I glared at my mum. "What?"

"You've sat there agonising over what's happened since the second we arrived. Take a minute to breathe, you'll be in better shape for her when she wakes up."

Was I in bad shape? Well, yeah, I fucking was, but I hadn't realised it was so obvious. Did I look as shit as I felt?

"I'm not leaving," I said.

"I can see you holding your breath, tensing your body. You're too tightly wound—"

"Mum," I said calmly but firmly. "I am not leaving this room unless it's with her. Okay?"

No one said a word after that, except Nell occasionally demanding that her best friend woke up immediately.

***

Mum and Dad left for the airport to pick Chloe's parents up and the rest of her family that stopped by during the two hour visiting time had left hours ago, promising to come back in the morning. I was left alone with Cassie, Nell and Jace – the three other people that refused to leave. I had a horrible feeling that tomorrow the nurses would try harder to get us to leave.

Chloe was still fast asleep. She was pale but apparently that was normal. That had better be normal. Besides the few times I'd quickly left to go to the bathroom I hadn't been away from her, and I didn't plan to, not until I knew for sure she was alright.

"I'm gonna get some drinks," Jace said. "Anyone want anything?"

"Coffee please," I replied, staring at Chlo's face for any sign that she was about to wake. "She'll want one. Should we get her one?" *Of fucking course not!* My brain was scrambled. Why the fuck would Chloe want coffee right after waking up from an emergency operation?

Jace looked to Cass and Nell for help. "She won't want anything yet, Logan," Nell said.

"I know."

Shit, I'm an idiot.

"Do you need to take a couple minutes?" Jace asked. "We'll stay."

"And if she wakes up?"

"One of us will come and get you."

I shook my head. "No. I need to be here when she wakes." If it were the other way around she would be the first person I'd want to see. "A *strong* coffee would be good though."

I stood up, stretching my aching legs. It was strange how you could do absolutely nothing and still ache, guess it didn't help that I was constantly holding myself in awkward positions, too tense to relax.

Brushing my fingertips over her hair, I said, "Come on, wake up, sweetheart."

"She will when she's ready, Logan," Cass said softly.

Nell gently nudged Chloe's leg. "Chlo loves her sleep."

I was just about done with the reassurance, too. They all meant well but the only person that could make this okay was Chloe. She *had* to wake up. I'd lost her too many times. She was finally mine and I hadn't even had the chance to make her nauseously happy yet.

I couldn't take my eyes off her; she looked so perfect it made my heart swell. "She's ready. She loved her sleep but when have you ever known her to sleep this long before?"

"He's right," Jace said. "Six hours and she was more than ready to get up."

She'd been getting less sleep than that recently. We'd both been running on four or five but it was so fucking worth it.

Nell smiled. "I know, but this is different. She's never been..."

"*Run over* before?" I said, feeling so fucking angry I wanted to find the prick that hit her and rip him apart.

Biting her lip, she looked down, wincing.

"Nell, Cassie, why don't you get the drinks?" Jace said, handing Cass his wallet.

With a nod, Cass took it and left the room. Nell followed after a heartbeat.

I ran my hands over my face. I hadn't meant to be so hostile to her. "Fuck it," I snapped, pulling my hair. "Why won't she just fucking wake up?" I was, quite literally, losing it.

Jace pulled my arm, making me look at him. "Calm down, Logan."

"I can't calm down. She was meant to wake up hours ago. Is she gonna die, Jace? Am I going to lose her?" Shit. I *couldn't* lose her.

"She's *not* going to die."

I was breathing heavily, trying to keep it together and stay strong when I had never felt so weak in my life.

"She can't die," he added.

She could, though. Everyone was going to die at some point, Chloe wasn't immune to death because I loved her, needed her. She was human and she'd been injured.

I turned away, not wanting to think about the worst outcome anymore.

***

Half an hour and a lot more stressing later, her hand finally flinched in mine. I leapt forward. "Chloe!" I said, studying her face.

"What?" Cass and Jace asked in unison.

"She moved her hand." I leant closer, using my other hand to stroke her cheek. "Chlo, sweetheart, can you hear me?"

She fluttered her eyes, frowning. And then they opened for the briefest second. She looked tired and groggy but she was still impossibly beautiful. "Logan?" she whispered.

I felt like fucking crying.

"Yeah," I said, smiling so wide it hurt. "I'm here, everything's okay. Can you open your eyes again?" *I need to see your eyes.*

She did and as soon as saw that bright amber staring back at me I could breathe again.

"Hey," I whispered.

"What happened?" Her voice was throaty and rough.

"Cass, can you get her some water and tell the nurse she's awake?" Nodding with tears in her eyes, my sister leapt up and headed for the door. "How're you feeling?"

"My stomach hurts and my throat is dry. What happened, Logan?"

"You were hit."

"I remember the car," she said as if she was miles away. What was going through her head?

"I'm so sorry, Chloe. If I hadn't come back or started that fight you wouldn't have been there."

"Shut up," I hissed. I'd had enough of this *I shouldn't come back, should've let you continue to believe I was dead* shit.

Chlo swallowed. "It's not your fault."

Jace opened his mouth to say something else but she shook her head. "Don't. You couldn't have known, no one could. I'm okay now. Are you?" she asked us both but looked up at me.

"We're both fine," I said, squeezing her hand. "Well, I am now."

"Bit worried, were ya?"

I smirked. "Just a little."

"I'll go see where Cass is," Jace said, ducking out of the room as quickly as he could. He hadn't really seen us as a couple that much so I understood that it was awkward and uncomfortable for him but she'd just woken up and I wasn't about to hold back.

"How badly hurt was I?"

"You're going to be fine but there was internal bleeding."

"Oh," she whispered. "That… sucks."

I laughed, feeling the prickle of tears working up from my gut. "Yeah, it sure does… suck. I was so scared, Chlo. Watching you fall to the floor like that was the most horrific thing I'd ever seen. You're not allowed to die before me. Got it?"

"Logan, I don't think you can choose."

"No, I can. I choose to go first, when we're old and grey and I can't get it up anymore. Actually, I might want to go the second I can't get it up but we'll cross that bridge when and if we come to it."

"Neither of us are going anywhere for a long time. I was promised forever and a day, remember?"

"I remember. I love you, sweetheart."

Her eyes danced even though she was clearly in some discomfort. "I love you, too."

I didn't get any longer to talk to her or do something big and possibly stupid like propose because Jace and Cass came back armed with a jug of fresh water and a nurse.

"Hi, Chloe, how are you feeling?"

"Sore and thirsty," she replied.

"Well, I can help with both of those," the nurse said, pouring a glass of water and getting me to help Chlo drink it while she administered a dose of morphine through the IV.

"I'll just step out and make a couple phone calls, let everyone know she's awake," Cassie said. "Glad you're back, Chlo. You scared the crap outta us."

Chloe released the straw from between her lips and smiled. "Yeah, sorry about that. Got run over and all…"

Okay, I wasn't at all ready for jokes. I put her drink on the side, ignoring the urge to snap. I didn't want to make her feel bad and I definitely didn't want her to be angry with me.

"I'll be back in a minute," Cass replied, giving Chloe's leg a little pat.

Nell stepped forwards from where she'd been standing, silently crying. "If you *ever* do anything like that again I will kick that tiny arse of yours into next year."

"Good to see you too, Nelly," Chlo whispered.

Nell pointed at her. "Imma let that one go."

Smiling like a moron, I laid my forehead on her hand, hiding a tear while she exchanged some colourful banter with her friend.

CHAPTER FORTY-SEVEN

Chloe

"Chloe!" Mum said, rushing through the door and almost knocking Logan over. He'd been pacing, trying to keep himself awake because he refused to sleep until I did and I wanted to wait up for my parents. It was half past one in the morning. Jace, Cassie and Nell had been kicked out an hour ago. Well, Nell had been kicked out half an hour ago because on the first round of kick outs she hid under the bed.

"Hey, Mum, Dad."

I was wrapped in two pretty tight but very careful hugs and inspected thoroughly. They must have decided I really was okay because they breathed a sigh of relief and sat back on the edge of the bed.

"How are you feeling? I'm so sorry we were so far away, love."

"Mum, chill. It's fine. I'm fine. Morphine's kicked in and I'm being looked after," I said, looking up at Logan. The only times he'd left my side was to get me fresh water and I was sure he ran to get it because I wasn't even alone for thirty seconds.

"God, we were so worried. Don't you ever do that again," Dad said. I'd not seen him cry before. I didn't like it.

"Dad, really, I'm okay. Tired but okay."

"Sleep if you're tired. We're not going anywhere," he replied, kissing the top of my head the way he'd done since I was little.

As tired as I was I didn't want to sleep. I was shaken up about the accident but Logan was being a baby about sleep so I knew if I wanted that stubborn boy to sleep I had to.

"You have to sleep, too," I said, raising my eyebrow, challenging him to disagree.

He nodded and patted the chair. "Got my bed ready." Leaning over, he gave me a soft, chaste kiss and settled in the chair.

The ward was as dark as it could be and it was quiet. Dad left after twenty minutes because there wasn't room for a fourth person to sleep in here and I was too exhausted to stay awake any longer.

Logan had pretended to be asleep as the nurse told my parents that only two people could stay so one of them had to leave. I tried to keep a straight face as I watched Logan sit still as a statue and breathe in and out evenly.

"Get some sleep," Mum whispered, kissing my cheek. She sat back and wrapped a blanket over her lap.

"Night, Mum."

"Good night, Chloe."

***

I woke up just as the sun was rising. Logan and my mum were still asleep in the two high back chairs on either side of the bed.

I pushed myself up with my arms, careful not to put any pressure on my stomach muscles. Jace gave me a lovely visual about stitches ripping open yesterday so I was extra cautious about moving slowly and not having the sealed cut on my stomach bursting.

It took me a little while to sit up but I managed it and

instantly felt a little better, a little less helpless.

Beside me, Logan stirred, his head at an awkward position. He groaned and rubbed his neck. He went from sleepy to wide-awake in an instant as he must have realised he was in hospital. Striking blue topaz eyes took me in.

"Hey, you okay?" he asked, moving from the chair to the side of the bed. "Been awake long?"

"Yeah, I'm fine. Just woke up. How did you sleep?"

He smiled, not answering my question so I knew that meant awful but he wasn't about to complain about it.

"Think you could speak to a nurse for me, I'd *really* like to be able to go to the toilet."

"You don't have to worry about that, sweetheart."

I took a deep breath. There was nothing I wanted more than to have this catheter out and I was promised this morning it could go. No one was going to convince me to have it in for another second. "Logan, I swear if you start talking about this I'm going to jump out of the window. Please, just go and get a nurse."

He smiled, amused, and kissed my forehead. "Sure. Do you want a coffee? I'll run to the machine too."

"The machine or Starbucks across the road?"

He chewed his lip nervously.

"Come on, my mum's with me and you need to get out of this hospital, even if it's just for five minutes." I pouted. "And I could really do with a decent cup of coffee. Please, Logan?"

"Okay. I'll get a nurse and then run down there."

"You're the best."

"Don't forget it."

"I love you."

I wasn't sure what I loved more, hearing him say it back or his reaction to when I said it. He looked so happy it made every part of me ache.

"I love you, too," he said and kissed me. "I'll be ten minutes, max."

"See you in a bit."

Mum woke up just as the nurse had finished removing the catheter, which was a particularly hideous experience.

"How're you feeling, love?"

"I'm fine, need a wee though, can you help me up?"

She was off her chair and by the side of the bed before I'd swung my legs over the side. I held onto her until I'd steadied myself, letting the initial head rush from laying and sitting for so long pass.

"Thanks, I'm okay now."

She didn't let go though; she walked with me to the bathroom. "Where's Logan?"

"Starbucks. I needed him gone while the catheter was being removed and I need a decent caffeine hit."

Logan was back when I'd finished in the bathroom. "Want help?" he asked.

"I can walk fine," I teased. "You're going to get an ulcer with all that worrying."

He shrugged and held his hand out. I let him because it was a lot easier than arguing. Logan helped people, he fixed things and if he couldn't he felt crappy about it.

When I was back in bed I was handed a large cappuccino. Mum watched us from her chair, sipping her skinny latte with a smile on her face.

"You spoken to Dad?" I asked.

"I texted him while you were in the bathroom. He'll be here at eight."

"How was your trip? You ready to tell me yet?"

I grabbed Logan's arm as he went to move away from me to go back to his chair. He took the hint, wrapping one arm around me as he sat on the bed. His other hand retrieved his coffee and he watched me and Mum, absentmindedly tracing circles on my forearm. It was really nice and very distracting.

"It was lovely, right up until we got the call telling us our child was in hospital, then a holiday was the last place in the world I wanted to be."

"Sorry."

I knew Logan would be frowning at me but I kept eye contact with Mum. "Don't apologise, Chloe! We're just so glad you're okay."

"Have the police been in touch?" I asked, looking at Logan.

"They spoke to me and Jace while you were in surgery and might want to talk to you today, if you're up for it. Don't worry about that now," he replied, kissing my shoulder.

"But I do worry about it," I said.

"Okay." He took my hand and squeezed. "The boy has admitted everything so he'll just be charged."

"That's good then." *I think.* I wasn't so sure. The driver deserved to pay for leaving after he'd hit me but it wasn't intentional. I smiled. They would want him to be locked up.

I took a deep breath and pushed the thoughts away. My whole life in the last few months had been a lot to take in and my brain was scrambled from trying to make sense of it all. I was pretty much ready to wake up from it or have Ashton Kutcher jump out and tell me I'd been Punk'd already.

"He won't get away with it. Everything's fine, Chloe." He kissed my hand and added, "I love you."

That was exactly what I needed to hear. Smiling, I mouthed *I love you, too.*

CHAPTER FORTY-EIGHT

Chloe

I was ready to leave the hospital about an hour after I woke up so by now I was going insane. All I wanted to do was to get home and put the accident behind me.

Logan squeezed my hand. Since first thing this morning he'd only left my side to go to the bathroom. It took a lot of convincing to get him to go get a coffee from downstairs and take another five minutes to breathe. He'd literally taken five minutes before he came back and he still looked a little stressed.

"I'm okay," I said.

He was having a hard time with that. Physically he knew I was okay but Logan worried about the people he loved excessively. He'd be stressing over my injuries and just about anything else his mind would conjure.

"Yeah," he replied, rubbing his eyes with the hand that hadn't been attached to mine since I woke up, before that too, probably.

"Why don't you go get some sleep? My parents will be back soon so I won't be alone."

He was already shaking his head before I'd finished. "I'm staying."

If I wanted him to go I was going to have to call security. Trouble was, I didn't really want him to leave.

"She's right, Logan," Jace said. "Me and Cass are leaving when Mum and Dad get here. Why don't you come with us and get a decent night's sleep. I'll bring you back here first thing."

"Look, I appreciate your concern, all of you, but I am not leaving this room. That's the end of it."

Sighing, I resigned myself to the knowledge that he was absolutely not going anywhere. Maybe I could get him to sleep in the bed with me tonight or he could have a camp bed in here.

"I can't wait to go home," I said, trying to change the subject from Logan's lack of personal wellbeing.

"Hopefully tomorrow, sweetheart," Logan said.

It had better be tomorrow.

"Logan, Cass, do you think you could give me and Jace a few minutes, please?" I asked.

Looking at me confused for a second, Logan released my hand. "Yeah, sure."

"I'll take Logan to the café and try holding him there for longer than five seconds. You want me to bring you anything?"

"No, thanks. Just make sure that one gets some fresh air," I replied, nodding towards Logan.

Jace stayed where he was by the window, until they'd left. As the door closed he walked over and sat on the bed. "Is everything okay?" he asked.

"That's what I want to talk about. I'm hoping that after everything that's happened we could find a way of being friends. It's kind of driving me crazy not having you in my life. I miss you, Jace. I thought you were dead and you're not and I want to be able to dance for joy and spend time with you but…"

"But I'm making it impossible."

Well, yeah, he was. Me and Logan hadn't helped but

nothing that happened we could have foreseen or controlled so there was no point in beating ourselves up about it.

"I am, too. When I put myself in your position it hurts so much and hurting you is the last thing I want."

"It's hard, Chloe. We were supposed to be for life."

"Jace, we were. I was with you and only you until the day I was made to believe you were dead. *Everything* changed that day. If I hadn't fallen in love with Logan we still wouldn't be together. There's too much that I couldn't forgive to go back to how it used to be."

He looked up to the ceiling. "The thought of being reunited with you was one of the things that kept me going. I almost called so many times but the fear of something happening to you or anyone else I love stopped me. When all I wanted to do was go home to you I pictured getting back together, sitting around the table with my family and holding your hand again."

"I wanted that, too, for a *long* time."

"So I was screwed either way. I could refuse to testify and maybe two terrorists would get off or go through with it and lose you."

"It's a shitty situation, Jace, but you're here now. Sometimes you have to sacrifice something you love in order to protect it. I'll never forget that the choice you made was to keep me and others safe. That matters."

"Where do we go from here? I don't know how to be your friend."

I smiled. "It's been a while, huh. We were good at it before we got together." Now I knew it wasn't going to be that easy, especially when there were feelings and a brother involved but I wasn't prepared to lose Jace again. "Can you do it? I don't want to hurt you more."

He took my hand, biting his lip. "I can do it. Like you said, we were friends before."

Easy as that...

"So what have you been up to while you were away?" I

asked.

"Ah, you know, studying to be a brain surgeon."

Smiling, I replied, "Yeah? How's that going?"

"Good. Saved my fiftieth patient last month."

I narrowed my eyes. "You played Xbox the entire time, didn't you?"

"Not the *entire* time. We had to live normal lives so we went to college. I'm working on my architectural degree."

"That's awesome, Jace." God, I was so happy to hear that. "You're transferring here?"

"Already have. I'm a year behind where I should be but it took a while to get back into… life."

That sounded familiar. "I'm applying for jobs in a few places in town, we could meet up on campus maybe?"

"Of fucking course we will." He frowned and laughed. "That was a very Logan thing to say."

"Yes. He does like that word. His best is five *fuckings* in one sentence."

"You keep count?"

"Me and Cassie might have a little wager going."

He laughed and it took me right back a few years. It was *so* good to hear that laugh again. "Of course you two do."

Fifty pounds to whoever counted the most in one sentence by the end of the year.

"Are you okay about me and Logan?"

"After…" He pointed to the spot on my stomach where I'd been operated on, not able to say the words. "I'm a lot better with it. Don't get me wrong, it's still…"

"Yeah, I understand."

He nodded once. "But I love you and I love him. He's changed."

You should've seen him after he thought you'd died then.

"He has changed."

"I was honestly concerned he'd die alone. I thought he was overly picky and looking for some kind of perfection that didn't exist. Makes sense now, though. His idea of perfect, and mine, is you. Can't blame him for that."

What do I say to that? One second all was great with Jace and the next he made me feel like a huge bitch again. He hadn't done it on purpose though, and there was going to be some awkwardness as we figured out a way to make a friendship work.

"Sorry," he said, "I didn't mean to make it weird."

"I know."

"Logan's happy. I want to be able to hate him, hate you both, but I can't. This won't be easy, Chloe, and there will be times we have conversations that are hard, but necessary, but I'm more than willing to go through all that shit if it means we can be in each others lives."

"Done. I'm so ready to have you back, Jace, no matter what we have to go through to get it." He leant forwards and kissed my cheek. "So tell me about the girl you lived with."

Frowning, he replied, "It wasn't like that."

"I know, but she was a big part of your life for over three years. I'd quite like to know more about her. Maybe meet her?" She was going to think I was a bitch for sure.

"Alyssa's cool. You'd like her."

"She's cool? That's all you have to say about her?"

With a smirk, he added, "She's tall, got dark red hair, brown eyes, and a small scar on her eyebrow where a piercing ripped out. She loves helping people and is training to be a nurse. When she got home the first thing she did was announce that she's gay, literally those were her first words. Apparently, her parents screamed, but because she was alive not because she's a lesbian, that they don't care about. When she told me she also said she was going back to Alyssa so I wasn't to call her April anymore, I've slipped up a few times so she's now taken to hitting me in the balls when I do."

I laughed, wincing as the morphine was beginning to wear off. "I think I will like her."

"You will. I might have to do damage control, though."

"You've been slagging me off to her? Arse!" I slapped his arm. There wasn't much room for me to be angry with him, though. He had a right to under the circumstances.

"It's cool, she'll understand."

I wasn't quite sure why it meant that much to me to get along with her. She'd been Jace's friend and the one person he could really lean on and talk to. It must have been so lonely for him so I was grateful for her.

Logan had clearly decided to take my 'can I have a few *minutes* with Jace' literally because he walked back into the room with Cass having given us less than a quarter of an hour.

"Everything okay?" he asked, handing me and Jace a coffee even though we'd said we were fine. He was always looking out for everyone else.

For the first time since Jace came back I felt like everything was okay. Or going to be anyway.

"Yeah, it is," Jace said, giving me the little smile I loved.

CHAPTER FORTY-NINE

Chloe

It had been a month since I got out of hospital and the only evidence of my injuries was a very small scar on my stomach, that was now healed and pain free. The driver got a fine and driving ban, which was about all I'd expected.

"No," Jace said into the phone and sighed. "I won't let her carry anything heavy… Yes, I'll make sure she takes it easy. Hello? Logan?" Jace made a crackling sound. "I can't hear you, bro, you're breaking up, bye." He hung up and put his phone in his pocket, rolling his eyes.

"Logan's on form then," I said as we walked down the Christmas decorated high street. We'd made the trip into the city to do some shopping. After I got out of hospital and we'd sorted through everything we made a pact to do something each week, even if it was just grabbing a quick coffee. Jace was important to me and I loved that we could be friends. It wasn't always easy but it was getting better.

"Yeah, I forgot how much of a worrier he is. I get it though, you sure you're okay to be shopping like this?"

"Yes, it's been a month, Jace, and I'm totally healed. I don't want to do all of my Christmas shopping online. Plus, you suck at getting your mum presents so I'm here to help you, and her, too."

"I want to get something for Alyssa as well. Any ideas?"

"I've met the girl a grand total of one time and you lived with her for three years. Why are you asking me? Ooh, book her in for that infinity tattoo she wants on her wrist."

"See!" He pointed to me. "That's exactly why I asked you. Remind me to call and book that later."

I was happy that he had such a great friend, most of his old ones had moved on. He had me but it wasn't the same. We were committed to making a friendship work but too much had happened for us to be best friends that shared everything.

Alyssa and I got along; we'd met briefly at Logan's house when Jace brought her over for the afternoon. It was after the accident, which put a lot into perspective for us all. Jace had admitted he still had feelings for me but he also admitted that he was happy seeing me and Logan happy. It was all kinds of screwed up but we were making it work for us so at the end of the day that was all that mattered.

"What're you getting Logan?" he asked.

I shrugged. "No clue. He was chatting about some new rowing machine thing."

"Why would he want that when he works at a gym and can use theirs whenever he wants?"

"Thank you!" I said, throwing my hands up. "But he wants it so I'll listen more and see if I can get it."

"I'll bring it up in conversation and let you know. It'll be obvious if you try getting it out of him now."

"He'll know anyway, but thanks, Jace." He was really trying and I loved that. I hadn't planned to shop for Logan at all today; it was just a little too weird getting the ex to help me pick out my boyfriend's present.

"So is Alyssa meeting us for lunch?" I asked, trying to change the subject as quickly as possible. We weren't quite ready for lengthily conversations about mine and Logan's relationship just yet.

"She might, I've got to text her in a bit and see if it's cool."

"You're waiting for me to tell you if it's cool, aren't you?"

He shrugged one shoulder lazily. "I wasn't sure if you'd want her there. I thought you wanted it to just be us."

"It's just us, I like the time we spend together, it's important to me, but we can meet up with Alyssa for lunch."

"I found that weird at first."

"Me wanting to spend time with you or Alyssa?"

He frowned and stopped outside in the freezing cold. The icy temperature had turned his nose and cheeks pink, mine, too, probably. "Well, both actually but I was talking about me."

"You know you're important. What we had was important and I couldn't ignore it even if I wanted to. And hey, you want to still be in my life after everything, too."

"Yeah, I do. It's not easy letting go of that much history, even if it would've been easier." I was about to question *easier* when he corrected himself. "Maybe that's not the right word for it. I don't know how to explain it."

"No, I get what you mean, Jace. We're still feeling our way through this. It'll get easier with time."

When he just loved me the way I loved him it would be a million times easier on everyone. I had to be patient with that, I'd had years to get over him and move on, he was only just starting to do it now, but I had no doubt that he would do it and go on to find who he was really supposed to be with.

"Think we can grab a hot chocolate from Starbucks before this starts to get really awkward," I said, grimacing.

Laughing, he nodded. "Yeah, I'm buying for being the one that started the awkward."

"Sounds good to me. Don't forget to text Alyssa."

We shopped all morning and planned a break for lunch at one. I had pretty much finished getting the presents I wanted, apart from Logan's rowing... whatever it was.

"Lyss can't make it, just us for lunch. That okay?" Jace said.

"Of course it's okay." I didn't need a third person to be with us. That would defeat the point of us trying to build a friendship anyway. "Where do you want to go?"

"You choose."

"Hmm, okay, maybe Giraffe? I fancy a burger."

With a little nod, he changed direction and we headed to the restaurant. He'd unloaded our bags back at the car so we could eat and get back to shopping. Although I was almost done when we listed the people Jace needed to buy for it was clear he wasn't.

We were seated quickly, considering the streets were packed with shoppers.

"What did you do for Christmas while I was away?" he asked.

Before he left we spent Christmas morning with our family, then in the evening he came over to pick me up, spent an hour with my parents and then we went back to his until I had to be home.

"Last year I did our usual but before that..." I shrugged. Before that no one felt that festive. "What about you?"

"Me and Lyss made our own version of a Christmas dinner and exchanged presents."

"Your own version being junk food?"

"Yeah."

"Thought so." I was too busy thinking of how awful that first Christmas was especially to think about what it was like for him. He was away from home, knowing we thought we'd never see him again. It was horrible.

"I'm sorry, Jace."

"Don't be. It was my fault, remember."

"No," I replied, finally getting it. "It wasn't your fault. You were put in a shitty position and you did what you thought was right. You did what *was* right. I was selfish to be mad at you for putting the lives of potentially hundreds of other people before me."

"It wasn't before you, Chloe."

"Right, sorry, that was put badly. What I'm saying is I understand why you did it and I'm really sorry for how I behaved when you came back. I guess the shock of seeing you again after going through losing you made me kind of… well, lose it."

"Wasn't all you. I could've handled coming back better. I could've also handled you and Logan better."

"Yeah, I don't think anyone can blame you for how you handled that."

"Cassie's right about one thing, if I really had died, I would've wanted it to be Logan. There was no one else I trusted to look out for you more than him. He loved me so I knew he'd protect you, turns out he protected you for another reason, too, but I can't blame him for that."

"Thank you," I said, on the verge of bloody tears. It meant so much to have him say that and to realise Jace had done what he had to, what I would've done to keep the people I loved safe. "God, I'm so glad we did this."

"Feels good to get shit sorted, doesn't it?" he replied.

"It does."

***

I lugged the bags of shopping upstairs instead of one by one like I'd promised Jace. They were more awkward than heavy, and I knew my own body, I was fine. I kicked the door open and immediately dropped the bags. Logan sat on my bed, looking less than amused that I'd carried so much.

"Chloe!" he said, getting off the bed. "What the hell? Why didn't Jace carry those?"

"He did and he offered to bring them upstairs but I declined. It was just a little too soon for him to be in my room. I promised to take them up a couple at a time but I couldn't be bothered to make the many trips. I'm fine, Logan. No pain, I swear."

He walked towards me, fighting a smile. "You're rambling, sweetheart. You don't have to explain yourself to me, just please, take better care. You might feel okay but you're healing still. I need you around and I need you to be okay. You're kind of everything."

I walked straight into his arms. "You're sweet and kind of everything, too. I'll be more careful until you realise I'm fine. When will that be by the way? It's been ages, Logan."

He shook his head in mock horror. "Is that all you think about, Miss Holland?" I rolled my eyes, clinging to him. "I worry about you. I don't want to hurt you."

"You won't hurt me. *I'm fine.* I miss you, Logan."

"You're on top. If it hurts you stop or it won't happen again for another fucking year."

At first I was stunned, both in the way he said it and that he'd actually agreed. I thought he'd wait until the scar was practically invisible before he touched me again.

"Logan, there is no way you could go a whole year."

He narrowed his eyes. "Fuck me, sweetheart."

It took only a few seconds for the shock to wear off and my body to burn with need. Well, who was I to say no to that?

EPILOGUE

Chloe

They say that moving house was one of the most stressful things you could do – they're totally right. It had been two weeks since we'd got the keys and I was desperate to move in. The place needed a new bathroom, kitchen, tiled kitchen flooring and carpet throughout though, so we decided to paint the two bedroom house and schedule all the work in those two weeks before we moved in.

As much as I just wanted to move I was glad we waited and didn't have to live around the mess as the work was being done. Finally though, fifteen days after the house was officially ours we were ready to move in.

Surprisingly, Logan had the most stuff. His parents' garage was full of gym equipment and furniture he'd bought over the last few years. The removal van was parked outside and our helpers were loading everything up.

Being impatient as hell, last night I dragged Cassie and Nell to mine where we boxed the final things up and took them to the house. I couldn't wait and knew that Logan's stuff would take forever. My things, which wasn't much, were already put neatly away.

"Logan!" I shouted. "Why are you still here? The sofa

is being delivered this morning and no one's there to—" He kissed me, which was both of our preferred way of shutting me up.

"I'm now going. Stop stressing, sweetheart."

I couldn't stop stressing; it was kind of what you were supposed to do when you moved. There were a million things going on at once and Logan was a little too laid back.

"Mum's going over in a minute with boxes of kitchen shit. She said she'd stay there now and unpack it. Want to go too, and decide where we're keeping stuff?" Logan's collection included everything we'd need to cook and eat. The boy had done good because over the last year all I'd bought for a house was three cake tins.

"Yeah, okay."

He kissed me again. "I'll see you over there in a few. Got your key?"

Once I'd forgotten my key but do you think he'd let it go?

"Yes," I replied, giving him a shove in the direction of the door. "Go! If you miss that delivery and we can't christen the sofa tonight I won't be happy."

That did it. His eyes widened, blistered and then he was jogging out of the door. Men were so easy.

"Chloe, want me to *accidentally* break this?" Jace asked, holding up Logan's framed old Jack Daniels poster.

That was such a tempting idea. The thing was ugly. "No," I said and sighed. "I appreciate the thought but I'll just make him have it somewhere it won't be seen. In the walk-in wardrobe behind the clothes maybe."

He laughed and said, "Alright." It had been a little over eight months since Jace came home and things were finally okay. He'd started seeing a lovely girl called Daphnee last month and I was thrilled for him. Jace had even reached the point where in an argument with Logan he could shut him up by saying *whatever, man, you stole my girlfriend*. It was quite effective, until Logan started giving him a dead arm.

"Daph stopping by tonight?"

"If she gets off work early enough."

"Cool," I replied. "Would be good to see her again." Despite the history and unique situation between me and Jace I got along with Daphnee really well. She was a bit of a gamer too, so a much better fit for Jace than I ever was.

"Don't you have some girlie night planned?"

"Next week, yes. Don't worry, I'll look after her."

He widened his eyes in mock horror.

Daphnee was a new addition to my group of friends that since Jace getting back and being run over had got a lot closer. I loved having the people I cared about closer together. Plus, I was on a mission to sort out Nell and Damon's idiocy and find Cassie a man that deserved her. Daphnee was a bit of a romantic so I knew together we'd make a great cupid team.

"Are all the boxes out of the garage yet?"

He grinned too wide for it to be genuine and that was my answer. "We've loaded about half. Good thing you have a big garage."

"That's the only reason all his stuff is coming with us."

I picked up a box labelled *DVDs* and carried it out to the front garden where we were chucking everything for my dad and Daryl to load it up.

Nell moved round the house like a whirlwind, dishing out orders and pulling funny faces to make me smile. She was the sole reason I hadn't killed today.

"Smile, Chlo Chlo, you'll be sleeping in your new house tonight," she said, dancing around me and bounding back towards the garage.

I did smile because she was right, all the stress of solicitors and estate agents was over, we'd packed up and all we had to do was finish getting everything in the van then unload it the other side. Tonight I could relax in my new house. And have a few hundred drinks.

***

There were about five people too many in the living room but I couldn't have cared less. All the people that meant the most to me were finishing off their fish and chips dinner in the living room of my first house, and first house with Logan, after helping us move all day. I didn't even care that after spending almost two thousand on a sofa I was sitting on the floor. Logan's arm was around me as he ate one handed so that helped me to not give a crap, too.

Daphnee had made it in time to eat which made things a little more complete. Over in the corner Nell was scowling at her phone. Last night she'd slept with Damon after holding back for over three months. Apparently, in all their wisdom they'd decided friends with benefits was a great idea again yesterday.

They could both have meaningless sex which was all well and good when you had that sort of agreement but things between them was anything but meaningless. My point being proven right now as she angrily tapped a reply to whatever he'd just said.

And she thought watching me run from Logan last year was frustrating.

She caught me shaking my head at her and glared, throwing her phone in her bag. Oh yeah, friends with benefits working out just fine.

Logan yawned loudly. "I'm tired. You tired, Chlo?"

"Very subtle, son," Daryl said.

"Nope, not tired at all," I said, grinning up at him.

"No, I'm sure you are."

Mum stood up and laughed. "I think that's our cue to leave."

"Oh, you don't have to, Bethany," Logan said, chuckling.

"I'm sure you two want a few minutes to yourself," she replied, biting her lip in amusement.

I could feel that Logan was about to bite back about lasting a lot longer than a few minutes so I slapped my hand over his mouth, earning laughs from everyone but my dad.

Logan just looked at me, all gorgeous and deep blue eyes, grinning behind my hand like a naughty child. God, I loved him.

"Yeah, we're out. You two make me sick," Nell said, turning her nose up.

I removed my hand, hoping Logan would behave and pointed to her. "We'll be talking tomorrow."

"Looking forward to it," she replied sarcastically and pulled me up for a hug.

"Come on, Nell, I'll give you a lift," Cass said as she kissed my cheek.

It couldn't have been two seconds after I closed the front door behind everyone that I was scooped up into Logan's arms. I squealed, not expecting it, and held on around his neck.

"We skipping the clean up?" I asked, pressing myself to him.

"I'll chuck the rubbish in the morning, right now I need to get you naked and horizontal in that big bed of ours."

"And what if I don't want to be horizontal?"

"Baby," he said, walking upstairs with me in his arms, "I'll take you anyway you want."

He bloody would too, the pervert.

"Hmm, that's okay, I don't mind being under you."

He put me down in our bedroom and I stopped by the bed, arching my back as Logan started his assault by kissing up my neck. "You're eager tonight," I said, gripping the muscular forearm that pinned me to his chest.

"I'm eager every night, Chlo."

Now that was true. At least now we had our own space and could make as much noise as we wanted. Although I was kind of going to miss his hand covering my mouth as I came.

I closed my eyes and my head hit his shoulder.

"Not getting into bed?" he asked.

"Enjoying this," I replied.

I was suddenly on my own and jumping as the loss of his body supporting mine almost made me fall over. He slapped my bum. "Get in bed, you."

"That was mean," I said.

"Oh, I plan on picking up where we left off the second you're laying down."

I gripped the cover and whipped it back. Something caught my eye and after taking a second to register what it was, I gasped. Sitting on the bed was an open, red velvet box with a gorgeous glistening ring nestled into it.

"Logan," I whispered. He was proposing! In an odd way but what else could I expect?

I was stunned to the spot so he reached over and picked it up. "Chloe Holland." I started crying, already, he'd only said my name and I was already bloody crying. "I've loved you for…" He gulped. His voice was thick with emotion and I could see the start of tears – his eyes had glazed. "I… Chloe…"

I smiled through my tears and gripped his shirt.

"Fuck it! Just marry me, sweetheart."

Now that was a Logan proposal. I sobbed and replied, "Of course, I will."

He picked the ring up, taking it out of the box and slipped it over my finger. Then I was in his arms, lifted off the floor and being crushed to his solid chest.

I laughed along with him, blinking through tears before his mouth found mine and he kissed me long and deep. He lowered us to the bed and taking it slow had been completely forgotten, we attacked each other like wild animals. Clothes were ripped – actually ripped off – and tossed on the floor.

My eyes rolled back into my head as he entered me sharply and quickly found a hard, fast, relentless pace. We were slick with sweat in a second. I clawed his back, moaning loudly. I could see the indecision in his face, he wanted to kiss me but he also wanted to hear me.

"Logan," I panted, fisting his hair and pulling his head down. He kissed me, tongue flicking into my mouth at the same pace he was pushing into me. Seconds later I came around him, kissing and biting him as I fell apart.

He wasn't done with me yet, he pulled out to flip me onto my stomach and everything below my waist clenched in anticipation.

"I love you," he said, entering me slowly, teasingly.

I was about to say it back when he pulled back and thrust hard, going deeper. "Shit," I hissed.

"Ahh," he whispered. "And I love hearing you." He lay down, covering my back and kissed my shoulder. His arm reached underneath me and his fingers found their goal immediately. I groaned into the pillow and fisted the sheets as Logan kissed and nipped on my neck, finding the punishing pace as before.

I was going crazy beneath him. I felt like he was everywhere. It was stimulation overload and I could barely take it. "Logan," I didn't know what I wanted to say – tell him to stop or to never stop. I was building again, so quickly. My body tightened and I fought to push back, to do something to deal with how he was making me feel.

I felt his smile against my skin. He clamped his mouth around my shoulder and bit down. I let go again, unexpectedly, and spiralled into one of the most intense orgasms I'd ever had where my body shook and my vision blurred. His fingers circled my clitoris, prolonging the torture.

He grunted behind me, moaning in my ear as he thrust hard and deep one last time.

Logan rolled me onto my back and then into his arms as I floated back to earth. We laid still, stuck together by sweat, trying to get our breath back. I snuggled against his chest, needing to be closer.

"Well," I said. "That was…" There were no words.

"I know. I don't mean to brag but I was fucking awesome."

I couldn't help laughing. *I don't mean to brag* my arse.

"Yeah, that definitely made up for the less than romantic proposal," I teased.

"Shit, you're right, that wasn't at all romantic, was it? I'm so sorry, Chlo, you deserved better than me swearing and demanding you marry me. God, I didn't even ask you."

"Don't," I said and kissed his soft lips. Why did I have to say that and make him feel bad? "Logan, it was perfect and it was very you. I love how you proposed – although when I tell my nan I'm missing out the part where you said *fuck it*. I wouldn't change a thing about that proposal."

He pressed me into the mattress and I wrapped my arms and legs around him. "This is going to be a short engagement. I'm getting another ring on that finger as soon as I can."

"Fine by me," I breathed just as his lips moulded to mine. "I love you," I murmured into the kiss.

He pulled back enough to see me properly but still close enough to drive me wild. His eyes had never looked so striking and so full of love. He'd never looked so content before and I was sure I had the same deliriously happy expression as he did.

He smiled and it made my heart ache. "Sweetheart, you have no fucking idea."

COMING LATE 2014

BOOK TWO IN THE CHANCE SERIES

OUR CHANCE

Nell Paisley believes that no good can come from love. Her grandparents screwed it up, her parents screwed it up, so why would it be any different for her? She would rather keep it casual and protect her heart.

Damon Masters was happy with casual through university but a couple years on and Nell is the only woman he wants.

With the aid of Nell's best friend, Chloe, Damon sets out to smash down the wall Nell's built around herself and show her that not all love is doomed to end in disaster.

MORE BOOKS BY NATASHA PRESTON

OUT NOW

SILENCE
(Book One in the Silence series)

Oakley Farrell stopped talking at the age of five and has remained in her own little world since. Her mum is desperate to find out what's wrong with her daughter, but does she really want to know?

Oakley's best friend, Cole has stuck by her. Their friendship is easy but as they start to become closer she is faced with a new set of issues to deal with.

BROKEN SILENCE
(Book One in the Silence series)

Four years after Oakley, her mum, and brother fled to Australia, the trial is ready to begin. Oakley makes the decision to return to England and face the people who hurt her in person.

Her love for Cole never faded, but how will he react to seeing her again? Will they be able to put everything behind them in order to get their happy ending?

COVERT

After seven friends take a trip to a secluded log cabin, a drunken night ends in the tragic and brutal murder of two of them. Mackenzie and four of her friends wake in a disorientated state to find the bodies of Josh and Courtney on the kitchen floor.

With the police determining that there was no forced entry or signs of a struggle, suspicion turns to the five survivors.

PLAYERS, BUMPS AND COCKTAIL SAUSAGES
(A companion novel to the Silence series)

Putting his player ways behind him, Jasper Dane is now strictly a one-woman man. Jasper, desperate to start a family with his wife, Abby, is devastated when she puts their baby plans on hold.

Holly has just arrived back in town for the summer, and after landing a job with Jasper, the two form an unlikely friendship.

Abby's immediate dislike of Holly and Jasper spending time together causes him to question his wife's fidelity. Broken hearted at Abby's sudden change of heart and suspicious of her reasons, Jasper takes action, sparking a chain of events that make his once well planned out life spiral out of control.

To get what he wants, he first has to lose everything.

THE CELLAR

Nothing ever happens in the town of Long Thorpe - that is, until sixteen-year-old Summer Robinson disappears without a trace. No family or police investigation can track her down.

Spending months inside the cellar of her kidnapper with several other girls, Summer learns of Colin's abusive past, and his thoughts of his victims being his family...his perfect, pure flowers.

But flowers can't survive long cut off from the sun, and time is running out...

COMING OCTOBER 2014

SAVE ME

Tegan Pennells used to care about everything: family, friends, boys, school, and music. Then her dad died and that stopped.

She doesn't care about her relationship with her mum and sister. She doesn't care that she's pushed almost all of her friends away. She doesn't care that she lost my virginity to her friend's brother in the backseat of his car. She doesn't care that she uses men or what people think about her *friends with benefits* agreement with Kai, a guy she met in a bar.

Tegan doesn't care about the man that received my father's heart. And she doesn't want to care about that man's son.

She doesn't want to care about anything ever again.

www.natashapreston.com

Printed in Great Britain
by Amazon.co.uk, Ltd.,
Marston Gate.